A Dragging

of Chains

The Seventh Otto Fischer Novel

Jim McDermott

Abbreviations used in the text

BfV – Bundesamt für Verfassunsschutz: Federal Office for the Protection of the Constitution, German domestic security agency

BVG - Berliner Verkehrsbetriebe Gesellschaft: Berlin Public Transport Company, responsible for u-bahn, bus, and, until the early1960s, tram services in West Berlin

CIA – Central Intelligence Agency: US foreign intelligence service

DDR – Deutsche Demokratische Republik: German Democratic Republic, or East Germany

GRU - Glavnoye Razvedyvatel'noye Upravleniye: Soviet military intelligence directorate

KGB - Komitet Gosudarstvennoy Bezopasnosti: state security agency of the Soviet Union, formed in 1954 by the amalgamation of former domestic (**MVD**) and foreign (**MGB**) security agencies

SDP – Ah, well, you'll have to read on

SPD - Sozialdemokratische Partei Deutschlands: German Social Democratic Party

StB - Státní Bezpečnost: Communist Czechoslovakia's state security agency

WASt – Wehrmachtsauskunftstelle: German Government agency maintaining records of servicemen killed or missing it action; now Deutsche Dienststelle

ZfH – Zentrale für Heimatdienst: Umbrella organization set up by Chancellor Adenauer to accommodate four departments that were intended to mature, eventually, into branches of the Federal Defence Ministry; one of these, Information Und Nachrichtendienst (an intelligence-gathering organization), would become known as the Friedrich-Wilhelm-Heinz-Amt (**FWHA**) after its appointed chief

Prologue: October 1954

He moved as he had done for as long as he could recall - lightly, on the balls of his feet, as delicately as a mine-field clearer - because scraped ground, ground that wasn't kept in mind, tended to betray a man. In the old, dangerous days they had laughed about it, called it *the ballerina's step*. It was a habit that had outlived all but him.

The enemy seemed not to care to be discreet, and he took this as a very good sign. The chase had started somewhere in Charlottenburg, probably even before his nerve-endings rose to the occasion, and a series of abrupt, random detours as he moved gradually into Wilmersdorf hadn't prised off his pursuer. He was anxious, naturally; but it occurred that if this was an assassination he wouldn't have been given so much field across which to run.

Once, he would have followed an agreed procedure, sprinting away abruptly through an alley (and preferably two or three), gaining a few moments to lift a sewer lid and go to ground where even Gestapo didn't care to follow. It was more difficult these days - the ruins were almost cleared now, and the wider, cleaner streets that had replaced them were unhelpful to flushed foxes. There would have been better opportunities across the line in East Berlin, where new concrete had flowed more slowly over the past decade, but over there they preferred too many of the old ways. He was safer in West Berlin, just.

His stride lengthened as the Preussenpark loomed. Trees and shrubs were allies (though not as much in October as even a month earlier), and the moment or two that any pursuer squanders before taking up a sprint might be enough. He was slower these days than back when every hour had to be taken as a possible last, but unless he was being followed by an amateur athlete he was certain his legs could do the business still.

As it happened, he didn't need to ask them for much. At the junction of Beyerischestrasse and Zähringerstrasse, his leading foot already in the air as he stepped off the kerb, the last un-preoccupied sliver of his attention caught something. He flung himself to the right, onto a half-cab bus, dragging the closing door out of the hand of its surprised conductor. He didn't bother turning to memorize the face of his shadow as the vehicle moved away. They wouldn't be so stupid as to send the same one, next time.

He sat down, almost pleased with himself. He was being carried in the right direction, north, back into Charlottenburg, as if the morning were doing its best to make up for the inconvenience he'd suffered. The feeling passed quickly, though, and his head began to work on who, and why now, today.

Was he a threat still? It wasn't as if he was uniquely informed about things, nor considered one of the more dangerous obstacles to what certain men wanted done. He was adrift, orphaned, a man for whom the professional obituary would have been written and printed by now, had he ever been important enough to deserve one. Was this about spite, or simply an orderly mind at work, gathering up the loose strands and tying them off?

He no longer had the contacts that might have told him, nor any idea how to acquire new ones. In effect, he was as alone as upon that terrible day he had stood outside Plötzensee Prison, shouting at the wall that they had missed one and didn't they have the balls to step outside and try to take him? It had been as ludicrous as every other aspect of the Reich's war on its own people that no one had heard him - or, worse, bothered to take up the challenge. A regime shaped to catch and expunge the outsider, the objector and renegade, had slowly, methodically hanged or beheaded his broken-bodied comrades for no better reason that they had tried to spoil Goebbel's filthy little exhibition at the Lustgarten, and all the while their perfectly healthy, untouched co-conspirator had waved fists that held full complements of intact fingers still, offering himself *gratis*, daring monsters to be men. Perhaps they weren't, nor ever had been; perhaps their appetites had been too sated to take a further morsel; perhaps some last shard of sanity had kept his voice too low to carry over the high prison walls (though loud enough not to torture him afterwards with *coward*).

That evening, he had returned to his cellar and waited, confident that he would soon be at the same peace as his comrades. He had been waiting ever since – thirteen years of backward glances and sideways steps, eased by short periods in which a sort of normalcy had taunted him with the pretence that it might be over.

It wasn't, though. He had survived National Socialism despite having pissed upon almost every one of its perverted principles, yet its unquiet corpse had assumed a new set of clothes and was shuffling behind him still, arm outstretched, having another go at finishing the job it could have concluded, easily and conveniently, against a wall at Plötzensee. A more pious man might have wondered if he were paying the price of past sins; someone with a better sense of humour would have enjoyed the irony of being chased for all the wrong reasons.

He got off the bus when it reached Ku'damm and stepped straight into a lunchtime crowd of office-workers, making himself as safe as a twig in a forest. Relief had become puzzlement, and now it was shading to anger. They couldn't know that he had no intention of exacting a price for what had been done, but their persistence hinted at the old arrogance - the assumption that they could do what they wanted, unhindered by the limits of the deep, dark holes into which they had crawled.

By the time he reached his shabby apartment block near the *krankenhaus* he was as agitated as he had been since the day the Allies arrived in Berlin. He had been told to wait, to be patient, to keep as grey a face as would turn attention elsewhere. It was sound advice, from a man he could trust as much as any, but in his present mood caution appealed as much as a winter plunge in the Westhafen. He wanted very much to light up something, and barely cared whether he'd be caught in the glare of it.

Which was why, when he had locked his apartment door, he picked up his tattered copy of Gindeley and forced himself to read a chapter. The edition he had bought as a young man hadn't survived his expulsion from university and every other faculty of the National Socialist State, but a lucky find while browsing dead people's furniture for his new home had restored a friend he had thought lost forever – a survey of Germany's earlier cataclysm, whose familiar toll of murder, starvation, rape and plague helped his own, hideous times fade to a sort of banality.

His mind was wandering through poor Magdeburg's besieged warrens once more, fancying vainly that at this time of reading the Swedish Army might somehow arrive in time to save the city, when a stray thought about consequences dragged him back forcibly to the broken now. The eternal problem was that those most deserving of restitution were least able to find it. The dead didn't make a fuss, point a finger, write memoirs or otherwise discommode those who had made them dead. A very few of the more important (or less fortunate) bastards had been show-tried and hanged, but the world had tired very quickly of pretending its righteous indignation. The DDR still made a few examples from time to time, but only because the effort was a cheap way of burnishing the Politburo's *kozi* principles. Adenauer's mob, in contrast, took care to step very carefully and widely around unpleasant historical truths. They used fading memories and natural mortality as a strategy, and quietly provided gainful employment to many of those who should have died or fled decently. In another decade or so, no one would care to recall their sins any more than they did those of Tilly and Pappenheim – not in Germany, at least.

He must have sensed this at some level for years, but bringing it out into the light put an edge to the day's discomforts, and his mind wouldn't return to the dimmer trials of 1628. He made some tea and ate a little, paced his bedroom-cum-study and half-determined to go out once more into the bright, dangerous world, and all the while a deadly whimsy churned what remained of his composure. He had no defence against persistence, other than camouflage. What he knew from back then might have the capacity to hurt some people still, but not necessarily the ones he wanted to deter. The trick – the marvellous but probably impossible trick – would be to get beneath the collars of men powerful enough to do something about his present tormentors in such a way as not to make his own removal seem the handiest solution. How the hell that might be done escaped him for the moment, but the weapon was there, ready to be used. It was a matter of finding a way to deploy and survive it.

1

Within moments of his arrival, the *kripo* decided that his foot badly needed an arse to occupy. His late father's assault battalion, fatally eager to get across no-man's-land on the first day of the Michael offensive, could hardly have churned ground more thoroughly than this. He looked up.

'Who found him?'

A young *polizeimeister* stepped forward. 'Me, sir.'

'And how many laps did you do before deciding you might be crushing the evidence?'

The lad reddened and stood straighter. 'I didn't. I determined the victim was deceased and then backed away in the footsteps I'd made on the way in.'

The *kripo* glanced around, and counted a further three pairs of legs with defrosted dew soaking their trousers and boots. One of them belonged to an *obermeister*, his vast belly and vaster slouch warmed by an outsized uniform and the air of immunity that a looming pension tends to encourage.

'Alright. Everyone who came to gawp, fuck off. Not you, son.'

The *kripo* stood from his crouch and waited for the pain in both knees to subside. He nodded at the spectacle.

'What do you think?'

Being asked an investigator's opinion was probably a new experience for the *polizeimeister*, but he didn't let the surprise show.

'He's cold and stiff, so it happened a few hours ago. There's a lot of blood. He wasn't killed somewhere else and brought here. I didn't see much of his hands ...'

'There doesn't look to have been a struggle.'

'Did he know the killer, then?'

'A good question. And how well?'

'I don't ...'

'I'm thinking aloud, son.'

'Right. Obviously, the killer took time to arrange the victim afterwards.'

'Which means that at least some of the blood transferred to hands and clothes.'

'Someone must have seen something, then.'

The *kripo* pulled a face. 'Not necessarily. It was freezing last night, there's no lighting around here and we're a long way from houses. If he – or they - had a car waiting close by, well ...'

He looked down once more upon the handiwork of persons unknown. The dead man was in his late forties or early fifties (and likely to remain that way), clean-shaven and formerly of adequate means, if his shoes could be trusted not to lie. On the slight slope his feet pointed towards and almost touched the waterline. His face was calm, the eyes closed; his clothes were sodden but neatly smoothed out, as if an undertaker had taken care to make the best of what he'd been given. Only the broad grin that a razor or similar had placed upon his throat spoiled the impression of peaceful repose, undisturbed by the large, clumsy feet that had ploughed up the crocus buds around him.

He turned to the younger man (whose presence he'd demanded only because his partner was on sick leave and peace of mind, no less than regulations, demanded that the task be shared) and patted his shoulder.

'Get back to your station and dry out. Write up a report and send it to me today. You did well.'

The lad looked pleased, though taunts about arse-kissing would no doubt rain down upon him later that morning. He disappeared through the bushes and was replaced almost immediately by the death-cart men and an older fellow with a leather briefcase, one act seamlessly following another on a depraved music-hall bill.

The attending Corpse Examiner was a former Waffen SS field-surgeon named Beltze, a familiar face. He nodded amiably at the *kripo*, who stepped to one side to give him access to the business.

'You won't be doing overtime on this one, Ernst. I'd guess the cause of death was large-scale transfer of bodily fluids from indoors to out.'

'Oh, don't spoil the fun, Melchior. The last real mystery I had was the wife leaving.'

'Why she didn't go earlier?'

The Examiner stabbed a forefinger at the mandatory punch-line and settled to his knees.

'Jesus, it's cold. How close did you get?'

'Not very. I thought I'd save you the sticky surprises.'

'Well ...' Beltze bent down and thrust his face closely to one that no longer minded the intimacy of strangers. '... he died quietly.'

'What do you mean?'

'Come here.'

The *kripo* got closer this time, and the faint smell was immediately recognizable.

'Chloroform.'

'A litre of the stuff, from the strength of it still. Very strange'

'Why?'

'Someone didn't want him to suffer, but killed him anyway.'

'It probably wasn't tenderness. He was meant to be a quiet, compliant victim.'

'Ah.' The examiner climbed to his feet and nodded at the ambulance men. 'Well, he was that, certainly. We're a little busy at the moment with the diphtheria thing, but I'll let you have something to give to the British by tomorrow evening. '

'Good. They like to have paperwork, even if they do nothing with it.'

The *kripo* watched as the ambulance men wrapped the body carefully. The dampness had settled on his war-wounded chest like an old, unwelcome friend, and he was beginning to miss his lost breakfast. He coughed and half-reached for a cigarette before the head reminded the hand that the habit was history.

The good doctor noticed the movement, reached into his bag and removed a flask.

'Brandy – cheap, but French.'

'God, thanks, Ernst.' The *kripo* took a deeper draught than was polite and only reluctantly replaced the cap. The Examiner repossessed his flask and sipped at it. He was looking around, at the river bank to either side of the crime scene and the broad expanse of the Havel before him. Its surface was half-frozen near the shore, but a thin drizzle was blurring the moving surface in midstream. The air was acoustically deadened, and deathly peaceful. He shook his head.

'It's too nice a place for this sort of shit.'

The *kripo* shrugged. 'So are many places. That didn't stop us shitting on them in the good old days.'

The other man turned and gave him a tired smile. 'I would offer you the usual line about duty and honour, but …'

'… you don't want to be kicked so early in the day.'

They laughed. That, and the victim's removal, lifted the mood slightly. The large patch where light snow had been muddied might have been a deer's bed the previous night, except for the bloodstains that rain would soon dilute to a smaller matter than they were. The brandy in the *kripo*'s stomach gave an illusion of warmth, the first he'd felt since leaving his home almost two hours earlier, and like all slivers of comfort it eased what had preceded it. A murder investigation would be opened and the perpetrators caught (or not), nothing would resurrect the dead man before the day came to them all, and that was the sum of what could be said or done for the moment. He turned, gave his surroundings a final glance (strange, that he lived so close to such beauty yet hadn't been here since before the war) and shook the examiner's hand.

'Let's leave the ducks to their ice-skating …'

The bushes rustled once more and the young *polizeimeister* emerged, his face redder than the unfortunate hair perched above it. The warm glow in the *kripo*'s gut faded more quickly than a winter sunset.

'What is it, lad?'

'A civilian called in at Moritzstrasse ten minutes ago. He's found another one, about half a kilometre upstream.'

2

Otto Fischer was humming tunelessly, staring through his magnifier into the privy parts of a Bifora, when young Renate's cough almost made him drop his dust blower.

'The storeroom's clean, Herr Director. I've rearranged the stock to match the invoice dates, so the first to be despatched is on the top shelf. I'll have my lunch now. Would you like me to bring soup?'

For several months now he had practised not wincing at *Herr Director*, but the hundred or so squandered *Call me Otto, please, Renate*s weighed on him still. She didn't seem to be deaf to anything else, so he assumed that her mother had given strict instructions in this particular regard. Strict was what the lady did best, he'd found.

'Thank you, Renate. Pea, please.'

For a moment it looked as if she might argue the point. Among the post that morning had been a pamphlet on nutrition, issued by the City Senate, identifying several foods as essential to good health which had previously been in short supply. Leading the list was tomatoes, and Renate, a model citizen, was more likely to defect to the East during her break than not have tomato soup today.

He was tempted to surrender and let her choose – a concession in lieu of the decent wage he didn't pay her. She had become too valuable to risk losing, though he hadn't thought himself in need of an assistant when her mother first volunteered her. For the gift of Renate at least, he was grateful. The other legacy of his four months' lodging at her family home (a temporary eviction from his shop on Curtius-Strasse during its conversion from bomb-damaged slum to state-of-the-times retail premises) was much less welcome. Frau Knipper's plans for her guest had matured in that brief pause, and no less remorselessly than those of a certain Austrian gentleman for Poland. Not usually of an optimistic bent, Fischer had put far too much faith in his mutilations' ability to fight off sentimental feelings (not realising that sentimentality played very little part in the lady's expectations), but a recent series of invitations to Sunday dinner at the Knipper home had put him right on the situation. It took no degree of paranoia to sense his knees being nailed into place beneath the dining table as he ate her excellent, ensnaring fare.

Renate was out of the door before he could change his mind about pea. He abandoned his mechanisms, put on a shop-coat and took up counter duties until she returned (which would be in twenty-nine minutes precisely, God and other natural disasters permitting). His working clocks had chimed noon some moments earlier, so he could expect a brief rush of busy customers, dropping off or collecting their prized (and usually worthless) heirlooms. Perhaps someone with a little spare time would pause to browse the small but carefully chosen selection of classical recordings he offered for sale, which would give him the opportunity to play something on one of his mended gramophones and speak of matters other than repairs and their cost. He enjoyed his work, but not nearly as much as he did the diversions.

Today brought no music lovers, however. He took three ailing clocks, wrote out tickets and was expecting Renate's return imminently when Udo Franke stepped in and greyed the day considerably. He was a retired bank manager who lived around the corner on villa-strewn Baselerstrasse, and possessed several virtues that made his acquaintance as attractive as that of haemorrhoids. He was a snob (and proud of it), a gossip, a man as certain of his opinions as Moses, and, worst of all, a fellow widower with all the time in the world to indulge himself. As a mere tradesman Fischer might have hoped to avoid his condescension, but wristwatches, clocks and gramophones appeared to occupy a fatally elevated position in Franke's league table of respectable purveyances. Whenever he sought ears for his opinions, *Fischer's Time-pieces and Gramophones* was prone to be burdened with a visit.

As always, he paused briefly to frown at the renovated stock (as if he might actually buy something) before getting down to the real business.

'Have you heard the news, Herr Fischer?'

During the past month, US ships had helped evacuate defeated Nationalist forces from the Chinese mainland to Taiwan, and the British had signed a pact with several Middle Eastern countries that shared an objection to Israel being Israel. More immediately relevant to Fischer, a brilliant young Canadian pianist had given his first concert to a US audience in Philadelphia, and Berlin's RCA agent had spread the word that the occasion had been recorded and would be available soon. It was very likely that none of these events had roused Franke from his warm home on a chill April day.

'What news is that?'

Franke nodded knowingly. 'Another one. The fifth.'

Putting a number on it dispelled the mist. Since the previous January, four men had been found murdered at various locations in the Borough of Spandau. An investigation was dragging its feet, and public concern was being amplified helpfully by a thousand rumours regarding the perpetrator and his motives (of which about nine hundred had been breeched on Baselerstrasse). Fischer began to long for Renate's brisk, unwelcoming presence.

'Ah, a tragedy. Have the police said anything new?'

'Of course not! They're confounded! It's as I've said, the murderer is one of their own, and can anticipate *every* possible line of enquiry.'

Fischer's memory couldn't drag out this theory from all the others he'd hardly listened to, so he said nothing. To his disinterested mind, the killings bore strong marks of gang-related business, of bad people disposing of their own. This was poor fare for the ardent gossip, however (being logical, unexceptional and expected), and Herr Franke had spurned it as all but witless.

He was saved the trouble of responding when the door opened once more and Frau Lemke entered. Whereas Franke was a mere gossip, the Pastor's wife had been known to embarrass radio masts (her status giving her unfettered access to the district's unwashed laundry, much of which she displayed assiduously). Her pronouncement on the killings had been early and definitive - the perpetrator was a man wronged by some secretive society upon whose members he was now taking his bloody revenge. Though she could not as yet speak to the specifics of this injustice, no doubt it fell out of some dark obligation, or blood-price unpaid, or demonic rite.

Fischer hadn't seen Frau Lemke for some weeks, but her theory had infected much of Lichterfelde and he was well aware of it. He found it only half-ludicrous, given the ample opportunities for lasting grudges that the times had thrown up, though it was curious that any German could imagine still that evil required satanic intervention. It made him wonder if her husband's sermons had given her a false optimism regarding human nature.

As her professional rival, Franke had derided Frau Lemke's theory often (and loudly), but not to her face. He smiled now and gave her a little bow, an acknowledgement of the social rank they shared. She returned it solemnly and removed a travelling clock from her bag. Fischer took it, examined it briefly and without comment placed it in a drawer beneath the counter. It was working perfectly, so she could only wish to sell it - a hint of financial straits that Franke would broadcast to the entire district within the hour, if he suspected. Fischer wrote out a repair ticket and gave it to the lady.

'Late afternoon today, Frau Lemke?'

She sniffed and turned to Franke. 'Have you heard? It's five, now.'

Fischer's morale was about to step off the cliff's edge once more when the doorbell announced Renate's return from lunch, a peal no less beautiful to his ears than that of the *Petersglocke*. Frau Lemke struggled briefly, but the magic of bloody murder had been dispelled. She closed her mouth, gave Franke a shake of the head that conveyed all her disgust, fear, revulsion and deep satisfaction at the world's depravities and shuffled out. Franke himself resisted for a few moments more, but he had tested Renate's indifference too often to be hopeful, and the near-inevitable appearance of Jonas Kleiber in the doorway behind her killed the moment entirely. Kleiber was a local journalist, a breed that gossips sought out as pilgrims did salvation; but he was an oddity, a hack who ignored all rumour until it gained evidential legs. He was also known to be brutally thrifty with his own news. If someone wanted to milk him for facts they were obliged to put hand in pocket and acquire the latest edition of the *Süd-west Berliner Zeitung*.

Defeated, Franke nodded morosely to Fischer and pointed himself at the door. Kleiber evacuated enough space to let him pass, stepped in and smiled nervously at the proprietor. He had been chased out of the shop too many times in recent weeks to take a welcome for granted, but today he had more than earned a loitering permit. Without a word, Fischer took his soup from Renate and left the young ones to their painfully-protracted courtship.

He had eaten only half of his lunch when Kleiber came into the workshop and offered his usual souvenir of a POW's extended vacation in Northern England.

'Ay up, Otto.'

'Has she told you to bugger off already?'

'No. Well, not quite. Did you hear about the murder?'

'You saw Franke. What do you think?'

'What did he say?'

'Why? You don't care.'

'I just want to know what folk think they know.'

'Really? Well, they're saying that this makes five, and that just about anyone and everyone probably did it.'

'Oh.'

Kleiber watched quietly while the pea soup was finished off. This was untypically restrained behaviour - so much so that Fischer almost felt the pressure of a lid wanting to be lifted. He wiped his mouth and looked up.

'What's wrong?'

'I don't know. But it's seven, not five. Bodies, I mean.'

'Are you sure?'

'I spoke to a *wachtmeister* I know in Spandau. He wouldn't say a word about the business until I got a few drinks into him, and then it was all nose-tapping and I-wouldn't-believe-what-he-knows. You know the sort - once they get that far they can't not say more. Anyway, the first two killings happened on the same day in January, as you'll recall.'

Fischer shook his head. 'The bodies were *found* on the same day. We haven't been told enough to conclude more.'

'Oh, right. Well, after that, another turned up later that month, one in February and now another one, yes?'

'That's what we hear.'

'Well, my fellow says that a further two were found last month that never got onto an incident sheet.'

'Why? I mean, how?'

'The police were still shuffling around the bodies – they were *found* together – when some nice Suits turned up, waved identity cards and closed it all down.'

'Can they do that?'

'I don't know, but they did. And within half an hour they had the evidence removed to somewhere that a police warrant or Berlin coroner can't follow. Obviously, rumours have been buzzing around the stations since.'

'That the dead men were special?'

'Yeah.'

'So why wasn't news of the other killings closed down also?'

Kleiber shrugged. 'The other corpses weren't special?'

'The Suits were Germans, I assume, or you would have said otherwise.'

'Yeah.'

'Possibly Intelligencers, then. How would they know that the others weren't *special* unless they investigated?'

'Well, *you* were one of them once. What do you think?'

Until that moment Fischer hadn't realised that he was a source, but it hardly bothered him. He would gladly give Kleiber everything he knew about the Gehlen Organization, because that was precisely nothing. Since they'd moved to Pullach he didn't even have an address.

'I worked for the Org for about ten minutes, back in '47. They were still trying to get their bearings at the time, so I didn't notice too much cold, ruthless efficiency. It looks like they've got better at what they do since then.'

'What do you think it is? I mean, these two missing bodies?'

'Jonas, I have no idea. Perhaps they were just criminal types who happened to have some sort of pull with Authority, who then reclaimed them.'

'Unlikely, surely?'

'I was only making the point that we can hardly guess who they were, or why they were made dead. It might be that someone who didn't like them took advantage of the other killings to put their own victims among them, hoping to lose any attention in a crowd of corpses.'

Kleiber brightened. 'I like that. It's sneaky.'

'It's just my head, playing games.'

'I won't quote you.'

Fischer picked up one of his tiny screwdrivers and squinted into his magnifying frame.

'Very wise. Herr Franke is as likely to have the right answer as me. Now, let me get on with this pig of a watch.'

'You aren't curious? You were police, once.'

'No, Jonas, I'm not. Bad things happen. You can certainly quote me on *that*.'

A small commotion in the shop made both men glance towards the doorway separating it from the repair room. Renate's plaintive voice warmed the back of the large man who filled it suddenly.

'This is not a public area!'

The *large* had no fat to it, being made up of sinew, muscle and bone, topped by a proportionate head. A well-knuckled hand removed the hat to reveal what had once been the average Prussian nobleman's preferred hair-style.

The apparition nodded respectfully. 'Herr Professor Doctor Fischer?'

Fischer sighed and replaced the screwdriver on his workbench.

'I was recommended to you?'

'You were, sir, yes.'

'The recommending party was a one-legged gentleman, a police officer in the Rhineland-Palatinate's *Landespolizei*?'

'He warned you, then?'

'I deduced it from the available evidence.'

The large man looked at Fischer with great respect. 'He said you were good.'

'I'm not. There's only one person of my acquaintance who'd oversell me so wilfully. That would be *Oberrat* Friedrich Holleman.'

Kleiber, who stood between the proprietor and the newcomer, turned to the former, his nerve-endings detonated by mention of the name. Two years earlier, he had (in his own words) *flung himself heroically* into the maelstrom of the East German Uprising to search for Holleman's wife, and even now it was only necessary to raise the memory of it for the resident twitch in his left eye to recommence transmissions. Hastily, Fischer sought some clarification that might calm the young man.

'If it's about the attempted break-in last month …'

'It's not. I'm not police.'

'What are you?'

'Luftwaffe, back then. It's how I know Freddie. I used to repair the 'planes he abused, until the day he forgot to bring one home.' The knuckles extended. 'Jens Lamsdorf.'

The grip was firm but not brutal, and Fischer's bad hand made no complaint. 'What are you now?'

'The same, in a way. Only I make parts for aircraft instead of begging them. This is me …'

He handed a card to Fischer. It was uninformative, a tastefully blank whiteness embossed only with *Fehr-Lamsdorf Flugzeugwerke GmbH* and a thin, black border.

'I didn't know the Allies allowed us to build aircraft.'

'They don't. We produce components for British and French companies.'

'You have the tooling for that?'

'We bought up what Messerschmitt no longer needed.'

Fischer returned the card. 'And how may *Fischer's Time-pieces and Gramophones* assist your company?'

'It can't. I just need the Fischer part.'

'For what?'

Lamsdorf glanced at Kleiber and thought about it for a moment. 'A disappearance.'

'I hardly ever dealt with missing persons.'

'No. I want you to arrange one.'

3

Unthinkingly, Fischer rubbed his 'lucky' shoulder - a designation
first applied, and very gently, by Jonas Kleiber. An area of his body
that, to date, had stopped half a tank of aviation fuel and two bullets
wouldn't have struck most people as being in the least fortunate, but
the most recent projectile, burrowing enthusiastically into already-
traumatized tissue, had thrown him backwards and spoiled his own,
uncertain aim, putting one of his last two bullets neatly into a would-
be assassin's eye. The constant ache of that two-year-old wound
intensified whenever stress accelerated the blood-flow through it - a
price he accepted gladly for its reminder that he could feel things
still.

He released the damaged article and swept a hand over the engine-
room of his commercial empire. 'I mend time-pieces and
gramophones - and sell them, sometimes. I don't do much removals
work.'

Lamsdorf glanced around at the evidence. He didn't seem
convinced.

'Freddie told me what you did for him back in '43. It would have
been much harder then than now, yet the Party never caught up with
him. Hell, the fact that he's breathing still is the best testimonial he
could offer.'

Kleiber's left eye was on the move once more. 'Right. I don't need to hear any more of this. I'll go and bother Renate.'

When he had gone, Fischer picked up his screwdriver and ailing Bifora once more, palely hoping that the hint would suffice. An envelope, landing heavily on the workbench, did for the last of his optimism. He looked up.

'I have plenty of work at the moment.'

'How many customers have you seen today?'

'Eight, so far.' He spoke defiantly, and it sounded pitiful even to his ear.

Lamsdorf nodded at the envelope. 'That's more than you'll take in six good months, probably. If you do things properly there'll be another like it when you're finished.'

'I'm not sentimental about National Socialism. Helping …'

'He isn't that, believe me. If he were, the envelope would be going to one of the rat-lines. They have all the expertise in the world.'

'Go to them anyway. Say that your man used to polish Mengele's proctoscope. It might get him a discount.'

'His foreskin might get in the way of that story.'

'He's misplaced it?'

'When they were both thirteen.'

Curiosity got a good grip before Fischer could smother it. 'Why is he still here, then? If he wants to be safe he need only go to the *Zentrairat* and apply for an Israeli passport. It'll take about half an hour, and they'll probably give him lunch while he waits.'

'He doesn't want to leave. It's just necessary that his present self disappears.'

'For how long?'

'Until he stops breathing.'

'That …' with an effort, Fischer stopped wondering who and what this was about. 'If he remains in Germany, he can't be certain that he won't be recognized.'

'It's a risk he accepts. At least it won't be family or old friends who make him.'

No, that wasn't likely. There were few Jews in western Germany these days, and most of those hailed originally from somewhere east of the Oder. Which begged the question …

'He's German?'

'Yes.'

'He should do something about his missing skin.'

'You're joking?'

'I mean, he needs a hospital record to show that it was removed other than ritually - he had phimosis and couldn't piss properly, something like that. It'll deflect attention if or when he's treated by a doctor, otherwise he'll be remembered.'

'That's clever.'

'It's a suggestion. Offer it to whoever you find to do this.'

If the other man was discouraged he hid it well, leaving the envelope where it was, letting its girth do the work for him. Fischer shook his head.

'Money isn't that important to me. I do well with very little.'

Lamsdorf picked up the package and held it, jigging his hand slightly as if gauging its weight. When he spoke once more it was almost a whisper.

'You don't even need to meet the man. It's an exercise, in camouflage - probably a few hours work, a little expenditure on the right sort of expertise to change a signature and frank a document. Wouldn't it be an interesting exercise, to help a man who deserves help?'

Fischer began to suspect that Herr Lamsdorf's previous employer had been Goebbels, not Göring. An appeal that managed to tease both his vanity and altruism, with a cherry denominated in Deutsche Marks to sweeten it further, wasn't something he'd had much practise fighting off. If he was honest, and despite his pretended indifference, a little windfall wasn't something to be spurned for no good reason. It would go a long way towards broadening his business, or give him the means to walk away if ever it became a mere job.

He tried to resist the burrowing worm, told himself that he had no cause to complain about his present life and routine. So they were hardly over-burdened by challenges, much less novelty – was that so bad? His present life was comfortable, fitting him as he'd fashioned it to do. Sleep and work consumed most of his time and preoccupations; otherwise, he went to the cinema (rarely), dined out at a small Italian restaurant in Steglitz (once a week, alone and modestly) or drank at his favourite bar in Schloss-Strasse (whenever the mood took him), and in between times fought off invitations to join the Luftwaffe Veterans' Association and local Rotary Club. There were far worse regimes a man could put himself through, but that was partly what was feeding the worm - the remorseless accumulation of days, blurring into uniform greyness, preyed upon him much as it did any ageing widower. He was more tempted, and less troubled, by a stranger's strange offer than he should have been.

'Do I have time to think about this?'

'An answer tomorrow would be helpful. The matter's becoming urgent.'

Fischer nodded. 'How old is the gentleman?'

'Forty-one, I believe.'

A very convenient age, for a certain kind of need. A whole generation of German men who otherwise would have been forty-one in 1955 had chosen instead to find anonymous graves in countless locations between home and the furthest points of the Reich's lunatic surge. From this disaster, bereaved families had gained paltry (and short-term) pensions, Slavic soil some vital nutrients and document-forgers a vast reservoir of unwanted identities.

'Any distinguishing marks? Scars?'

'Apart from the gone foreskin, none.'

Fischer wanted to stop there, because a further show of interest was another way of saying yes; but his mind had begun to shuffle the various possibilities into line. A good identity was one that couldn't be sniffed out easily. It would require that a dead soldier or sailor be found whose demise hadn't been caught by WASt as more than a missing-in-action (and someone, ideally, who hailed from East Germany, in order to lessen the chance of an old friend bumping into the right name with the wrong face in years to come). Of course, WASt had been permitted to continue to function after the war, so it was possible that a few lost souls had been recaptured by random twitches of fate over the past decade. He – someone - would need to be careful, and a visit to the War Graves Commission might be necessary, too. If it was to be done right, the many possible stumbles averted, whoever took the job would be put to more inconvenience than Lamsdorf seemed to imagine. Every officious little clerk he approached would squint and want to know why; every form submitted would be pored over for the slightest discrepancy; and finding the right – that is, competent and discrete – papers-man would involve at least a partial descent into the underbelly of a city that was only just beginning to rediscover its respectability. Looked at from every side, it wasn't a job for anyone who didn't really appreciate the money, or who preferred the quiet life, or who had the sense not to invite the sort of trouble that couldn't be measured until it was already chewing a man's ankles.

Fischer glanced around at his safe haven, its many broken mechanisms pleading for his tender, reasonably well-recompensed attention, and sighed.

'I'll need a photograph. At least three copies. And not a recent one, obviously.'

4

Rolf Hoeschler examined the evidence carefully. He felt as if he were betraying a trust by doing so, though she had offered it freely, without being asked. Really, he shouldn't have felt guilty, but there it was. And there *it* was.

He'd married into money. Wealth, in fact - the sort that sits on a man's waist, or side by side in his large garage, or displays itself wantonly in every one of the many rooms of his tastefully furnished demi-mansion - the sort that ordinary men never hope or expect to sniff in passing, much less have paraded for their edification and approval.

Fuck me Up and Down.

Her hand stroked the back of his neck. 'I didn't want you to want me for more than me.'

He wondered how she could even have thought it. She was beautiful, witty and did things out of uniform that were probably illegal in God-fearing societies; yet she'd waited almost two months to break the news as if her courage had needed to be summoned. A few years earlier she had almost had him killed, and that hadn't turned out to be an impediment to their present happiness. How could she imagine that money might be?

Like most ex-paratroopers, former spies and defected policemen he knew very little about book-keeping, but the quantity of zeroes that kept company with each other didn't need much parsing. Her stock of properties was listed in the ledger's frontispiece, and required the best part of the page to itself. He'd known that she made money from rents, but this was spectacular. He was looking at what must have been half of Schöneberg, with a fat slice of Dahlem to keep it company.

'How ...?' The likely answer suggested itself while his mouth was still open. 'You stole General Myasnik's money?'

She shook her head. 'The day he was summoned to Karlshorst he knew he was a dead man. Before he left he gave me what he called my back-wages. It was in dollars, a lot of dollars, more than I could have earned in ten years any legal way.'

'Why would he do that?' Hoeschler had no right to be jealous about a historical arrangement (of whatever degree of moistness), but no new husband cares to decide whether he prefers to be a recovering cuckold or pimp.

She shrugged. 'He used to tell me that I was his daughter. The first time he said it I thought, here comes the sick stuff; but it never did. He was ... strange with me. He could have a man dismembered without twitching, and then, ten minutes later, cry when I sang *Bayu Bayushki Bayu* to him. He didn't have family, so I suppose I filled a hole.'

Hoeschler had almost become one of the General's dismemberments (and been put in one or more of a different of kind of hole thereafter), so he didn't think of disbelieving her. Still, it was strange that she had stayed here, in Berlin's American Zone, where her former crimes – against Americans, principally - had been committed.

'You didn't think to run with the money?'

'Run where? I don't know anywhere else. This is where I could put it to best use.'

'You just bought up properties?'

'Not immediately; but having so much cash and nowhere to hide it made me nervous. They say that bricks and mortar are always a safe bet, so I looked for half-ruins that the Americans hadn't commandeered, hired a few decent men I knew from Tempelhof to do the renovations and paid them decently. They've stayed loyal and I give them more work as it comes up.'

'And you get rents.'

She gave him the shrug again. 'People need a roof. It's not a business that has bad years. Sometimes tenants get on in the world and want to buy their places, and I always say yes. The money goes into new properties and renovations.'

He glanced around their apartment. It was warm, comfortable, a little too small for two people (and an actual squeeze when his boy was home from college), and until now he hadn't thought it anything but adequate. But he recalled their wedding feast here and the slight twinkle in the eye of his best man as he cast his eye around the fixtures and fittings. Hoeschler had assumed at the time that it had been about his entering the staid, respectable state of matrimony; but Otto Fischer had a fine detective's eye and could spot things that amateurs couldn't, so perhaps the twinkle had been more to do with what all former members of *Fallschirmjäger* appreciated - a luxuriously soft landing.

He closed the ledger. She was waiting to be reassured, and he hardly knew how to do it. He wasn't going to resent her success, or become impotent because it wasn't he who was bringing home the potatoes - hell, if she asked him to collect the rents he'd do it happily, knowing that the cash going into his pocket would stay there, so to speak. It was just that he wasn't familiar with the protocols of praise, not regarding commercial matters. *This is all very satisfactory* didn't seem enough.

He tipped his head to one side and regarded her. 'The first time I ever saw you I knew you were trouble.'

She laughed and hugged him. 'I am, always.'

'You pay your taxes?'

'Religiously, and resentfully.'

'There's no-one looking to break your legs?'

'I don't deal with bad people. If you find anything in there that's crooked I'll retire.'

He sighed. 'Well, that's all good, then. But don't ask *me* to retire.'

For fifteen months now he'd been working as a clerk at BVG's headquarters on Potsdamerstrasse, one of the heroic cadre of men and women who made the trams and buses run, and sometimes on time. It was a pleasantly boring job, one in which no one thought or needed to aim a gun at his head in the hours between clocking in and out. If he kept his head down, worked hard and put in a little extra he might even achieve some sort of promotion in the next ten or twenty years; in the meantime, it had financed his boy's mechanical engineering course in Frankfurt and left him enough money to eat, most days. For a while that had been enough, but then he had become lonely in his vast, two-room hovel and gone looking for company – specifically, to test the sincerity of a woman who had once told him to not to be a stranger.

These days, Germans knew better than to employ the phrase *it's a funny old world*, but it held enough truth still to trip a man. He had thought that it would be difficult - a matter of dogged detection, of stirring old dust. He could recall her address of course, and with the help of only a little alcohol had found the courage to knock on its door. When an old lady opened it, he had asked without much hope if she knew the present whereabouts of one Mila Henze.

I should do, she had told him; *I pay rent to her every month. And if you see her before I do, tell her my boiler needs mending.*

So, little more than two hours after he had made the decision to excavate his past he was sitting in Mila's new, nicer apartment, sipping tea politely and asking after her health as if they were slightly distant acquaintances who had never banged each other; as if she had never wrapped her naked legs around him while the General's thugs coshed and tied him; as if eight years had been the turn of a single, unstained page between then and now. She had been equally formal, speaking of her *modest* business and enquiring about the minor matter of his defection to the west, carefully avoiding any mention of her former occupation or connections. This civilized exchange had continued for about twenty minutes, after which she had kissed him passionately and then straddled him on the floor between their chairs. The old world had seemed *funny* for all the right reasons, that day.

Five weeks later they were married, she having proposed to him while he was distracted by a menu in the most expensive restaurant he'd ever visited. He'd said yes of course, because no gentleman wants to disappoint a lady, and since then his life had become the warm, confusing confection that a farewell to bachelorhood usually is. Until today, that is.

It was a first-in-class of a revelation. Added to his other blessings, it made him wonder if he was being lofted on silken pillows towards the mother of all falls. The Hoeschlers, sons and daughters of the (not very fertile) soil, had never been lucky historically, veering between smallholding and outright serfdom, leavened by just enough education to send the occasional male into town work. He was probably the most fortunate of his line (coming out of the war with hardly a scratch to boast of), but that was to say very little. The ledger he held in his slightly damp hands was saying something more.

She was waiting with a sort of Christmas morning expectation, daring him not to be delighted.

'You've done ... very well. The money's in a safe place?'

'Everything that's not for day-to-day expenses goes to an account at the Hamburgische Landesbank.'

'Hamburg? Why?'

'I don't trust the Russians and Americans not to fight over Berlin. It's better to have money where it can't be burned.'

That was it - his entire stock of sensible questions exhausted. Not knowing what else to say he hugged her, which was obviously the correct thing to do because she didn't let go for almost a minute. He used the time to wonder how life was when the struggle went away, and how easily he'd be able to adapt to it. For some reason, the weight of either question didn't press too brutally.

He should have known better. When she released him he saw the look again, the one she'd worn when handing him the ledger. It was the sort of look that makes a man expect news of an affair or impending triplets, but he doubted the first, and, as she was fifty-two years old, would have put her on a circus-bill for the latter. This was something else, and before she could tell him he was feeling what might almost have been a sense of relief at there being a price for his undeserved good fortune.

'About the Americans …'

5

During his final year in Sachsenhausen, Fischer had shared a hut with one of Dönitz's senior officers, a man who had graduated from a school of such hard knocks that a mere NKVD Special Camp must have seemed like a recuperation detail. His name was Wilhelm, and even several years after the fact he remained puzzled by his wartime elevation from the North Atlantic to paperwork (though by then so many U-boats had been sunk beneath him that a desk was probably the only available command remaining). Pondering the vast panorama of hut ceiling from their bunks, the two veterans had swapped stories of their service days and discovered a mutual loathing of plummeting, though Fischer had to concede that crushing pressure, foul air, claustrophobia and a single shitter between forty-five men probably trumped his own, largely theoretical fear of parachutes remaining snug in their packs. In the years since, whenever he recalled those conversations it was with a slight sense of awe at the inventiveness of their race, that men could find so many different and exotic ways of killing themselves badly.

At the moment he was thinking of Wilhelm's particular *bête noire*, ASDIC, because his own instrument was pinging rapidly. It had become more sensitive with age, though its lack of directionality made it more tormenting than useful. All it told him was that something wasn't right, when what he needed to know was where to jump to avoid the likely mess.

The money-padded envelope was locked in his safe but he could hear it clearly still, whistling an uncomfortably half-syncopated tune. Why had he said yes? Why had Freddie Holleman recommended him on the strength of a false identity that on several occasions had bitten both their arses? If there was one industry in Germany that had thrived since the war it was that which made a man someone else. There were hundreds of craftsmen in well-equipped cellars, expertly altering old documents, tea-staining new ones or excising damning evidence from those that should have gone up in smoke with the rest of the Reich. Why would Otto Fischer be pushed to the front of that parade?

He hadn't spoken to Freddie for almost two months. Despite loving the man, he had tired of hearing what was wrong with Trier, with the probationary assignment to the city's regular police force (rather than the *Landeskriminalamt*) and with the unspectacular view from the new Holleman home (in the eastern part of the city, too far from the river). Above all, he was sick of the rants about the local Occupying 'Power' – which, surreally in 1955, remained … Luxembourg. His old friend regarded it as Germany's greatest shame, to be administered by a State that couldn't put together a football league without recourse to kidnapping Belgians. Whenever they spoke, he had some new, bad joke about the place.

Otto, listen - what does a Luxembourgeois driving instructor say to his pupil'

I don't know, Freddie.

'Claude, tomorrow you'll be doing a three-point-turn, so don't forget your passport.' Ha!

So he had taken to avoiding the telephone, and Holleman, busily trying to cram new police protocols, hardly ever thought to pick up the receiver. His wife Kristin called occasionally and that was always a pleasure, but otherwise Fischer was content to know that they were safe enough to be bored with life not-quite-overlooking the Moselle.

Yet a call to Freddie was now unavoidable, and it couldn't be put off until his mood improved. He had hardly dialled the final number for *Direktion* Trier when Renate came – staggered - into the workshop with what a glance told him was a late 1920s Vox table-top gramophone (an instrument he could repair with his eyes closed and which almost certainly had a bad case of grating metal governors). He shook his head, pointed at the receiver, and she about-faced with comical precision. By this time the voice on the other end of the 'phone had repeated its question impatiently. Fischer asked for *Polizeioberrat* Holleman, and was told to wait.

The voice returned some twenty seconds later. 'He's out of the office. Is this police business?'

Any 'business' of a superior officer might well involve the sort of people who could make life hard for a duty *meister*, so the curtness was cut with a tinge of respect. Needing the message to get through, Fischer lied cheerfully.

'Of course. A matter of some urgency, but confidential. He has my number.'

'Your name, please?'

'Professor Doctor Fischer, speaking from Berlin.'

It pleased him that he'd managed both to return the facetious joke and do Freddie Holleman a small favour (matters that crossed several jurisdictions could hardly fail to burnish a new man's reputation). He also felt the slight, craven relief of having tried to discharge a chore and had it put off. The matter of the envelope and fugitive Jews deferred, he went into the shop to discuss the Vox's repair with its owner, a middle-aged gentleman whose finely-cut clothes suggested that he might have borne the cost of a new machine with little difficulty.

'It was a gift from my wife, to mark the release of my orchestra's first recording – the first with me as a member, that is. That was in '32.'

A naked nymph couldn't have seized Fischer's attention more completely. For the next few minutes he interrogated his customer politely but thoroughly, lamenting the viola's limited repertoire and sympathising sincerely with the gentleman's subsequent, enforced descent (due entirely to artistic differences with the Third Reich) into the debased world of music hall accompaniment. It was time wasted of course, and Fischer could feel Renate's accusing gaze warming the side of his face as the two men meandered through half-recalled glades in Germany's flattened cultural woodlands; but conversations like this were as close to a holiday as he was ever likely to wander. It made the interruption all the more painful.

Renate went to answer the telephone and *Herr Director*'d him at a parade sergeant's volume. He made his excuses to the Violist, shoo'd her back into the shop and lifted the receiver.

'Hello, Otto.'

Fischer's ASDIC pinged once more. A normal conversation with Freddie Holleman required some preliminary patience while a head of steam was given the space and time to vent. *Hello, Otto* sounded serious.

'Hello, Freddie. How's Trier?'

'Fine. The job's something that little Otto could do in his spare time off the potty, and Kristin's like a stuck needle about the house they found for us; but the money's good and I should get into Criminal Division soon. They told me you called.'

A concise, informative answer that wandered almost nowhere - this was definitely Freddie Worried.

'You recommended me to an old comrade. To disappear someone. Why?'

'Yeah. Jens was ground staff at our field in Belgium, a good guy. He said he had a mate who needed to be someone else. I told him that I'd been in the same place and that you'd got me out of it.'

'He can be trusted not to put one between my shoulders?'

'Um, yes – definitely, yes.'

Strangely, Fischer wasn't reassured. 'What is it, Freddie?'

The long silence that followed made him grateful that the public-service budget of the Rhine-Palatinate was shouldering the call.

'He, ah, he's a sharp one, is Jens. Back in '40 the squadron couldn't have kept going without him. We were pushing forward fast and getting shot up pretty badly, so repairs were critical. He and his cronies in other ground crews in Luftflotte 2 had a sort of arrangement to barter spares as and when desperately needed. I say barter; it was an open secret that equipment movements were accounted for but some sort of commission was being skimmed off. No one minded, not even Headquarters – it seemed fair enough, seeing that we were being kept in the air. I never saw him again after I got shot down, but mates who visited the one-legged ward told me he'd gone too far and been investigated.'

'Obviously, he managed to avoid the firing post.'

'More than that. One of Kesselring's staff officers put in a word for him, said he was an unsung fucking hero. The last word I had was that he'd been transferred to a unit in Luftflotte 3 and went with it to Italy. That would have been in '43, just before the Allied landings, and I don't doubt he made another packet out of what followed. War just seems to suit some people.'

Fischer's peasant's prejudices told him that great wealth never came honestly, so Jens Lamsdorf's *curriculum vitae* didn't worry him unduly; but a man who could emerge from the twentieth-century's greatest human catastrophe smelling of lavender wasn't to be trusted solely on the strength of his frank, open face.

'So I may be working for a seven-fingered juggler?'

The shrug was almost audible. 'Yeah, possibly. How much has he offered you?'

Fischer told him.

'Christ! We could both retire on that.'

'The job won't be too difficult - it isn't as though there aren't still large, undiscovered holes where men used to be. And this is Germany, so the right paperwork counts for more than a mother's memory. It's just that ...'

'If a guilty party's ever needed, there'll be plenty of witnesses to a half-faced fellow, rummaging through service records for the right missing corpse.'

'Something like that. But then I tell myself that he paid upfront, and he's lit himself up by talking to you about the business beforehand.' Fischer returned the sigh. 'You spoke by 'phone, yes?

'About four weeks since.'

'You're sure that this *is* the Lamsdorf you knew?'

'No doubt. His voice has more gravel to it than a *kaserne* parade-ground.'

'Alright.'

'Hell, Otto – just do a quick job and stick the cash in a hole somewhere. If things go to fuck it'll get you to somewhere warm where old Nazis are welcome.'

'Then what? Endless reminiscences over fake beer in fake beer-cellars?'

'Yeah, but *real* steak. And ladies with tan lines, too.'

Fischer laughed. A man who thought too much about things needed to know someone like Freddie Holleman, who rarely could be bothered to think at all. Somewhere between them lay an even, happy ground.

'I'll see how easy it is. Things may have changed at WASt in the decade since I last bothered them.'

'The French run it, don't they?'

'Not since '51. It's officially an office of the Federal Republic.'

'Ah. Us pretending to rule ourselves. What do you think of it all?'

All was the great, looming day - the open secret that the Federal Republic was about to acquire full sovereignty and have its former occupiers become allies. The newspapers had been speculating since the Soviet Union officially ended its state of war with Germany earlier that year, allowing the Four Powers finally to agree a general peace treaty. It was what every German wanted of course, and what most of them feared – feared, because it posed a question: What Next? Germans had great reason to fear *nexts*.

'I don't. Things will be the same or they won't, and nothing that Otto Henry Fischer thinks, says or does about it will be worth a cat turd.'

'We'll be a country without an army. How will that work?'

Fischer should have said nothing, but temptation dragged it out before he could consider the consequences.

'Perhaps Luxembourg could rent us theirs.'

The telephone receiver almost melted under the sustained blast of obscenities that followed. Fischer removed it from his ear and glanced into the shop. The Violist had disappeared and Renate was busying herself with a feather duster, trying to clean what she had already made pristine an hour earlier. Really, he had no reason not to do this thing. At most he was getting ten customers a day, of whom perhaps two or three had business that his assistant couldn't deal with immediately. If he spent a little time finding an identity for Lamsdorf's Jewish friend, what did it matter?

Ping.

The invective had slowed slightly, giving him the chance to interrupt. 'Freddie, how busy are you?'

'Not very.'

'And your uniform? How impressive is it?'

'Not greatly. I've lost some bars and moved from one shade of green to another.'

'It'll have to do.'

'For what?'

'For covering my back.'

6

Why Spandau?

The question had been rhetorical, but the *kripo* (his name was Melchior Fux) had thought about it a great deal in the three days since his boss had posed it. All the bodies had been found within the borough, including those that didn't exist, officially – two on the banks of the Havel (one above and one below its confluence with the Spree), another in east Staaken, two in Wilhelmstadt, one in Haselhorst and the latest close to the perimeter of Gatow airfield. All were male, aged between forty and fifty, the cause of death in every instance but one a cut throat. The oddity was the 'plane-spotter, whose sightless vigil had been hampered slightly by a bullet hole in the left eye. The killer (or killers) had laid out each of them with a degree of care that hinted equally at some perverted sense of respect or private derangement, and to date that was all that anyone could say as to motive. None of the empty-pocketed victims had been identified as yet, which meant either that they were lost souls or that someone had taken particular care to make them appear so.

Why Spandau? It wasn't as if the bodies were clustered. The borough was one of Berlin's largest (though least populated), and the killer(s) had taken considerable advantage of the space it afforded. All the victims had died where they were found; none appeared to have anticipated their demise. They came willingly, or at least obliviously, to the sites of their executions.

As the officer responding to the first killings, the *kripo* had inherited the remainder (all of them gratefully surrendered to his care), which meant that he had a small multitude peering over his shoulder – his immediate superiors, the would-be Voices of the People at Senate Hall and perhaps even the British, all of them letting the sand run down to the moment at which he could be fingered as the cause of nothing much happening. It was fair enough, given that he headed a team of one, occasionally supplemented by however many *anwärter*s could be spared at a given moment (to date, one also). He needed more men, a line of telephones, a database, inspiration and the hand of God shoving him towards an underserved resolution, and he was as likely to get any as all.

What he lacked the most was *expertise*, because no-one at Friesenstrasse's Police Praesidium could offer any. West Berlin's police force had been in existence for seven years now, and still its principal efforts extended to the preservation of public order and the free movement of traffic. The *kripo*'s title and job description were proof that a Criminal Investigations Department existed, but domestic violence, the occasional shanking in an alleyway and black-marketeering were the limits of its present expertise. Nor could he pick up the 'phone to Wiesbaden and ask help from the *Bundeskriminalamt*, because the Federals' writ didn't extend to Berlin. The Allies weren't too fond of the idea of a centralized

German police force, not when memories of the Gestapo's fine work were still fresh.

Fux looked around his 'office', a cleared cupboard on the second-floor. It was more than his rank deserved, a small acknowledgement of the burden he'd assumed. Apart from a desk that would shame a school classroom it housed a chair and a small bookcase, presently occupied by a single box-file, the Department's entire library on method-murder (its contents a pile of press-clippings and a modest collection of surviving pre-war case notes). He had asked for and been refused a telephone line, so the floorboards between his desk and the nearest receiver in the Bulls' Pen were losing their shine at a far faster pace than the case was progressing. He'd speculated already about whether the cost of a pot of varnish would be deducted from his severance pay.

He wanted to succeed, but the prospects weren't good. His prior career in shipping administration and wartime service with the Pioneers weren't ideal preparation for police work – in fact, had entry standards been more rigorous he probably wouldn't have got into Criminal Investigations at all. But the tidal flow of defecting *VolksPolizei* who'd crossed the line in '48 had seized the majority of lower-level vacancies and lowered the median standard of recruitment to the new Force, making what previously might have seemed merely mediocre look fairly sharp by comparison. He was grateful to the *kozis* for that, at least.

He had built a fairly good record in his four years here, but his only homicides to date had been small stuff (if not to their victims), perpetrated by men too stupid not to flag themselves so obviously that confessions had hardly been required. A *kripo*'s success was measured by his closed cases, and he wasn't sure that statistics were the best yardstick. Boxes had been ticked, procedures followed, no corners cut and still it felt like he'd mastered a knack rather than grown a proper policeman's head. If he had any intuitive feel for his job, it was wearing damn fine camouflage.

Not that the distilled spirit of Sherlock Holmes, hovering directly overhead, would have been enough for this case. The investigation should have had men on the streets for weeks now, knocking on doors, bothering passers-by, raking through undergrowth near the murder sites, putting out requests for information on every form of media and generally giving the impression that a righteous steam-roller was in motion. It didn't and hadn't, though. There had been hints that his superiors were just beginning to think that this was a serious business when the men in suits arrived to remove two of the victims from both the scene of their deaths and the public record, and suddenly the Braid didn't know whether their own careers would be better served by pushing forward or treading water. It was why this one-man mini-circus was proceeding, unhindered by resources, until the view was clearer. He was beginning to wish that the Control Commission would take an interest and put a foot up some arses to move it along, but Germans killing other Germans didn't seem to be a matter that disturbed their sleep.

He thought about that for a little while, then forced his mind back to the day's business. A lady had walked into Moritzstrasse station that morning and admitted to having almost fallen over the latest body while walking her schnauzer. Until that moment, it had been assumed that first sight of the corpse was made by British MPs during their patrol of the airfield perimeter, but … he checked his notes … Frau Geneva Weck's testimony almost certainly made her the first post-mortem witness. He had hurried across West Berlin to interview her, and by doing so wasted the best part of a morning. As upset as she had been by the spectacle, fear of Authority had obviously preyed more, and anything useful she might have offered had been forgotten somewhere in the weeks between and amid ceaseless fretting about whether she had made herself an accessory by default. Had her husband not threatened to carry her to Moritzstrasse over his shoulder she might never have come forward.

No, she couldn't recall having seen anyone in the minutes before little Buffi found the body and tried to pee on it. No, there didn't seem to be anything unusual about the ground around it, but then it was much too close to the perimeter of a British air station for any sensible German to be wantonly curious. Yes, the man had quite definitely been dead when Buffi found him, because he had continued to stare into the sky with complete indifference to the dampness beneath him, the wet snuffling in his ear and her timid enquiries as to his health.

It was all so pitifully useless that Fux lost the urge to be unpleasant about her tardiness and sent her home with a bland exhortation to recall her duty as a citizen next time (as if she made a habit of falling over corpses). When she had gone he remained at Moritzstrasse for another hour, speaking to local officers about what they were hearing on the streets. Within ten minutes he'd established that rumours were circulating about the two lost corpses, which meant that at least one member of Spandau's force (and probably more) was opening his big mouth at random. He wasn't too troubled by this. Public outrage, or at least apprehension, was what the business needed urgently, whatever the men in well-fitting suits intended. He just hoped no-one assumed it was his mouth that was doing the moving.

Why Spandau? One answer sprang to mind, and as much as he wished to dismiss it out of hand the thought kept returning, making his stomach turn uncomfortably. More than half the Borough's boundary comprised the western extremity of 'free' Berlin, the armoured line between two dogmas. In other circumstances that wouldn't have been a cause for concern - the Soviets kept a fairly close eye on what passed across the line in either direction, and someone with a taste for killing (even if it was sanctioned by some form of authority) would stick inconveniently in too many memories. But Spandau's westernmost district, Staaken, was an oddity. At the end of the war, the British, wanting to keep all of the Gatow site within their Zone, had traded off Staaken's western extremities to the Soviets, but until 1950 the area had continued to be administered from Borough Hall, so west Staakeners had been regarded as a breed between, and even allowed to vote in West Berlin elections. When the DDR was established it took full control of the administration and moved the security border eastwards to sunder Staaken fully; yet even five years later, the border control along this small stretch of the 'Iron Curtain' remained slightly more porous than what flanked it.

He had spoken to enough former *vopos* to know that their pay and prospects left a gap, one that a fat bribe would fill conveniently, so the men on the border might have been encouraged to look the other way, in which case the motives (or mental disorders) that had birthed these deaths would be incapable of investigation, at least by him. It might be why it hadn't been possible to make identifications. It might be another reason why his bosses were pushing him with long poles, anxious not to get too close to something that could bite off their hands. But then it occurred to him that if he made this theory convincing enough they'd have no choice but to take it from him and give it to General Gehlen's people, because trouble between the two Germanies was not bread-and-butter police business. The thought cheered him slightly. Perhaps they were just waiting for him to make the case so they could dump the business without seeming too eager. He could think of at least three of them – including his immediate superior – whose career paths were very much plotted to avoid potential thickets. They would want to push this thing as far as possible from the Unsolved file.

But the oddities – the two *removed* victims – bothered him still. Were they nothing or everything to do with the others? Until he knew more he couldn't be sure that washing his hands of the rest wouldn't come back upon him, badly. It would be best to discuss it with someone first – but who? He had no close colleagues in the Criminal Investigations Department, and even his usual partner was a half-stranger still, a man with whom he shared little off-duty time (and whose drawn-out recovery from what had seemed to be no more than a sprained back suggested that he was avoiding contamination no less carefully than their superiors). Who else was there who might listen? His wife? A priest?

He picked up Frau Weck's non-testimony and opened the desk drawer in which resided several similar gems - the fruit of much legwork, little inspiration and even less luck. There hadn't been a new killing for almost a month now, and he wondered if he should put his hopes in time's ability to distract, to shuffle the pack of priorities and make this business something less than what it presently was. They couldn't accuse him of indolence, or obvious incompetence; they certainly couldn't say that a single piece of paperwork was missing or incomplete; and until some presently unforeseeable event jumped up to surprise them all it wasn't likely that anyone would want to step forward and take responsibility for pressing the accelerator.

The clock in the Bulls' Pen chimed five, the appointed time for him to go upstairs and make his report to *Oberrat* Genschler. Nothing in it would shake the floorboards, being in almost every part identical to the ones he'd been making every two days for several weeks now – every two days, because when someone prodded Genschler in turn he wanted to be able to show that he'd been keeping on top of his investigator. As with most senior Policeman's workloads, it was all about how it looked, not how it was going. Fux stood, straightened his tie, and picked up a piece of paper from his desk. It contained nothing to do with today's 'progress', but a man making a report from memory could be suspected of indifference - or, worse, improvisation. In any case, his investigation had reached the stage at which it needed all the props it could muster.

7

Rolf Hoeschler paused outside the entrance doors to Föhrenweg 19, a pleasant, three-storey red brick building that had been poor Ludwig Beck's headquarters during the years he had headed the General Staff. It was the sort of pedigree that could make a man thoughtful.

On the way here he'd decided that things could go badly in at least four ways, and it took an effort of will to present himself and state his business to the military policeman on guard duty, an enormous fellow with a face that would have frightened the spikes off a hedgehog. He was nodded through as far as a turnstile, where another giant took the piece of paper from him, read it and frowned even more deeply.

Hastily, Hoeschler explained the discrepancy. 'She isn't well today. I'm her husband.' He removed his identity card and marriage certificate from his breast pocket and presented them. They were studied for almost two minutes, the frown wavering slightly during this time to hint at irritation, frank disbelief and – Hoeschler suspected – an impending migraine. Eventually, the monster returned them and told him to wait, pointing to a rank of three wooden stand-chairs that stood beneath a modest, gold-framed photograph of Dwight Eisenhower in civilian clothes. The visitor obeyed meekly.

Ten minutes later, an athletically-built man in his mid-thirties and obligatory mid-grey suit strode through the turnstile, smiled pleasantly at Hoeschler and beckoned.

'It's a nice day. Let's walk.' His German was perfect, untainted by any trace of an American drawl. As they left the building his hand remained on Hoeschler's shoulder, a gentle but firm presence. They walked southwards along the narrow, tree-lined footpath as far as Thielpark, when the hand applied a little more pressure to guide Hoeschler to the left, into its western gate.

On a work-day morning there were plenty of visitors already, most of them walking at a pace that suggested they had no particularly urgent business. At an empty bench beside a pond the grip relaxed and the American sat down. Hoeschler joined him, leaving a body-sized gap between them.

For a while the CIA agent said nothing, He glanced around, taking in the park's wooded, hilly terrain with what seemed to be genuine appreciation. Even ten years after the war, there remained too few vehicles on Berlin's roads to oppress the air on the days when coal fires weren't necessary, and both men breathed deeply (one to catch the early spring fragrances, the other to calm his nerves).

The American cleared his throat. 'The Soviets have someone named Thomas Braun in custody, at Karlshorst.'

Frantically, Hoeschler tried to recall the name.

'I … don't know him.'

'He was General Myasnik's lead Kraut at Tempelhof, in charge of the pilfering. You've heard of Myasnik?'

Was supposed to know the name? He didn't know what admitting it to an American agent would do to his prospects for a quiet life; but Mila had also been one of Myasnik's 'Krauts', so there was no utility in denying things.

'The Ivans put him against a wall, didn't they? About seven years ago?'

'They did. But KGB like to be thorough. As you most definitely know, a number of his Germans managed to avoid the shit as it splashed. This Braun guy must be an idiot, because he stayed in East Berlin rather than find a deep hole somewhere, and now they've got him.'

'He won't last long, I expect.'

'No, but he's trying to do something about that.'

Christ. Whatever booty Braun had managed to extract from the wreckage of the General's operation must have been spent by now, so he would have only one thing of value to barter.

'What's he saying?'

'Plenty of things. Mila Henze, for two. Obviously, KGB can't do anything about her, not without risking an incident. That's why they passed a message to us. They thought we might object to her having helped the General unload so many of our cargoes back then.'

'And do you?' CIA might have sent a couple of soldiers to pick her up, but instead had requested her presence at Föhrenweg 19 politely, by letter. It didn't smack of vindictiveness.

The American scratched his nose and paid attention to a small boy who was trying to lower a toy boat into the pond. Hoeschler wanted very much to grab a lapel and start shaking, but being a part of the entertainment he thought better of it.

Eventually, the other man's attention drifted back. 'The Berlin Airlift was a vast propaganda win for us, probably the biggest we've had. In the years since it's sort of acquired a lick of glory, like Valley Forge, or Guam, and like any story that wrote itself it didn't spare the gilt trimmings. Re-writes that make us look less great, or careless, or even dumb, aren't smart. We flew thousands of tons of stuff into Berlin, and if some of it got re-routed by our Tempelhof handlers, well ...'

He turned to Hoeschler. 'I assume she's being a model citizen, these days?'

'You probably know already. She has a respectable business, renting out properties and nothing else. All her accounts are filed on time, without omissions. Berlin's more than getting back in taxes than what was taken - allegedly – at Tempelhof.'

'Good, then. Obviously, she needed to be warned about this. What she and you do about it is your business. Here ...'

He handed a card to Hoeschler. It contained only a name – Gregory Smith – and a telephone number on the Dahlem exchange.

'… if you need to speak to me further, call this number. Don't leave a message if I'm not available.'

Without a further word, Herr Smith was off the bench and walking briskly back along the path towards Föhrenweg. The interview's conclusion was so sudden that Hoeschler didn't have the legs to move for several moments. He stared at the card, trying to think what it all meant. Clearly, none of his feared bad endings had reported for duty, but neither had the expected feeling of elation. He should have felt better about this than he did.

The apartment was only two kilometres from Thielpark, and he decided to try to walk off his feelings. The American had been as accommodating as he might have hoped, but why? The Western Allies' hand-over of sovereignty to the new Federal Republic was weeks away at most, but the CIA had every right to continue to pursue past crimes against American interests, particularly in Berlin – so why wouldn't they? Smith's explanation had seemed convincing, but perhaps only because its audience had wanted so very much to be convinced. The United States was a wealthy country that enjoyed making it obvious to the world; but no-one was sanguine about theft, particularly when it was organized by and for the benefit of sworn enemies. General Myasnik had been a rogue element of the Soviet State and paid the penalty for it, yet the ledger was hardly closed by his death. A significant proportion of what he had taken from the Americans – both product and intelligence - had fallen into Moscow's hands, something that Washington must have hated like death. Wouldn't they try at least to recapture the loose change, even if it were only to make a point?

And why hadn't Smith been disappointed not to have seen Mila herself? Why the walk in the park, rather than a warmer interview in an interrogation room? Hoeschler wasn't familiar with CIA protocols, but he didn't doubt that the organization proceeded as much by a book as any other. Quiet, courteous words in ears couldn't be standard intelligencers' procedure, even for those of a nation that prided itself on its idiosyncrasies.

Don't leave a message if I'm not available.

By the time he reached his apartment building, he was fully as nervous as when leaving it earlier than morning. He nodded to Helmut the *portier* without really seeing him, took the stairs two at a time and let himself into the Hoeschler residence without shouting his usual greeting. Mila was in the kitchen, baking (a recent interest, possibly goaded by the conventional swerve that her life had taken). As he entered she leaned towards him and kissed his cheek, her hand transferring a quantity of flour to the sleeve of his dark suit. He didn't notice it.

'That was over quickly. What did they say?'

Briefly, he gave her the summary. When he mentioned Myasnik her face fell (no matter that she had wholly expected the summons to

Föhrenweg to be about her former relationship with the General), but rose considerably thereafter, and the interview's sudden, surprising conclusion - the best news imaginable - might have transported her halfway to the ceiling had she not been watching her husband's face carefully.

'What is it?'

'I can't think it's what it seems.'

'Why not?'

'I don't know. Are we that lucky? Is anyone?'

'You think we're being played with?'

'I … no, not that.' Hoeschler stared at the floury mess on the table in front of him. 'I tried to make sense of it on the way home, and only one thing occurs to me that explains what happened today – the *way* it happened. How this turns out depends on something, I think.'

She was wiping her hands on her apron, frowning, her mood as flat as his now.

'On what, Rolf?'

'On how much money Herr Smith wants to make it to go away.'

Fischer had known that he wouldn't be successful immediately, but it surprised him that his patience had worn so thin with age, or creeping sanity.

Naturally, it would be easiest to invent an identity, and if no-one ever cared to delve into the past life of Lamsdorf's friend it would probably be sufficient; but a persistent search would stumble right into a lack of evidence to flesh out the wraith. The gold option would be to find someone whose existence could be verified by one of the administrative check-points through which his life had passed, but whose death had not been recorded, much less notified to family by WASt. It needed to belong to one of the many thousands of German soldiers whose demise had gone unrecorded, either because it occurred during an operation that had failed so disastrously that the staff-work had gone up in the same flames as everything else, or because the winners hadn't thought to notify the Red Cross of those they'd slaughtered or captured. In either case, it meant the Eastern Front.

Hundreds of thousands of German soldiers had been swept up there, from when the line stood at the outskirts of Moscow to its final redrawing at the Berlin Chancellery. At the time, most of them had probably thought they'd been lucky to survive the fighting, but the feeling couldn't have lasted. In the years that followed, the Ivans had creatively culled their massive POW population through indifference, overwork and underfeeding, and notifications of deaths had been rare, and usually accidental. Fischer – and anyone else who cared to make the effort - had a vast potential reservoir of lost souls from which to make a choice of resurrection.

The problem was, he had to go at it from the wrong direction. He had no access to lists of missing men against which he could check WASt files to satisfy himself that they remained missing. Was he able simply to walk into Eichborndamm 179 with a division's worth of names from units he knew to have been annihilated and then cross-check until one of them didn't come up, he might have earned his fat envelope in a single morning (having disbursed only the price of a bus ride to Reinickendorf). WASt didn't welcome day-trippers, though. Civilians had to apply in writing, giving a name or names (though a reason for making the request was not required) and then wait for the tectonic majesty of the system to give satisfaction. Even if he did it in batches, he might be dead before hitting the lucky coconut in the dark.

He thought around the problem until his head hurt, and Renate, fearing his mood, began to find reasons not to disturb him. It was only when he overheard her recommending the recording of Quadri's *Tosca* over de Sabata's to a browsing old gentleman that he realised the damage his preoccupations might cause. He hastened to correct her and then spent almost an hour attending to shop business rather than the matter of lost souls. The thing was well lodged in his head, however, and later that afternoon he managed to mend an ailing *Bulova* without once thinking about what he was doing.

He recalled that towards the end of the war, some newspapers had been allowed to carry official lists of missing men (Goebbels had urged it to offset popular anger at WASt's growing failure to provide timely information to their relations directly). He went to Lichterfelde Library to trawl old copies of the *Berliner Morgenpost,* but ten seconds' effort told him what he should have guessed already – that no details of units or other operational data were offered, only the districts (but not addresses) from which the missing men hailed. His other obvious options weren't any more promising. One ostensibly fertile source was the surviving HIAG card index of missing Waffen SS personnel (which held all the data that newspaper reports didn't), but the chances of Himmler's Finest ever having recruited someone who was missing a foreskin were probably zero. Naturally, an approach to the Soviet Authorities to access their records would achieve as much as a fart into a milk bottle, while petitioning the DDR's Ministry of the Interior for access to its archives at Potsdam and Dornburg would provide all the satisfaction of the fart and the bonus of unwanted attention from *Stasi* (who doubtless would regard a *night and fog* abduction from Lichterfelde as a nice day out of the office).

I've done this before, he told himself; but that had been at a time when he'd had easy access to Luftwaffe records and the luck to find a serviceman who had died, not in combat but in his home, burned with his family during one the first British terror raids on Hamburg. That conflagration had – it seemed – removed all the family's personal papers, which made the job of resurrecting them much easier. Two hours' creative reworking of Luftwaffe personnel data had allowed Freddie Holleman to step into the life and cadaver of Kurt Beckendorp without any bells sounding, and the plummeting fortunes of war thereafter had kept attentions elsewhere. For his deliverance Holleman had thanked Fischer often and effusively, to which the latter had always given the same response – that the false Beckendorp should direct his gratitude instead to Arthur Harris and bureaucratic dissolution.

Peace made things more difficult. Unlike a professional identity thief, Fischer had no hinterland of useful contacts from whom to bribe, coerce or beg favours. Almost everything he did would have his name – and, worse, his face – attached to it. Five or six years earlier he might have been lost in the vast crowd of persistent optimists who held out small hopes still of recovering a lost son, father or brother, or at least of getting word of their fate. Optimism had faded, though, and with it the volume of approaches to WASt. He thought about how wonderful it would be to access some of these past applications to the organization, pick half a dozen of the disappointed wretches who had received no satisfaction and then present their disappeared kin to Jens Lamsdorf to make his choice at leisure. And then he chided himself. Ten days' non-movement was frustrating; it wasn't nearly an excuse for heartless shittery.

Inspiration came on day eleven - an idea that, with hindsight, seemed so obvious that he wished he could borrow Holleman's tin leg to kick himself with. He realised that he had personal access to a small but perfectly formed set of ghosts whose fates were known only to God and whoever manned Purgatory's gates – his comrades in his final field posting: 2nd Battalion, 181st Artillery, who almost to a man had been killed or captured on 14 January 1942, a matter of hours after the flayed, screaming corpse-in-waiting of Otto Fischer had been evacuated from Andreapol. What remained of the German forces at Okhvat had then retreated hastily and established a new line (about thirty metres long) on what became the Rzhev Salient. His comrades' deaths had been assumed but never confirmed; they waited in warriors' limbo, lost and half-forgotten, requiring only the necromancy of an efficient memory to be resurrected.

He required all that efficiency now, because what he needed to recall was mundane to a degree. Soldiers tend to talk a lot – to relieve homesickness, or boredom, or the terror of what they might be doing in the hours in which they aren't talking. Fischer had never been like that. In *Fallschirmjäger* 1 Regiment he'd had a reputation as a surly bastard (he preferred to think of himself as coolly taciturn, but hadn't been given a vote), a comrade best left alone in his corner of the Mess. His ears had worked too perfectly, though, and much of what he hadn't want to hear had been heard anyway – about lives, loves, family, ambitions, preoccupations and … *heimats*. A man hadn't known war until he'd been obliged to suffer lengthy expositions on *why* – why Saxons were the salt of the earth, East Prussians the bedrock of German civilization and why it was that no-one on God's fertile Earth works harder than a Coburger. Even now, Fischer recalled much of the meat of that drivel, but putting it to individual faces and names was more difficult. But there was one in particular, a monologue on *kulibiak* and how the Danziger recipe was the Matron's Tits however the fucking French or the fucking Russians made it, that pushed itself front and centre. He recalled this mainly due to the fact he had never tasted the dish and needed to ask its ingredients, but also because it had been one of the few reminiscences of a sentimental soldier that had made him laugh. Then again, he had almost always laughed when that silly bastard …

Rudi Bandelin. A brute of a man in charge of three guns, a rare second-lieutenant raised from the non-com ranks on the strength of his ability to get on with his men, mainly by making them laugh. Not a joker, though - that sort staled very quickly, but Rudi could tell an anecdote or express an opinion about anything and make it amusing. Fischer had transferred into 2nd Battalion only three months before his very last day at the Front, and a new man (particularly a surly, keeps-to-himself bastard) isn't allowed into confidences immediately; but Rudy's mouth had been sufficiently muscular to throw a quip all the way across the Mess.

He was an ideal choice, all other things being equal - a native of a part of Germany that wasn't even Germany any more: a place from which all histories had been expunged. His gun-crews had been next to Fischer's on that day at Okhvat, so he had almost certainly either gone on to his good reward or flung up his arms at the advancing Ivans (not that they ever took too many prisoners in the heat of a fight). But did someone mourn him still? And if they did, where were they now?

He paused, forcing himself to slow down. There were military records to consider first. The *Reichswehr*'s central personnel records had been destroyed in February 1945, courtesy of USAAF. Some duplications might have survived in those German States that, stubbornly, had continued to keep their own records after 1867 (in that year all military administration had been centralized by the new Reich), though he need hardly worry in the case of West Prussia, which had been wiped from geography. *If* Rudi's Länder records had ever existed, *if* they survived and *if* they had been recaptured officially (almost certainly by the Soviets) they were most likely to reside now in the DDR's Central Archive at Potsdam, and therefore be inaccessible to people wishing to check upon Lamsdorf's mysterious friend. The faint alternative he wasn't too worried about. To date, the Federal Republic hadn't established a military records department in their Bundesarchiv at Koblenz, so even if some sleight of fate had wafted Prussian Länder records further westwards, there was as yet no place for them to … land. There remained WASt, of course, which curated whatever it had managed to scrape together from the conflagration that attended the end of the war; but he could check there very easily, now that he had a name and unit to present. Otherwise, the only military likeness of Rudi would be that pasted into his *soldbuch*, which Fischer would bet his fat envelope upon not having survived until the sun set on 14 February, 1942.

Which left only troublesome priests. Some pastors had maintained records of those of their parishioners who had gone to war. It was invariably an individual initiative, a comfort to the families who might never again see or have word of their loved ones – a physical memorial, in some cases with photographs, of those the State had rendered less than mist. He didn't know if the Danzig parish in which Rudy had lived enjoyed the services of such a man – and again, the fact that the parish no longer existed was reassuring (to Fischer at least). But some pastors had fled the Soviet advance, and one who cared so deeply for his flock might have attempted to preserve their posterity also. It could have been carried in a single ledger, after all. If the paperwork had come west, Rudi Bandelin might not be a safe choice.

Which brought him neatly to Rudi's family and friends. The forced migration of refugees from what was now western Poland was his biggest, most opaque concern. Obviously, the Bandelins weren't a Jewish tribe, so the most industrious and efficient harvester of identities, the Zionist Jewish Agency, wouldn't hold information on them. Otherwise, the papers of those refugees who survived the march westwards had first been examined at Allied military relief centres and later copied by the local municipal and *Kreis* authorities in which they settled. An Office of Expellees, Refugees and War Victims was established in 1949, in Frankfurt, and they would have taken in any information that survived still; but as Bandelin hadn't been a common surname even east of the Oder, he wasn't too concerned about the effort required. In any case, if some relatives had survived until now they would know about their pastor and what he held, so the disappointments would come all at once. If Rudi was fit to be resurrected, Fischer would know soon enough.

On the day that inspiration arrived, so did the photograph - three copies, as he'd requested, all nicely creased to seem older than they were. Their subject matter looked Aryan - not ReichsHeini's big, blond, Viking template, but a perfectly nondescript German male, certainly not one to turn minds even fleetingly to promised lands, much less the savage caricature of *Jüd Suss*. The gentleman's frame appeared to be less sturdy then Rudi Bandelin's, but that hardly mattered. If the identity was clean the two men could be as dissimilar as Julius Caesar and Julius Streicher. No-one would know.

So he wrote his two letters, one to WASt, the other to the Expellees' Office, and, expecting the wheels of German bureaucracy to turn at their customary millimetric pace, put the business from mind. It was a relief to return to distressed gramophones, clocks and wristwatches, a ward-full of which had accumulated during his days of meditation, and Renate seemed glad to have her employer's head back where it should be. Unfortunately, she took this apparent end to his preoccupations as an opportunity to broach a pressing but unwelcome matter.

'My mother asks if you'd like to have lunch with us this Sunday, Herr Director.'

Fischer managed to stifle the bowel-deep groan - and, for a few moments, made a show of finding the (non) movement of a Langendorf more interesting than it could possibly be. It gave him a little space to search for something credible that didn't hint at his preference for spending the day - and the three to either side of it – fasting rather than fall once more into proximity with Frau Knipper. Its elusiveness reminded him once more that he should always have a small selection of plausible excuses primed and ready to be delivered, glibly, at a moment's notice.

'Er, yes, thank you, Renate. That would be splendid.'

This being only Monday, he had plenty of time to dread Sunday, but his anguish was interrupted an hour later by the astonishing arrival of a reply from WASt, some thirty-six hours after he sent off his letter. It was a short, almost regretfully-expressed note to tell him that no further information had been received regarding the fate of Rudolph Bandelin since his regimental commander had posted him missing on 17 January 1942. Made slightly dizzy – and optimistic - by this early success, he found the telephone number for the Expellees' Office and called immediately. To a rather terse receptionist he explained that a recently deceased gentleman in Westphalia had left a small remembrance in his will to members of a family named Bandelin, formerly of Danzig. He had written to the Office in the correct manner, but as there was some dispute regarding other bequests, he wondered if he might obtain a verbal assurance that the Bandelins – or at least *a* Bandelin – had managed to flee westwards, and, if someone might be so kind as to check, an address?

He was transferred and obliged to repeat, word for word, his request, and sensed a considerable degree of satisfaction in the refusal he received. The Office, he was told, had wound down its active function in the previous year and acted now only as a repository of information for the Federal Government's use (or not). It had been assumed that all personal applications regarding missing relatives would have been made by now, and, consequently, a decision had been made not to maintain a vestigial service for the very rare approach – such as his – that might yet occur.

Fischer almost laughed aloud. Whatever he said next, no surviving member of Bandelin's family could ever have their hopes raised by it.

'I understand. I assume that you still record information provided?'

'We do, yes.'

'I received word that a member of the Bandelin family, one Ernst Rudolph, formerly of 2nd Battalion, 181st Artillery Regiment, was seen in the Dortmund area about four years ago. I can't testify to the accuracy of this, naturally, but I retained the letter stating the claim. It's anonymous, unfortunately.'

'Please repeat those details.'

Fischer did so, slowly. Having been excised from the bureaucratic firmament, Rudy Bandelin was now being restored to it - cleanly, unverifiably, untraceably. Barring an extraordinary twist of malignant fate – a chance meeting of strangers, names exchanged and a distant memory jarred to the point at which someone might make something of it – an old comrade in arms was not going to make any difficulties about being exhumed.

As Fischer replaced the receiver he let the forward impetus of his unexpected successes do its work. One of only two matters remaining was a substantial one – to find someone who could produce convincing paperwork. His own intimacy with the criminal underworld had ended in 1937, while Freddie Holleman's undoubtedly more up-to-date contacts now enjoyed a drawn iron-curtain between them and any inconvenience he might visit upon them. The Berlin business directory was up and running, but as far as he knew forgers didn't have a section in it as yet. Which left only an approach to someone who might know a man - someone whose bread was habitually buttered in the darker, more contemptible strata of human society.

'Renate?'

She pushed her head through the beads that separated the shop and workroom.

'Yes, Herr Director?'

'Would you mind taking over for half an hour? I'd like to go out for lunch today.'

If she was surprised by this stark swerve from normalcy she didn't let it show (other than in the set of her shoulders, which squared slightly to meet the challenges of her temporary promotion). He put on his old hunter's jacket, stepped into the street, turned left, and, twenty metres further on, left again, into the premises of Lichterfelde's premier local newspaper.

The journalists' office was a fragile wood and glass structure perched on a mezzanine of iron pillars above the print room, accessed by a set of stairs that shouldn't have held a cat. As whenever he scaled them, Fischer felt their every creak and groan in his bones, and grasped at the door handle at their summit as a climber would a crampon. Once it was secured he stepped hastily into the bustle of the newsroom.

Herr Grabner, owner-editor of the *Süd-west Berliner Zeitung*, was not at his desk. At the only other one, Jonas Kleiber stooped over a typewriter, frowning as if he didn't believe a word of what he'd written. When he looked up the frown cleared and he sat back, goading a complaint from his chair that made the staircase sound almost content with its lot.

'Ay up, *Fischer's Time-pieces*! No clocks to mend?'

'A few. How many criminals do you know?'

Kleiber pursed his lips and stared at the typewriter. 'About a battalion's worth. Mostly locked up now, or running. Why?'

'That business with the big fellow. The disappearance.'

'Oh. You want a papers man.' Despite his best efforts to convince otherwise, Kleiber was as sharp as a rat's elbow when he could be bothered to think. 'Presumably, one who's neither – locked up, I mean, or ...'

'If possible.'

The frown returned for a few moments, followed by a slow shake of the head. 'I knew a genius of a man, a former engraver who could whip up a reference to get you past St Michael.'

'What's the problem?'

'He's dead, mainly. Apart from that ...' Kleiber's face cleared. 'Norbert Roth!'

'Local?

'He is, very. In fact, his main source of income's in the borough.'

'He's discreet?'

'As a sphinx. What he does is illegal, but the police ignore it. He wouldn't wreck that sweet arrangement by talking.'

'He must lay out a lot in bribes.'

Kleiber shook his head. 'He doesn't need to. He has a speciality – marriage certificates. In Lichterfelde it's big business.'

Fischer took the point immediately. 'Camp Andrews.'

'Yep. Too many local girls getting an American deposit in their accounts. Then the daddies fuck off home without leaving a forwarding address. As you'd imagine, most of the new mothers need help, but the Missions don't like to encourage fornication, and if they go to the main Churches they get the foster home speech, so ...'

'It helps if they have paper to confirm their respectability.'

'Tremendously. Norbert's doing an important social service. The police look the other way because of that, and the fact that he doesn't charge much – and, of course, because it puts a stick up American arses. One day, there's going to be a shit-slide of paternity cases in the USA, all backed up by impeccably forged evidence. And it serves the horny bastards right.'

'Horny?'

'An Americanism. Referring to the condition of not being able to keep a cock in pants.'

'Ah. Where can I find Herr Roth?'

'Oh, don't do that!'

'What?

'Let me speak to him first, to get him in the right mood.'

'He's shy?'

'No. He has a temper like a kicked boar. It's why his wife left - that, and him throwing her through a window.'

'Then I shall come wreathed in smiles and goodwill.'

'And money - come wreathed in money. It improves Norbert's mood wonderfully.'

9

If there was one good thing about this, Rolf Hoeschler told himself (though there probably wasn't), it was that he used to be good at it.

Prised from a Soviet POW camp and trained to be one of the creatures who spied upon their own countrymen, he had discovered a faculty for not been noticed as he shuffled through his nation's apocalyptic new landscapes. Even Otto Fischer, with whom he'd had a slight prior acquaintance and whose remaining neck-hair could be teased awake by the threat of drizzle, had remained oblivious to his attention during several days in which it seemed they might be, or become, enemies. He was the best sort of shadow – not only discreet but of average height and looks (Mila would disagree, bless her), with nothing in his manner or gait that would catch an eye or otherwise mark him as anything other than a nondescript of the great, grey breed of Berliners.

This was different, though. Following citizenry wasn't difficult because most of them were oblivious to the fact; tracking a man who assumed the worst, always, required a more deft technique, particularly when pursuer and prey had met only recently and memories were fresh.

He had thought about some sort of disguise, but couldn't be certain he wouldn't catch a glimpse of his reflection, laugh aloud and make the exercise as pointless as it was absurd. So he combed his hair a different way, put on some of his older clothes and the sort of thick belt that a manual worker might effect and left it at that. He told himself that deflection required only that he seem to be other than what he was, and that he not put himself where eyes might expect to see him. It sounded good in his head, and half-convinced him.

If he just wants money, why are you doing this, Rolf?

It was a damn good question, and he hadn't wanted to worry her with the answer - that Mister Smith might prefer neat endings. Taking Mila's money and then doing or saying nothing more might well leave him exposed to a pointed finger. It wasn't likely that his victims would ever find the courage or idiocy to fling accusations, but who besides Smith himself knew that he had been given information by the Ivans? And what would they say if he seemed to be doing nothing with it? Might he not consider it safer to squeeze out what he wanted and then arrange a taxi ride across the line for the only two people who knew that he was a blackmailer? It was what a different sort of Rolf Hoeschler would have done.

So he told her that he needed to make sure no-one else was involved – that someone from Karlshorst wasn't following Smith to get to her. That was so like what most people imagined spies did that she just nodded and said nothing more about it. But then he wondered if he might have stumbled upon another problem to add to the rest. The line between East and West Berlin was permeable, crossed by thousands of workers in both directions each day and however many intelligencers had clandestine business to transact. What better way for KGB to arrange a risk-free search for Mila Henze than to tip off the CIA and then follow comfortably in the slipstream? This was so very much what spies did that the moment it came to him he wanted to drag her to Zoo Bahnhof, jump on a train to Hamburg, clear out her bank account and take the first ship to where folk spoke neither English nor German.

He doubted that she would ever run, though, which was why he was doing this – and because doing nothing was as fine an admission of helplessness as he could conceive. Waiting for Smith to press his demands wouldn't necessarily make them more vulnerable, but only in the same way that closing one's eyes didn't alter a firing squad's schedule. A plan – even if it didn't deserve the name – brought the illusion of holding an initiative.

But where and how was he to start? Smith lived in a compound only some two hundred metres from his workplace, and for all that Hoeschler knew the two were connected through the gardens that lay behind the staid, railing-topped wall. CIA and other American agencies had requisitioned all of this pretty stretch of Föhrenweg, making a German the alien here, not them. He couldn't just hang around, pretending to smoke and read a newspaper, not if he wasn't to break both of the only-just-conceived Hoeschler Rules of Surveillance.

His fervent hope was that Mila wasn't Herr Smith's only object of personal interest. Berlin was a city of dark histories, and a man whose professional hours were ringed by denunciation, betrayal and innuendo could assemble an army of squeezed marks, if he chose to do so. He would need to be very careful, though. Hoeschler had been guided out of the office, to a place where an implied threat could be aired safely. That had been in nice weather, when a walk in the park was a natural, expected recourse. What about other times?

Hoeschler's own experience of clandestine liaisons had occurred largely in or near cafés, and for good reason. They were places where loitering was expected, where intelligencers could meet with their local contacts, their *rats*, without anyone noticing. There, matters could be discussed discreetly in plain sight, packages could be transferred between knees and threats or promises dispensed without fear of discovery. If another CIA man walked in and witnessed the exchange, what did it matter? His colleague would be in the right place, doing what seemed to be his job.

So, it needn't be somewhere too distant from Föhrenweg 19 – why would it be, if busy men needed to get back to their office? There was nothing on the street itself, but he found two small cafés a few hundred metres to the north, on Königin-Luise-Strasse, and it had already occurred to him that there was an easy way to determine which of these was more likely to be favoured by Herr Smith and his kind.

Following a half-hour's careful reconnaissance, he spent less than ten minutes in *Café Leon*. The second establishment, *Tortenstube Alfi*, required an even briefer visit, its 'coffee' resembling an execrable blend of forest floor scrapings and chicory. *Café Leon*'s offering had been bland and inoffensive, the sort of brew amenable to American palates, so he retraced his steps, took a table away from the window and resigned himself to several hours of nerve-stretching, stomach-tormenting leisure.

He had telephoned his workplace that morning to take sick-leave, the first in his time with BVG. His supervisor had been surprised but made no fuss about it, and even offered his best wishes for a speedy recovery. Hoeschler feared it would be anything but that. In his experience, surveillance was a job less suited to men than the more patient varieties of shrubbery. He expected to be unlucky for at least a week, and had armed himself with a copy of the latest *Deutsche Bundesbahn* rolling-stock manual, a work guaranteed to make the most inquisitive eyes glaze over should his prolonged presence draw attention. He opened it as his first coffee arrived. The café was quiet, waiting for the lunchtime press, and none of the seven other customers glanced in his direction.

Within minutes of the wall-clock striking twelve he knew that his guess had been correct. There was a shine to American suits that German tailors either couldn't or didn't care to copy, and even had the haircuts not given away their owners he was reasonably confident that at least two men who entered with the crowd worked somewhere on the northern stretch of Föhrenweg. They sat together, chatting quietly, uninterested in their fellow diners, and paid and departed as soon as their meal was done.

Just before one o'clock another shiny suit arrived and took a two-seat table close to the door. This one was dining on his nerve-endings, casting his eyes around the café every minute or so, and Hoeschler had to pretend an interest in the dimensions and weight-bearing capabilities of the *Offener Güterwagen* that its designer could hardly have carried off. After a few minutes he began to feel exposed, and had almost decided to take a short, circular tour of nearby streets when the Suit was joined by a middle-aged man in a trench coat. The newcomer dropped his hat on the table, sat down and scanned the room brazenly, as if he were either a cadet spy on his first day's outing or someone who really didn't care who noticed.

They spoke intently, voices low, and neither seemed too happy about what was being said. Hoeschler imagined a promised package that hadn't been delivered, a secret somehow misplaced between *there* and *here,* a potential turncoat who hadn't turned - any or none were equally likely, he wasn't interested or ever likely to know which. After five minutes the Coat stood up, retrieved his hat and walked out of the café. The Suit remained for a further five, glancing at his watch occasionally, the frown on his face still. When he left there were no coins on the table to express his satisfaction with the service.

A familiar, paralysing boredom slowed Hoeschler's head, making time drag further. Back when he'd first come to Berlin it had taken very little experience of the intelligencer's life to make him wonder how anyone could stand it for more than a few days. Its alternating periods of anxiety, outright terror and waking coma, added to the inevitably solitary nature of a life lived apart from company, seemed wonderfully designed to crack the most even temperaments (not to consider what innumerable cups of coffee did to an otherwise unnourished stomach). It was a job for dullards, or the vocation of fanatics.

Two lunch hours passed like the wait before a dawn offensive. By 2.30pm he could hardly recall life outside the *Café Leon* except as a pleasant hallucination, and the weight of caffeine made his need (and efforts not) to fart almost painful. If further CIA personnel had entered since the twitchy one departed they were disguised beyond his ability to recognize them, and his resolve was slipping badly when, just a few minutes before 3pm, he noticed something that made the entire exercise seem futile.

A man wearing much the same fashion in worker's clothes as himself walked in, went to the counter and handed to one of the male employees a small package. The waiter placed it out of sight without a word and carried on with his cup-drying duties. The other gentleman, equally reticent, turned and walked out of the café. The entire transaction had taken some ten seconds, and only Hoeschler had noticed it.

It struck him that if he was right about what he had just witnessed, none of the Americans who worked at Föhrenweg 19 need ever leave their building. A safe drop-off avoided the necessity of faces being seen with each other until a conversation became necessary, and even then a telephone would probably do the job nine times in every ten. He might wait here forever, slowly turning as brown as the muck he was drinking, and see nothing to his advantage. Herr Smith could probably run as many of his contacts remotely as he chose – excepting those, of course, he was welcoming to his coterie of victims. He had the ability to be seen only when he chose to be, and always on his terms.

Hoeschler stood and picked up his book. He was tired, dispirited and had no idea how he was going to explain his abject failure to Mila (whose confidence in him was as touching as it was incomprehensible, given the ease with which she once had betrayed him to her General). All that remained was either to wait for Smith to squeeze them poor or to flee Berlin, hoping that the American would think himself too exposed to mount a prolonged search. That last, feebly optimistic thought distracted him, and at the door of the café he almost barged into someone. He lifted his gaze to apologize (though it had been no-one's fault), stumbled towards the three-step stoop and was saved from a fall only by the swift reaction of the other party, who threw out an arm and held him long enough for him to regain his balance.

His saviour laughed. 'Watch it, mate. You'll cause heart attacks in here, going down suddenly. Everyone's expecting a knife in the back.'

Red-faced, Hoeschler thanked him and went out onto Königin-Luise-Strasse. His clever strategy had been a comedy – obvious, probably, to anyone who'd cared to glance in his direction. If the clientele could joke about who they were, what chance had he of passing for an innocent? He decided not to tell Mila about his day – it was much better to let her continue to believe that her husband was a man of subtle parts, rather than a court jester. In any case, it was too early to go home, so he had time to walk and consider what, if anything, came after his search for a deep bin in which to place his newly-crafted Rules of Surveillance.

10

On that day that Fischer decided to risk proceeding without the comfort of a little reassurance, Freddie Holleman telephoned to provide it.

'They're a registered GmbH. The Head Office and premises are at Regensburg.'

'That's logical. If they bought plant from Messerschmitt they'd probably want to locate nearby and hire old hands too.' Fischer took the business card from his desk drawer and examined it once more. 'Do you know who the Fehr half of the partnership is?'

'No, I can't trace him. But there *was* a firm, *Fehr Machinenwerke*, that supplied parts to Messerschmitt before the war - in fact, back in the days when they were still BFW. I assume it's the same fellow, though he must be white-haired by now.'

'That's probably him. So, Jens Lamsdorf's at least partly kosher, then.'

Holleman laughed. 'It's all he ever was.'

'Thanks, Freddie. That's useful.'

'There's something else.'

'What?'

'I looked at *Fehr-Lamsdorf* quite closely. They've filed accounts for two years to date. It's just that they don't … do anything.'

'He told me they supply parts to Allied aircraft manufacturers.'

'Yeah, well, they don't. They *did*, but the last job was finished and paid for three years ago, apparently. At the moment they have no turnover, just small capital injections and a few minor purchases. The balance sheet shows one live contract, and it hasn't been met as yet. The thing is, it's for uniforms.'

'Uniforms? For whom? We don't have an army.'

'It doesn't mention armies, just uniforms. The accounts state that it's with *ZfH*.'

'Who's that?'

'I have no idea.'

'If they've nothing to do with aircraft parts, why the hell are they still called *Fehr-Lamsdorf Flugzeugwerke*? And why submit accounts if they're doing nothing?'

'What I just said, doubled.'

The answer to the second of his questions struck Fischer almost before it was out of his mouth: *legitimacy*. A registered company fulfilling - more than fulfilling - its filing obligations was assumed to be respectable. If Holleman hadn't actually looked into the accounts, Fischer would have made that assumption himself. Even now, he couldn't say that this wasn't all above board, despite Lamsdorf's little lie. Wouldn't he want to impress a man from whom he needed a favour? The contract for uniforms was harder to understand, but being mentioned in company accounts indicated that it wasn't something ... what did the British say, *iffy*?

He scratched his cheek. 'I suppose it's nothing to do with me. If he's incorporated, pays or intends to pay taxes and offers me a fat fee in advance, why should I care?'

Ping.

'You shouldn't, mate. Get the job done and bank the cash is my advice. Then think about a comfortable retirement.'

'I'm fifty-nine, Freddie. I need to be occupied still.'

'Then travel. Get a nice motor. Find an indecent young lady, the sort who'd ...'

'I know the sort. But I've never enjoyed having time on my hands.'

He could hear the sigh all the way from Trier. 'You're a strange one, Otto. Do you know what Kristin says? That you're never happy unless it's raining. Your ship's finally coming in – enjoy the feeling!'

'It might find a reef first.'

'Argh!'

Fischer stared at the disconnected receiver without really seeing it. Freddie was probably right (and the Kristin diagnosis almost certainly was): a rare and unexpected windfall was no less for being either, and he hadn't been able to put a finger upon any of his bad feelings about it. At worse, he might be abetting a fugitive, and how many Germans could say the same? Adenauer's myopia regarding the previous Regime was an example to his nation - their Germany was forward-looking, so determined to bury its recent past that, without anything explicit being said or done to effect it, a generation was allowing memory to dissipate like a miasma meeting a westerly. Who would care if the man about to become Rudi Bandelin had particular reason to flee a personal history?

Otto Fischer for one, but the well-packed envelope and its promised sibling were easing that care considerably. His own past was hardly something to inscribe upon a monument; it made shame less of a balm than a gross indulgence, so he put his doubts back in their box, put himself into his jacket and asked Renate to assume supreme command of the shop for the rest of the day (which, being Saturday, amounted to ninety minutes before early-closing). Her delighted smile and half-leap to attention almost cheered him.

Jonas Kleiber was discussing something with the *Süd-west Berliner Zeitung*'s only compositor, so he waited in the premises' shabby foyer and scanned the previous day's front page. It was all as expected - more syndicated speculation on the Spandau murders, a when-will-it-happen piece on the Federal Republic's assumption of full sovereignty, a hearty congratulations to Amelie Bruckmann, widow of Murtenerstrasse, Lichterfelde, one hundred years old yesterday (*poor bitch*, thought Fischer, idly) and a large advertisement for hair-restorer. He was still considering the latter's implausible claims when Kleiber appeared, struggling into his own jacket.

'Have you brought some cash, Otto?'

'One hundred Deutsche Marks, a down-payment.'

'Yeah, that should do it.'

They walked south and west, towards the Parkfriedhof. At Finkensteinallee (only a street away from the remarkable Frau Bruckmann, Fischer realised) Kleiber took an arm and turned left, stopping almost immediately at the gate to a small but comfortable house that was set well back in a large garden. A downstairs curtain twitched as they walked up the path to the front door.

It was opened by a thin, elderly man in a collarless shirt, thick-lensed spectacles and a scowl so set that the corners of his mouth pointed straight down towards the hollow chest below. The beaked nose, its nostrils stuffed generously with hair, sniffed.

Kleiber smiled radiantly. 'Norbert!'

'Is this him?'

'It is - Otto Fischer, a good friend: Norbert Roth.'

'Um.' The gentleman nodded slightly, turned and retreated into the house. His two visitors followed for a few paces until Fischer paused to unleash several huge, wet sneezes.

Norbert turned. 'That'll be Himmler,' he said, glumly. 'He sheds like a leper.'

A jet-black head appeared briefly around an open door, checked the disturbance and retreated. Fischer clasped his handkerchief to his nose and followed the other humans into a sitting room whose décor hadn't been disturbed since the days of Kaiser Frederick. In one corner, a writer's bureau was stacked with stationery boxes, jarring the otherwise domestic atmosphere.

Roth turned, lifted a finger and waved it at his guests. 'I don't do work for Nazis.'

'He isn't one, I promise you.'

'I hate Nazis.'

'He's Jewish, actually.'

'I hate Jews, too.'

Beaming still, Kleiber explained. 'Norbert isn't prejudiced. Really, he hates almost everyone - even the girls he helps.'

'Whores.'

Fischer sneezed once more, waited a few moments and tried again. 'Then why …?'

'I hate Americans more. Loud, unpleasant goats, to a man.'

Fischer began to like Norbert. 'Our Jew, he wants to stay in Germany, but it isn't safe. He's earned the right to be safe, hasn't he?'

Roth sniffed. 'Who's after him?'

'The same sort who were after his kind back then, I assume.'

'The Master Race? I hope he fucked one of their mothers. What does he need?'

'I've found a strong identity, so it's just a matter of the paper to prove it.'

'Berliner green?'

'Federal grey, if possible.'

'It is. Place of birth?'

'Danzig, 1914.'

'Ah, good. A date?'

'Your choice.'

'It's five hundred Deutsche Marks.'

The sum wasn't phrased as a negotiation. Fischer took out his wallet. 'I've brought one hundred. Is that enough for now?'

'And photographs. Two would be better, in case the first doesn't take to being distressed. It happens sometimes.'

Fischer extracted them from the wallet. 'Height and eye colour are pencilled on the back of this one. No permanent distinguishing features, apparently. Anything else?'

'No. They'll be ready in three days. It would be two, but I have a couple of marriage certificates to finish. How old should it be?'

'Something early, but not notably so. 1951?'

'Right. I've a supply of cards from Duisburg, Hanover and Schweinfurt district offices. Do you have a preference?'

'Hanover. The British Zone is the most crowded. I like that.'

'Hanover it is. I'll alter the card number to correspond to a 1951 issue date. It will duplicate an original, obviously, but you can locate that one at your leisure and lift it from the local registers, if you feel it's necessary.'

'It shouldn't be.'

'One more thing. How good is your memory?'

Fischer shook his head regretfully. 'It's terrible. I have trouble recalling things, particularly names, faces and addresses. I imagine that today is going to be a complete blur by tomorrow.'

Satisfied, Roth placed the money and photographs on the bureau. 'Would you like tea?'

The question was so unexpected that neither of his guests spoke for several moments. Eventually, Kleiber nodded. 'Please, Norbert.'

The further surprise was the intact, gold-leafed Seltmann porcelain (a wedding present, surely, that Frau Roth forgot to take with her on the day she was defenestrated) in which a fine blend was served. Fischer sat quietly, sipping his tea, listening to an incongruous discussion on newly-promoted BFC Südring's thin chances of survival in the Oberliga, and had managed to drain most of his cup before Himmler reappeared and squatted next to the immune system he'd dismantled earlier.

The conversation couldn't survive the frequent explosions that followed, and within three minutes Fischer and Kleiber were out on Finkensteinallee. Gradually, the former recovered his breath and was able to stand fully upright (having been ineffectually assisted in the meantime by gentle pats on the back). He dabbed his eyes and sniffed deeply, taking in enough air to speak.

'He wasn't as bad as you painted him.'

Kleiber shrugged. 'He gave your face the benefit of the doubt. Norbert respects wounds, probably because he spent the war playing with train time-tables.'

'I assume that *his* memory's equally poor?'

'He's closer than death, I promise. You've nothing to worry about.'

Fischer blew his nose to give himself time to think. It was all but done, now. He would collect Rudy Bandelin's new identity card in three days, wait for Lamsdorf to call to arrange the pickup and then carefully hide both halves of his generous fee, having stepped smartly away from any stain of what might be a criminal association. And snow was angels' dandruff. He had taken enough of life's harder knocks to know that unasked-for gifts rarely came without at least one needle poking through the wrapping - he just couldn't see where it might be, for the present.

'I *always* worry.'

'I know, it's tragic. You've a solid business, a beautiful assistant and now a golden pot to piss in during your retirement years, and still you're gloomier than a wet Monday.'

Fischer had received the diagnosis twice now in the space of an hour, which made it hard to argue or ignore. He shook his head and sighed. 'There's the darker side, too.'

'Your wounds? This is a nation of wounds. You've come out of it with a lot more than many.'

'Not that. There are worse things than wounds.'

'What?'

'Dinner at Frau Knipper's house. Tomorrow.'

Kleiber beamed. 'Have you ever thought about it?'

'What?'

'That if I manage to scale Renate's walls I might be calling you Father, one day?'

'Jonas, you know that I was taught to break necks?'

'It could be one of those double weddings that English romantic authoresses find appealing.'

'And that I need the practise?'

11

Everyone was celebrating the good news when *kripo* Melchior Fux received the bad.

A few minutes earlier the radio room had sent word around the building that Adenauer had announced the date – 5 May – when the western Allies would formally end their military occupation, thereby recognizing, bestowing or relinquishing (whichever the constitutional lawyers said it was) full sovereignty of, upon or to the Federal Republic. Men who hadn't appeared to give much of a damn about anything for years were cavorting around the Bulls' Pen, embracing, slapping backs, punching shoulders more playfully than they did their suspects' heads and generally behaving as half-drunken fathers do outside birthing wards. One of them was trying to get the *Deutschland Lied* going, though as yet he had only the assistance of an *unterkommissar* whose singing voice was a perfect half-tone shy of where it should have been. Fux was gamely joining the fray, pretending good fellowship with men he hardly knew, when *Oberrat* Genschler caught his attention from the doorway and tossed his head. He followed, relieved to be distracted.

Genschler waved him to a chair, which was not usual (the previous day's non-progress report on the Spandau cases had been delivered, as always, while standing to near-attention), and offered a cigarette. He took it silently, wondering what he'd done or failed to do. The

Oberrat seemed to be of the same mind, as it took him several attempts to begin the conversation.

'The murders ...'

'Nothing since yesterday, Sir.'

'No, I didn't ...' His superior squirmed in his seat, half-picked up and replaced his own cigarette, glanced at the closed door to his office and then, when none of these inspired or prompted a form of words, scratched his nose. Fux, who had more than enough experience of not knowing what to say about the Spandau business, was content to wait patiently for whatever emerged - in fact, the longer it took the less he worried that his demotion might be the point of it. Genschler had never been reticent about giving out that sort of bad news.

'The ... the cases are to be closed, with immediate effect.'

Closed? For a few moments Fux said nothing as he tried to put his head around the word. They had a file for unresolved cases, regarding which no forward movement had occurred for a number of months or years. There was one for unresolved cases, where insufficient evidence had been compiled to offer a realistic chance of conviction. But the only *closed* files were those for cases that had been solved. He hadn't, until this moment, realised that an investigation could be deemed to be over in the absence of some form of resolution.

'I don't understand, Sir.'

'We have orders not to pursue the matter further.'

'But … there are seven corpses that …'

'Five. You've been investigating five killings. What the other two are or were isn't our business. From this moment, we proceed as if none of them are. Assemble all your notes and evidence and leave them with me.'

Fux was half-aware that his mouth was open, but he did nothing about it. This was hardly possible. He had half-feared, half-hoped that the cases or cases would be taken from him and given to someone else. It might have hurt his career; but not so much, probably, as failing outright. He could always point to his lack of resources and the failure of witnesses to come forward, while the Department's lack of experience of method-murders would make his successor's task as joyless as his had been. An honest, dutiful effort, however futile, was nothing to be ashamed of.

This, though – this was inarguable yet almost blasphemous, as if Luke and John were to be excised from the New Testament for being after-the-event, circumstantial evidence. It was something the Soviets might and probably could do - over there, almost all realities were what the Party said they were; but here, in what was claimed to be an open, democratic society, the dogged pursuit of criminality was part of what made the system work. He was being told, officially, to collude in …

What? He couldn't ask, of course. Genschler would have explained already, were it something that a *kriminalkommissar* should or could be privy to. It occurred to him that his boss might be even more uncomfortable about it than himself, given that he must know something more than nothing. Whatever the reason for it, this must have come down a lot further than there were floors at Friesenstrasse.

'Will this reflect in my professional appraisal?'

The Oberrat shook his head. 'It's nothing to do with your work. I wish it was.'

'Excuse me?'

'It doesn't matter. You'll be reassigned, to assist *Oberkommissar* Eckardt with the Neukölln burglaries. He's lost a couple of men to promotions recently, so he'll be glad of the help.' Genschler tried a smile, unconvincingly. 'At least you won't be spending half your time getting to and from the crime scenes.'

'No, sir.'

'Well, that's all. Let me have the paperwork by lunchtime. And Melchior …?'

He had never used Fux's given name before. It sounded wrong, like *darling* from a bank manager.

'Sir?'

'Not a word - to colleagues, friends, the wife, anyone. If a question's asked about anything to do with the business, shake your head, shrug, change the subject or just laugh and ignore it. Our mouths, like the cases, are closed.'

Fux went straight back to his cupboard-office, ignoring the continuing celebrations in the Bulls' Pen. It wouldn't take long to assemble the corpus of work that now wasn't work at all - a small briefcase could have held it quite comfortably, but the lack of physical consequence didn't make him feel any better. He was betraying his oath and every principle he had imagined he held, trampling on his duty to the city and not even knowing why. Whatever the circumstances that had caused the deaths of seven (or five) men, it was unthinkable that they not be investigated until some form of truth emerge, if only for it to be placed in a locked box thereafter.

And he couldn't even discuss it. He wanted to tell his wife, if only for the hug that would solve nothing and sooth almost everything; but if somehow it was discovered she'd be stained by the crime as much as he. Whoever had done this – *could* do this – was not to be tested. He was no coward, but it would take a majestic fool to seek to make an enemy he couldn't even see, whose power he wasn't capable of measuring. Silence was impossible, and the only option he had.

He gathered his briefcase-worth of painstaking work and put it in the middle of the small desk. It didn't look like much, even to its proud father. His generation had seen and done some terrible things, reduced life's meaning to a point of insignificance, but that was all supposed to be done with. Seven men – good men, perhaps, or very bad – had been erased, and now all recollection of them was to go the same way. It made him think of how he used to feel about the things that flowed past him, crimes by any name other than war. He had reassured himself back then that his hands were unsoiled, and it had convinced as much as it did now. He was complicit, an accessory to something, an abettor, an accomplice, as faithful to instructions as a rudder setting a new course when the wheel turned. What shit it all was.

But I have a good job. Its salary paid the rent, fed and clothed his family, took them all to Ruhpolding each year and left enough to put towards a retirement that wouldn't be hand-to-mouth. If the price for that was not to be remembered as a moral colossus, why should it rob him of sleep? He was a few short rungs up a long professional ladder, which meant that his slice of responsibility for anything, good or bad, was thin enough to cut cake. *Do what you're told*, he told himself, *and don't think too much about it.*

This was uncommonly good advice, and made him feel slightly less wretched about the day. He scooped up his paperwork, opened the door and stepped out into the Pen, where nationalist fervour had subsided to a few stupid grins and a perambulating schnapps bottle. As he crossed the room he tried to smile when his eyes met others, but his heart hadn't come fully around yet to what the head so sensibly proposed. At the last desk before the corridor that led to his *Oberrat*'s office he paused to avoid a leg pushed out to trip him. It belonged to Jürgen Ledermann, the sort of playful cock that almost every organization needs to keep its median IQ from skewing the statistics. He was wearing his habitual smirk of self-appreciation, and Fux felt more than usually inclined to wipe it with a slap.

'You had a call, Melchior.'

Fux waited, determined not to feed the routine with easy lines. Eventually, the smirk wilted and disappeared.

'From Waffen Ernst. He says can you stroll across to Forensics? It's urgent, apparently.'

12

The reckoning arrived in the morning post. Hoeschler was shaving in the bathroom and didn't hear Mila's stifled curse, but when he emerged it took no great surge of intuition to read the look on her face.

She handed the paper to him. The typed instructions were concise and clear; they gave a bank address, account name and account number, and below that the terms. There was of course no signature.

He read it twice, and looked up. 'This could be worse.'

'Worse? He wants eight hundred! *Every* month!'

'We can afford it for a while. Better still, it's not a one-off demand.'

She stared furiously at him. 'How is that *better*?'

'It means he isn't planning to betray you to the Ivans - not yet, at least. We're going to be supplementing his salary. It gives us time to think about what to do.'

'Do? I'll have him stabbed! Fuck!'

He hadn't ever seen her angry – not *really* angry. They had fought just the one time, about him keeping his job; but that had been a polite exchange of views, and she'd conceded graciously to the set of his jaw. This was a detonation, a beautiful fifty-kilogram landmine going off, and he decided that telling her to think straight, not stupidly, probably wasn't the keenest strategy. So he waited, letting the debris fall slowly to earth, listening to a lot of the same sort of language he'd learned in barracks, until she paused for breath.

'Germans don't arrange accidents for CIA men, not unless they're *Stasi*. We can't take on the USA, sweetheart.'

'So we just give in?'

'No, we don't. We bear it for a little while. Think of it as the ground rents going up drastically. It isn't fair, but then not much is. We can take our time to find the best way out of this; then, we spend the rest of our lives looking back on it, calling him names, drinking Christmas toasts to his rotting testicles, complaining that the toilet's blocked by an extra-large Smith ...'

She laughed, but he knew it wouldn't last. Her seed-stock might have been rotten money, but what had grown from it had required hard, honest work. She wasn't the sort to let smug bastards dip their manicured hands in her jar.

The smile was still on her face when she spoke once more, probably to give her room to pretend that she wasn't being serious. '*You* could deal with him. You've done it before.'

It was expected, but he was disappointed. 'I've killed two men in my life, apart from those who were trying to kill me. The first was a terrible mistake that I've never stopped regretting, even for a minute. The second seemed a necessity at the time, and I don't dwell on whether I was wrong about that, too. I couldn't find the stomach to do it again. But what if I did - I mean, having persuaded Smith to meet me again, and in a place where it could be done with a chance of me getting away afterwards? What then? We can't ever know for certain that there's nothing – *nothing* – in his possessions or friends' confidences that wouldn't give the Americans a straight, chalked line from his body to this apartment. There must be a bank-book at least - how else could he get at the money? How much effort would it take the CIA to access the bank's personal files and find us? Shit, they'd probably just *buy* the bank if anyone tried to stand on a point of customer privacy.'

Her lower lip had set while he was speaking. She knew she shouldn't even have considered the option (much less suggested it), and probably that made her angrier still. He kept his own irritation tightly reined in and told himself that she felt cornered; that it was principally her neck and cash on the block, not his.

Without a further word she turned and went into the kitchen. He could hear the kettle being filled, which was as a welcome a distraction as he could have hoped for. The next part would be the worst, and he assumed she was thinking about those particular six of his words that had flagged it: *the best way out of this*. For him it was obvious - for her, unacceptable except in extremis. The problem, apart from Smith himself, was West Berlin. The city was a stockade, a place excluded from the new rules that applied elsewhere in Germany. Here, the war wasn't really over, even if the protagonists had changed; here, the Allies would continue to exercise the real authority until such time as the Soviets went home and left their German *kozis* to make the best of it (which wouldn't be soon, if ever). The CIA's Berlin Station recognized the authority only of Eisenhower and Dulles - all else was either competition, antagonist or supine herd. Out in the other Germany, inconvenient legalities ensured that cowboys couldn't range so widely - Smith would have had far fewer opportunities in Frankfurt or Bremen, where contacts were shared among agencies and paperwork couldn't be pushed back, sideways or misplaced entirely. Nor would the implicit threat of broadcasting the whereabouts of Mila Hoeschler *née* Henze carry much weight in places where KGB couldn't commute to an execution.

She knew all of this, but having lived in and survived the company of monsters she regarded Smith as manageable. He wasn't, though - a man didn't need to be deranged to do casual evil, as any of their countrymen could attest. The American might even experience a twinge of regret at tossing her to the wolves, but it would doubtless be salved by a decent lunch, or a round of golf, or in pleasant contemplation of his other, cowed sources of extramural income.

Hoeschler read the short note once more as the kettle's whistle began its complaints: *Gewerbebank, Belenstrasse 10, Dortmund; account of Martin Ruprecht Janssen.* There would be half a dozen steps of disassociation between Janssen and Smith - a laundromat's-worth of cleansing of the trail of dirty monies. Any accusation that the Hoeschlers could think to make against him would at best be laughed out of Föhrenweg 19 and more likely investigated as a slur devised by Soviet agents. A complaint made directly to the city's police would be met with a shrug at most, and more probably disbelief that the effort had been made at all. The Hoeschlers had nothing to say, or do, that could conceivably deter Herr Smith. Hell, it might not be his real name – just one that CIA operatives in Berlin dragged from a drawer as required.

Mila gave him his coffee, took his shoulder with the freed hand and kissed his cheek, making the truce official.

'Then what?'

Run like hell. He shrugged. 'I don't know yet. We need time to find possibilities. Perhaps Smith will be recalled to the US. Or one of his other victims – if there *are* others – will betray him. What he's doing is dangerous, even for an American in Berlin. We're all supposed to be friends now, so I can't see that General McAuliffe would be happy about his people blackmailing the natives.'

'Natives?'

'Us, the Krauts.'

'I don't like that word.'

'You're not meant to. Still, if Smith manages to avoid the salt-mines, we need to find an exit.'

'Berlin is home.'

'I know, but you've been preparing for something like this - otherwise, your excess cash wouldn't be in a vault in Hamburg.'

She shook her head. 'Taking precautions doesn't mean you ever want it to happen. If we ran we'd lose every pfennig that's tied up in bricks and mortar. That's thirty-nine well-paying properties, gone in the mist because one swine thinks he has a right to our money.'

He thought about that for a few moments. He was already wealthier than ever he could have expected, but she was right – abandoning a fat goose because a fox gets into the yard didn't sit well in the gut.

'Could you deed them to someone else? Someone you could trust? They'd be your agent in Berlin until it was safe to return. Smith can't stay here forever, and if your appointee has no wrong history he has no hold on them anyway.'

She sat on the sofa and sipped tea, staring at some point between her nose and the wall opposite. The thought had surprised him, mainly because he couldn't see an obviously dumb side to it. He waited, watching her walk the proposal.

'What if he has the properties seized? He could make up a charge.'

'How? Even in Berlin, what jurisdiction could CIA have over German residential properties, unless they could find evidence to show the landlord lived at Karlshorst? And even if some reason could be found, Smith would light himself up by even suggesting it. No, his only power is what he knows, and that has to be used discreetly.'

She thought a little more and then frowned. 'It doesn't matter. The only person I'd trust enough to do it is you, and that's no good.'

'What about friends?'

'Who? Gisella can't keep her lips together for two seconds. Margret's a sweetheart, but she has no more idea about business than I have about stripping a tank engine. And poor little Doruţa would burst into tears every time one of my tenants told her that it had been a tight month and could they pay double the next time? The only people I'd really trust to do it couldn't be trusted with the temptation.'

She was talking about her old Tempelhof colleagues, the ones who had worked for the General, and he agreed entirely with that particular assessment. It was no good putting their precious immoveable wealth into the hands of someone who'd hire muscle and guns to keep it.

'What about *your* friends?'

'Eh?'

'What about Otto Fischer? Wouldn't he do it? He's a business man, after all.'

The suggestion was so unexpected that he forgot to be pleased she was taking his idea seriously.

'Christ, no!'

'Why not?'

'Because ...' On paper, Otto was ideal for the job. He'd be assiduous, painstaking and not give the slightest damn about all the money passing through his hands that wasn't his to spend. The Hoeschlers could enjoy a few years of comfortable *faux* retirement somewhere far from Smith's ability to hurt them and then return in the sure knowledge that, barring earthquakes or the Americans and Soviets having had it out in Berlin in the meantime, their nest-egg would have fattened pleasingly. The thing was, *paper* was no medium on which to make this particular calculation.

' ... the poor devil's done enough.'

She sniffed. 'We could give him a percentage of the rents.'

'What good is that? He wouldn't know what to do with the money. All he wants is a little peace, and we of all people shouldn't steal it. He spent three years in Sachsenhausen for no good reason, thanks to your General.'

'That wasn't my fault. Or yours.'

'No, but every time shit's being flung from a spade he's in its way, and his friends get the benefit of the cover. You know what his luck's like - if we ask him to do this he'll probably groan inside and say yes, of course, and then one of our buildings will fall on him while he's trying to collect the rent.'

She almost managed not to smile. 'Alright, not Otto. Anyone else?'

'There's Freddie Holleman, but he can't ever come back to Berlin except to be fitted for a coffin. I don't know Gerd Branssler well enough to ask, and in any case he's already giving Engi free bed and board in Frankfurt. Otherwise, I discuss the weather with the old fellow in the kiosk on the corner and football with my workmates. That's it.'

She sighed.' We're not the best-connected people.'

'Never mind. It was probably a stupid idea.'

'No, it wasn't. It just isn't practical, not for us.'

'Could – should – we sell off the properties?'

'I thought about that, but it would take time.'

And Smith would want his slice of that, too. Hoeschler began to think that her first idea was the best of a bad crop, even if he wasn't capable of making it happen. He shrugged.

'Well, let's pay the first instalment, and think some more about it.'

'Eight hundred Deutsche Marks!'

'It's bearable, if it gives us time. But we need to do something else immediately.'

She looked at him, the lower lip setting once more, and he hurried on.

'No, it has to be done. Even if Smith doesn't give you away, we can't assume that the Ivans won't take a hand themselves. You need to be harder to find.'

'How? I'm not leaving the city without you.'

'I don't know yet, but Otto might have an idea. He won't mind me asking his advice – it'll be a nice distraction from his clocks.'

13

Not wishing to revisit the consequences of Himmler's affections, Fischer asked Jonas Kleiber to pick up the identity card and pay the balance of monies owed to Norbert Roth.

'What if it's rubbish?' Kleiber asked, reasonably.

'You recommended him. Is it likely?'

'No, but I wouldn't know good work from bad.'

'Neither would I. Bring it here and we can compare it to ours. If he's stamped it with a frank from the Brazilian Interior Ministry, or fixed the photograph upside down - well, we know where he lives.'

Kleiber took the cash and returned within the hour. It took no more than a few moments' peering at the card of one Rudy Bandelin (born in Danzig but now, apparently, residing somewhere in Hanover's administrative district) for Fischer to satisfy himself that if this was a poor piece of work it was beyond his wit and ability to see it. Both he and Kleiber carried the green Berliners' card and this was a Federal item, but other than in its expected idiosyncrasies it looked every bit as much the genuine article as their own. This business wasn't going to fall on a point of paperwork.

There was nothing more to do now than wait for Herr Lamsdorf's call and arrange for the item to be collected. If the promised second tranche of payment materialized, his little safe would contain more money than he had ever possessed in a single, accessible sum. It would buy him a comfortable retirement (provided he didn't linger too long), or a year or two of hugely enjoyable prodigality, or an incremental worry to add to the others that people of substance tortured themselves with. He would need to think about a savings account, more insurance and even, perhaps, investments in other men's speculations. With what he knew of such things, roulette wheels and depraved women might be the sensible options.

He considered writing to Earl Kuhn in Bremen to ask his advice. Back in their dangerous Stettin days his old friend had kept his monies wrapped in plastic beneath the floorboards with a large collection of ex-military hardware, but family life and respectability had resettled it in what he called his *portfolio* (which to Fischer sounded very artistic but probably wasn't), so he would know a sound opportunity from suicide by speculation.

And then he thought again, about eggs and hatchings. There was so much that he was trusting to be as it seemed to be, when all reason and experience prodded him hard in the back, told him to bury Lamsdorf's money in the sort of well-armed hole that Earl Kuhn used to swear by and not even think of it as being *his* until all possible bad endings had disappeared over a far horizon. Goodbyes were far easier to bear when expected.

This gloomy truth cheered him slightly, and he returned to his repairs with a clear head, untroubled by anything other than the festering matter of Renate's mother. The previous Sunday lunch at

Haus Knipper had been every bit the ordeal he had anticipated, the delicious fare garnished horribly with arch looks, long sighs, accidental yet lingering contact between hands and other collateral horrors of a middle-aged woman shedding thirty years of carefully-acquired maturity. What her daughter thought of the performance he couldn't say (blank walls being expressive by comparison), but at one point over the *kaiserschmarrn* he imagined he caught a glimpse of the same sort of cold contempt she reserved for customers who brought in broken wristwatches and asked if they might collect them before closing time.

In the three days since he had tried to push it from mind, with much the same success as a prisoner awaiting the guillotine. The woman was implacable, immune to hints that his affections lay elsewhere, if anywhere at all. Spurning subtlety, he had seized the conversation at one point and spoken of his dead wife more, and with more feeling, than he had in the past five years. The regretful noises that met these reminiscences were delivered with what he could only interpret as grim satisfaction.

He was acutely aware of time pressing, because certain sorts of assault acquire moral weight by reason of their persistence. If he rejected her she would say that he had played her cruelly, and the world would believe it. If he emptied his safe and fled, his reputation would be less than that of Martin Bormann. If he carried on as before, feigning blithe ignorance of what she was doing, the wedding arrangements would doubtless proceed anyway and he'd be enlightened when his button-hole arrived. Other than admitting a yearning for young boys or willing goats he couldn't see an obvious way out.

He tried to dismiss the matter from mind, but repaired two Siemens factory clocks and a Schaub Supraphon and then couldn't recall their ailments when writing out the invoices. In fact, most of the rest of the day passed as a sort of blurred, grey background to the pronounced problem of Frau Gertrude Knipper's expectations of Otto Henry Fischer, and it was only when an unusually white-faced Renate stepped into the repairs room about an hour before closing time that he was able to extract his head from affairs of the reluctant heart. The cause, strangely, was Frau Lemke, the Pastor's wife.

She was standing beside his plastic Doxa display, a steadying hand upon it, trying not to cry. Sensing immediately that some discretion was required he turned to Renate, quietly told her to take an early evening, helped her with her coat and locked the shop door behind her. All the while, Frau Lemke stood in attitude, a tableau of Tragedy, Bravely Borne, staring down at the counter top with moist eyes. He brought a stand chair and placed it in readiness.

'Please sit, Frau Lemke. I'll make some tea.'

He had no idea whether she wanted or even enjoyed the beverage, but his head needed time to drift in from its former preoccupations. When he returned from the kitchen she was seated, and weeping openly. He placed her cup on the counter, hoping that it would give her an opportunity to calm herself, but whatever moved her had built a head of steam.

'It's Abel, he's ruined us!'

Abel - Pastor Lemke – was not, to Fischer's knowledge, a gambler, drinker or whore-monger, so he didn't know what to make of this.

'In what way?'

The question was simple enough but she took her time, lips rehearsing, marshalling something into shape.

'He's not an *easy* man, Abel.'

This was undoubtedly true. A virulent anti-communist and as certain of his opinions as any pharaoh, the Pastor made for difficult company. Fischer had long found it easiest to agree with everything he said and hope that concurrence would wear him down or send him off to find more disagreeable targets.

She coughed and started again. 'It hasn't been the same since the war. Abel didn't mind the Party marching into Church affairs – he thought it brought some clarity, and discouraged disputatious habits ...'

Again, Fischer had to agree. Executing troublesome clergymen had quite removed their inclination to squabble about doctrine and stuff, and what remained certainly counted as a sort of clarity, if thinly-shared.

'... but since the Peace he's disagreed with just about everything and everyone. He's always saying that he's *old* Old-Prussian Union, and he's against the Westphalians, the Dahlemites, the Barmensians *and* the Dibelians, and he refuses even to acknowledge the Supreme Church Council's replacement by the Church Chancery. He preaches what he thinks, you know that, and the Senate's got word of it. So they warned him, and then they warned him again, and now ...'

'He's been sacked?'

'Oh, no! They'd never do that - well, not unless he pledged himself to Satan during a sermon. No, they've ... they've ...'

'Frau Lemke?'

The tears flooded forth once more. 'They've stopped his salary. It's been weeks now, and we've spent all our savings. We're penniless!'

She grabbed his hand. 'Herr Fischer, you're a good man, without a gram of gossip to you. It's why I can trust you. Please help us! The General Synod's sending someone to talk sense into Abel - God knows I can't - but it'll be weeks yet before it happens. Might you assist us in the meantime? Please?'

Fischer had bought her unbroken clock, so he knew that all wasn't well with the Lemke finances. This was unexpected, though, and despite his own faith being weaker than a consumptive lung on a frosty day, there was something about the humbling of over-righteous, self-appointed pillars of the local community that pleased him far less than it should have. He patted her shoulder.

'Of course. Excuse me.'

He went into the back room, opened his safe and removed some money. When he returned to the shop she had stood up and was anxiously scanning the front window for evidence of onlookers.

'Is this enough?'

The expression of pathetic gratitude answered that eloquently. She took the bundle and jammed it into her bag.

'I'll give you a receipt, naturally. We'll repay you as soon as possible, and with interest of ...'

'Never mind that, Frau Lemke. I trust you to repay me whenever it's convenient, but no interest, please. Friends aren't usurers.'

He knew he'd gone too far when she took his hand and kissed it. It required ten minutes of think-nothing-of-its and of-course-you'd-do-the-same-for-mes to eject her into the street, and even then she lingered for a further five, staring into the window, hand on heart, expressing her thanks silently, before he could pull down the blinds and decommission the business for that evening.

Exhausted, he went upstairs to his apartment. He had given her almost a thousand marks - more than he kept in ready cash - so he was already shaving the money he didn't yet own, the bundle he'd told himself wasn't his until everything was done – no, *safely* done. It wasn't necessarily a Rubicon crossed (he could divert some of the next few days' takings to make up the shortfall); just one more sliver of unquietness to add to what had kept him from seven solid hours of unconsciousness in recent nights.

Later, he wished that God, Fate or weather-front could have left it at that, but before his supper had warmed in its pan the telephone rang. He went downstairs to answer it, and that was when a poor day became a bad one.

14

Ernst Beltze had offered the choice to Fux, who, not relishing the prospect of their being seen together, suggested the *Friedrichswerderscher II.* It was close enough to both their workplaces, not visited much either by police or corpse examiners, and, being a cemetery, of great convenience if their luck soured.

The day was quite warm, but Beltze was wearing his usual overcoat, a garment that could have peeled the glamour from Bruno Kastner. He was waiting, as arranged, beside the comforting bulk of the Spinn Chapel, sucking on a cigarette. When he saw Fux approach he dropped it and ground the gravel with his foot.

'Hello, Melchior.'

'Ernst.'

The *kripo* put his back against the stone and leaned. 'What is it?' he asked, knowing perfectly well what *it* was.

Beltze glanced around. 'Have they taken you off it?'

'Yesterday.'

'Me too. I mean, yesterday. The Chief Examiner removed the case numbers from the active list - five souls, uncreated at the stroke of a pen, like it was God's fucking will. My notes were requested – that's the way he put it, though giving me five minutes to get them made it more of a confiscation.'

'Really? I wasn't rushed. The *Oberrat* let me stroll downstairs to get my files. He seemed as nervous about it as I was.'

'I don't think I've ever seen Gröller nervous - but then, he served his apprenticeship in Neukölln, in the twenties. That sort of experience tends either to calm or destroy nerves. He was shifty, though. I couldn't get a straight answer from him, and then I realised I shouldn't have been trying. This is something that everyone wants gone, and quickly.'

'But *why*, Ernst? Hell, none of it was going anywhere, was it? I'd interviewed every possible witness, filled the forms, tread water and hoped that it would be passed off. Why kill something overtly, when it was comatose already?'

Beltze shrugged. 'I can't think why. It was straightforward enough – four cut throats and a shooting, no struggles - and, according to you, no identification. What the other two were, the two that were snatched away by parties unknown, I couldn't say.'

'Something about them's loosened some exalted bowels, that's for sure.'

'From which conclusion we should draw the obvious lesson and become very forgetful. It hasn't hurt your standing in the Department?'

'No. I've been moved to a case that has some chance of resolution. Which, to be honest, is what I've wanted for weeks now.'

'Have you? I've been offered a new post, a promotion - Kreuzberg District Examiner. What I've done to earn it is something else I can't say.'

Fux rubbed his nose. 'So we should be happy.'

Beltze sighed. 'Delighted, even. We're in a new world, Melchior. Germany - well, half of it – officially gets back to her feet next week, and we're both rising men in our professions. What wouldn't we like about all of that?'

They stared at the gravel beneath them, trying to find comfort in a question that had only one rational answer. Neither man had any reason to wish the investigation other than a relieved farewell, and the manner of its passing couldn't have put a lid on its capacity to harm their future careers more emphatically. No-one, it seemed, wanted anything to do with the unfortunate men who had been laid to early but very careful rest in the Borough of Spandau.

And yet the *kripo* couldn't shake the sense that he was colluding in something. Like Beltze, he had spent enough time in uniform to know that orders aren't to be questioned, but usually they involved doing things, rather than being told to back away. It didn't sit easily, to regard murder as an administrative inconvenience.

Beltze removed another cigarette and tapped it against its case. 'I'm not comfortable, but it's what it is.'

'We've both done worse, Ernst.' Fux regretted the comment before it was fully out. As a Pioneer he had assisted operations on the Eastern

Front that wouldn't have earned a place on any battle honours board, but Beltze had served in 8th SS Division *Florian Geyer* and seen things that he'd carry to the grave – perhaps beyond, if the Jews turned out to be right about God. He glanced at his friend, who seemed to have taken the implied slur as a statement of fact and was nodding slowly.

'We have - but that was war. This is supposed to be peace, and peace holds men to higher standards. Or it's supposed to. Still, I don't doubt that my new office and salary will help to blur the discomfort.'

The gravel beneath them received further attention. Nothing more could be said usefully, and the *kripo* should have left it at that; but it was the way of an unsettled mind to pick at loose, troublesome threads. He cleared his throat.

'Do you think about the two that went missing?'

'The world's unluckiest men?'

'Why do you say that?'

'They were murdered and *then* kidnapped. I wouldn't call it winning the lottery.'

Fux smiled. 'I mean, why it happened?'

Beltze shrugged. 'Because they might have been identified.'

'Yes, but by whom? And *as* whom?'

'How the hell can we know? By the Amis, as Abbott and Costello?'

'They died in the British Zone.'

'Flanagan and Allen, then. It doesn't matter; it isn't our business anymore.'

'I thought about *you*, Ernst. You have the tattoo?'

Not everyone who served in the Waffen SS had his blood group marked on the upper arm. In the early days it was more or less compulsorily applied, but as the Service expanded massively the practice became inconsistent. Beltze had transferred into *SS Florian Geyer* when it was formed in '42, so he might have been able to forego the opportunity.

'I have, and so do many others. I doubt that being former Waffen SS was reason enough to have the bodies disappeared. It doesn't do a man any favours on a CV these days, but unless someone's come forward to point a finger it's hardly a sensation, is it? Christ, the 8th's reserve battalion was involved in wiping out the Warsaw Ghetto, and not even the Zionists have looked sideways at us for it. In any case, wouldn't the Allies consider two murdered ex-Waffen men to be something of a result, rather than to be disappeared?'

'You're probably right. I shouldn't care, but it pokes me. The other five went through a process, even if it's being closed down. Those two ...'

'... Are very likely to be reason why the rest is being erased now. Have you thought of that?'

'Of course.'

Beltze smiled. 'We should put it all in a giant file marked *Unknown*. It's what it is, all of it.'

'Again, you're right.' Fux glanced around. About fifty metres from the mausoleum, an ageing parks employee was hacking at shrubbery that had half-concealed a grave. Further away, a woman was kneeling at another grave, tidying out old flowers and replacing them with new, letting the world know that her dead husband or son hadn't been overlooked. How fortunate everyone here was, he thought, to be recalled as someone; to be other than a case number that was about fall from all human memory.

Beltze was buttoning his threadbare overcoat. 'I have to get back to the office, Melchior. We probably won't be sharing any more damp meadows, but try to keep in touch.'

They shook hands. The corpse examiner turned, towards the adjacent Jerusalem and New Church Cemetery and his office beyond. Fux watched him for a few moments, trying and failing to be sensible.

'Ernst?'

Beltze's shoulders stiffened, but he turned back. 'What is it?'

'Why Spandau?'

'Because it's pretty. Our murderers preferred their work to be framed in an aesthetically pleasing manner.'

'Or because it's the British Zone. Who might want to get up British nostrils?'

'Who doesn't? But they haven't even twitched about it, from what I hear.'

The *kripo*'s brief, hopeful moment of inspiration fluttered and died. 'No. As far as I know, they haven't asked a single question since the investigation started.'

'There you are, then. Goodbye, Melchior.'

'Are you doing anything next week? The celebrations, I mean?'

Beltze laughed. 'Gröller's let everyone know that it's compulsory attendance. He's making a speech - about the Republic's rising destiny, apparently. No doubt he'll be as pompous as a Hohenzollern, but we've been promised champers to dull the pain.'

'Come along to our office afterwards. We're having beer and pastries. And no speeches.'

'Ah, thank you; but our being seen together probably isn't wise - we were the entire investigation, after all. When the dead are properly forgotten, eh?'

15

'Good morning, Renate.'

'Hello, Jonas.'

'You're looking particularly ravishing today.'

'Um.'

'Where's Otto?'

'He isn't here.'

'Where, then?'

Renate considered Kleiber, her unlooked-for suitor, for a few moments. Being by now a proficient reader of her moods, he thought he detected a slight disturbance in the adamantine facade that his efforts usually broke upon. Encouraged (or rather, made less fearful) by this, he put on his tenderly concerned face.

'Is something the matter, little mouse?'

'He wasn't here when I arrived this morning. I had to let myself in - *and* open the safe to get the cash float. He's never not here.'

'Did he leave a note?'

She looked at him as she might an idiot's slower brother. 'If he had, I would have said so.'

'Oh.' Kleiber hadn't known that she was trusted with the combination to the Chubb. A witticism about elopement came briefly to mind, but he didn't want to put a bullet into prospects that were already dying on their feet. She was correct of course – the proprietor never spent the night off the premises. He had neither lady admirers (Renate's predatory *mutti* aside) nor hard-drinking acquaintances with whom he might choose to pass an all-night lock-in. As a friend, Kleiber should have been more worried, but the normal rules didn't seem to apply to Otto Fischer. His life-path had been so strewn with rose thorns (where it wasn't mined) that he seemed not so much unlucky as tragically invincible. Still, this was not usual, and a headlining image of an already-mutilated wretch lying injured in gutter somewhere teased the journalistic mind.

'Should we call the police, Jonas?'

In the entire course of their quasi-relationship, Renate had never asked Kleiber his advice (and hardly ever called him by his name). He was both flattered and unnerved.

'N … no, not yet. There could be any number of reasons he's not here.'

'I can't think of one.'

Neither could Kleiber, but that admission wouldn't impress her. 'He might have gone for a walk.'

'It's becoming a very long walk.'

'You know Otto – he's ... philosophical. He might have lost track of time.'

'And it's raining.'

'But it's *warm* rain.' Kleiber regarded her severely. 'A man who fought his way to Moscow and back – well, he was carried back – isn't going to be cowed by a little dampness, not if he's got stuff on his mind.'

Renate sniffed. 'Well, it's not something he's done before. I'm worried.'

'It might just be an unexpected errand. Or a favour asked by one of his neighbours - half of them are tottering, you know that. Perhaps Frau Schäfer's finally had that aneurism she's been threatening, and needed to go to hospital.'

Another sniff. Though not an outright pessimist, Renate preferred not to be surprised by turns for the worse. Kleiber considered it to be her least attractive quality (that, and being the daughter of Frau Knipper), but in this case he could think of nothing that was likely to move her other than Otto's swift and happy return.

He had just decided not to say any more on the subject when the door opened and the missing item stepped in, closely followed by another man.

Renate let her relief show by gibbering. 'Herr Director! We thought you'd been murdered!'

'No, we didn't ...'

The man who had followed Fischer into the shop stepped to one side, giving a clear view. He was a stranger, but Kleiber recognized him instantly from his photograph. From three identical photographs, in fact.

Fischer half-turned. 'Jonas, I think you know … Rudy Bandelin. Renate, this is a friend, from the war.'

The man now to be known as Rudolph Bandelin nodded. He was about Fischer's height, as slightly built but with a much darker complexion. He looked to be forty years old or thereabouts, but his clear skin and regular features made the best of it. Kleiber decided immediately that this might be competition.

Renate held out her hand in greeting. She never did that, in anyone's direction; she disliked contact with other people intensely and deployed a near-instinctive manoeuvre, little more than a shrug, which carried her away from threatened intimacy with everyone, including her hapless *beau*.

Bandelin took her hand and smiled, making himself even more damnably attractive. It struck Kleiber that this imposter had undeservedly inherited a noble combat record in several of the Eastern Front's most parlous clashes, while he himself had managed to surrender to the British after less than a full morning in a too-large uniform. What a young, impressionable girl might make of that he hated to imagine, but did so anyway.

'Fraulein.'

At least the bastard didn't click his heels or kiss her hand. She returned the smile (Kleiber considered it a simper) and didn't seem to be in a great hurry to release his …

'Jonas?'

Fischer was looking curiously at him.

'Yes, Otto?'

'Could you come into the back, please? Renate, I'm afraid you'll have to look after the shop for a while.'

'Of course. Would you like tea?'

'No, thank you.'

Kleiber followed Fischer and Bandelin through the repairs room and into the stock cupboard. His friend looked troubled, or at least preoccupied. He had a habit of rubbing the scarred side of his scalp whenever his thinking accelerated, and it was receiving some attention now.

'Jonas, you recall Herr Lamsdorf?'

'The Money? How could I forget?'

Fischer glanced at the newcomer, whose face was as impassive as the wall behind it.

'He's was arrested, three days ago.'

'For what?'

'War pillaging, and embezzlement.'

'*Which* war?'

'The obvious one.'

'That was ten years ago. Who gives a f …?'

'Apparently a lot of, ah, *cultural* items disappeared from churches and galleries during the retreat to the Alps in early '45. The Italian government made approaches to Adenauer last year, and somehow they managed to put the finger on Lamsdorf as one of the culprits. From what Holleman told me of his wartime activities, it's feasible.'

Bandelin coughed. 'Jens sold some stuff, definitely. But that was lomg before he started up in business. I can't understand how the trail remained visible.'

'It was all unofficial? The thefts, I mean.'

'Definitely. This wasn't Rosenberg's *Kunstraub,* just a few quick fellows taking advantage of the confusion to pilfer stuff that could be hidden in rucksacks.'

'Hm.' Fischer stared at the clocks on his To Do shelf. 'It isn't likely, is it?'

'What?'

'Firstly, that the Italian Government has enough time on its hands to go looking for the petty stuff; secondly, that any evidence could stain the perpetrators this long after the event. And even if someone got very lucky, what's the point of it? The loot's gone, long gone, and if what Lamsdorf did was a crime, it was on the old Regime's books. Why would *this* one raise old dust by pretending it cared? If a few million dead Jews, Gypsies and florenzers don't spoil its sleep, why should this?'

'So … what, then?'

'Jonas, what do gangsters call it when a man's culpability is … arranged?'

'A set-up.'

'Thank you. Does he have enemies?'

Bandelin considered this for too long, and Fischer sensed that something wasn't going to be said.

'He has … competitors. What businessmen don't? He's not the sort to go looking for trouble.'

'Not since he sold off his war booty?'

'No.'

'How long have you known him?'

'Since … 1950.'

Fischer took his time, giving the clock shelf more attention. Kleiber watched, wanting him to just ask the obvious damn questions, but then the wisdom of *not* asking occurred to him. Having more understanding of the business would be to wade further out into a swamp that wasn't advertising its depth.

Eventually, Fischer woke from his trance and went across to his safe. He returned with the radioactive item and handed it to Bandelin, who scanned the details.

'Danzig. I've never visited the city.'

'It doesn't matter. If anyone ever tries to reminisce, tell them that some things are too painful to discuss. It isn't even Germany any more, you can't ever return, something like that. I'll give you some details about your war service, though I doubt you'll encounter any more of the handful of men who came out of the Okhvat fight alive.'

'Thank you.' Bandelin tucked the card into his jacket's inside pocket.

'Will you stay in Berlin?'

'No. I have the promise of a job in Wuppertal.'

It was a tired old joke, but Kleiber couldn't resist. 'Don't stand under the elephant.'

Bandelin smiled thinly. 'I won't.'

Fischer was watching his face carefully. 'Are you going to do anything? About Lamsdorf, I mean.'

'What *can* I do? I don't even know if he did what he's been accused of.'

'No, of course not. Is there anything else you need?'

'Could you exchange some dollars? I need enough for a hotel tonight and the train fare tomorrow. I don't want to be conspicuous.'

Fischer gave him what he imagined was a fair fistful of Deutsche Marks in exchange, shook his hand and said goodbye. Kleiber managed a nod that wasn't overtly hostile and chaperoned him to the front door. Renate said nothing, but her wistful gaze struck the younger man like a penalty kick to the groin.

When he returned, Fischer was putting his new dollars in the safe.

'I don't like him. Otto.'

'You made it quite obvious.'

'Why didn't you ask him ...?'

'What? How he knows Lamsdorf? Why he needs to be someone else, and why Lamsdorf's financing it? Who, exactly, is looking for him, and could it drag us into the same shit?'

'All of those, yes.'

'It isn't my business.'

'What if he's not being straight with you?'

'Then whatever I asked would have earned a bent answer, which makes it a waste of breath.'

'You could have made him drop his trousers, at least.'

Fischer laughed. 'I don't know the correct rabbinical forms for that.'

'And what if Lamsdorf confesses to all of this? You'll be in the firing line.'

'What a brilliant strategy that would be – to ease the pain of two alleged offences by admitting to a third.'

Exasperated, Kleiber kicked the leg of the workbench, an unforgiving bulk. 'Ow! You don't seem to be worried.'

Fischer picked up a Venus and read its repair label. 'I was, for most of last night. But then it struck me that I was fretting about the things I can't see, which is the least useful occupation a sane man can put himself to. I have no idea if this can hurt me. All I know about Lamsdorf is a small part of his war record. Of the new Rudy Bandelin I know nothing. Who is interested in either or both of them is equally a mystery. Unless you have a pack of tarot cards or some chicken guts, you know as much as me. If I have to give back the money, I've lost nothing. If I'm charged with desecrating a fallen hero's eternal sleep and abetting a fugitive I'll have to deal with it, though I'd be amazed if the police scour the streets for me for want of better things to do. It all comes to nothing much that I can see or do anything about.'

Fischer placed the Venus carefully on the workbench and looked up. 'I tell you what, Jonas.'

'What, Otto?'

'Let's go and have lunch. My treat, at *Lorenzo's*.'

'I have to work.'

'Tell Herr Grabner that you're on to something - a gang, possible involved in identity theft.'

'Very amusing. Do you think that I could?'

'Why not? Let's be irresponsible for an hour - God knows when I last was. And we'll have an excellent topic to discuss while we eat.'

'Which is?'

'Why the man now known as Rudy Bandelin insisted that I met him this morning outside Camp Andrews' main gate, directly under the gaze of two American sentries.'

16

It had been some years since Rolf Hoeschler had felt eyes (real or imagined) on his back, so it was difficult to put himself back into the skin of a self-made stranger. When he boarded the s-bahn at Schöneberg he had intended to disembark at Lichterfelde West, the most convenient halt; but then he thought about what the old Hoeschler might have done, and decided to leave it a stop early at the Botanical Gardens and take a circuitous route from there to *Fischer's Time-pieces and Gramophones*. A few minutes later his inner rabbit squeaked a little louder, urging him to disembark as early as Feuerbachstrasse station and give himself all the time he might need to spot a pursuer. It struck him later that he might as well have saved the train fare and walked all the way.

As he moved south and westwards, subtly checking reflections in shop windows and occasionally giving his shoe-laces some pretended attention, he wondered how he might broach the subject.

Hello, Otto. You're looking well. How are things? And business? Have you managed to persuade your assistant to call you anything other than Mein Führer yet? Ha Ha! So, I need to get Mila out of sight for a few days, possibly weeks, in case KGB try to put one in the back of her head. Any ideas?

It was going to be awkward. No-one had said anything about it since, but to Hoeschler's mind a certain fraught day almost two years past should have been their gold-watch moment, the one at which a final boundary was crossed between Trouble and the gentle, sure decay of years that comes to anyone who survives the former. He was fairly certain that Fischer felt the same way. Naturally, a rogue CIA agent seeking to pad his pension couldn't have been anticipated, but that was - should have been - the Hoeschlers' problem. Yet he couldn't not tell Otto why he was asking the question; he would want to know when, why, how and everything between, and only later would he give himself the space to consider how unfortunate he was in his choice of friends.

That prospect didn't alter Hoeschler's course by a centimetre. He was going to impose himself horribly upon Otto Fischer because the man was the ranking expert on dark pits in which sharp, pointed things grew. He would ask a half-innocent question with a wholly cynical purpose, which was to recruit help – help to see a way out of this that didn't involve either murder, poverty or taking up permanent residence overseas. A new husband shouldn't need to admit to himself that he couldn't protect his wife, but when the problem came from one (and possibly both) of the World's most powerful Intelligence Agencies, he had to own to his limits and find reinforcements.

He had reassured Mila without believing a word of what he told her. Smith wanted his tribute in instalments, but what did that really mean? It might be that he was merely testing their willingness to pay by asking for relatively little at first. Once they were in the habit of parting with their money, would he lean on them for more? If he began to worry about being exposed – perhaps by a colleague, or another victim, or even perhaps because nothing had gone wrong to date and he was beginning to feel heat beneath his collar – might he not demand one final, ruinous payment and then toss them to the Soviet wolves? Nothing could be anticipated, beyond the certainty that they were going to become poorer.

Otto would help, if he could. He wasn't God, but his head went places that most didn't. He could read people, and circumstances, and if there was anything to be done he might see it, lurking in cloudy waters at periscope depth. He might see a *chance*, at least.

On Rothenburgstrasse, watching life moving behind him through the window of a shoe shop, Hoeschler thought he saw a face for a second time in half an hour. This required a further, tortuous detour that brought him back up on to Könegin-Luise-Strasse near the Botanical Gardens and a kilometre east of the café in which, forlornly, he had tested his intelligencer skills a few days earlier. At the small semi-circular approach to the Gardens' northern gate he paused, glanced behind and failed to find his new friend in the scattering of pedestrians. His breathing slowed and he allowed himself a few moments' rest. From here he could cut through directly to Curtius-Strasse and Fischer's shop, a matter of twenty minutes' brisk walk at most. He entered the Gardens, found a bench, and sat.

It was a warm May day, the greenery in its first growth, and little of this place's dark history impressed itself upon him. Both Fischer and Freddie Holleman had mentioned the Lichterfelde murders - the tiny, cruel excisions hidden beneath early 1945's frenzy of butchery. He had been a hundred kilometres to the east at that time, one of hundreds of thousands of German soldiers tensed to receive the Soviets' final, overwhelming push into Berlin. Had a comrade told him then that a couple of Luftwaffe invalids were wandering around one of southern Berlin's finer suburbs on the trail of a murderer of old ladies he would have laughed as at any good joke, but like almost everyone else his sense of perspective had been dulled by several years' surfeit of horror. That was another thing that made Fischer unusual - there weren't many men who could see very worst of war and plot a sane course through it.

He forced himself to stay on the bench, pondering method-murders as he watched passers-by. No-one seemed to be interested in him. He was sitting at the junction of three paths opposite the Botanical Museum, so even an adept pursuer walking past nonchalantly would at some point need to glance back to ensure that the target had not disappeared. In almost forty minutes, not a single head turned. Most of them belonged to women, but he wasn't entirely reassured; all that surveillance required to be effective was a good pair of eyes, steady nerves and the stomach not to care for the consequences of one's efforts.

When his arse had numbed sufficiently he stood and took the western path, into the heart of the Gardens. Within a few metres he was under trees, where it commenced to wind like a tense anaconda, making it almost impossible for him to know whether anyone followed. Still, he was beginning to feel more at ease - he told himself that Smith could hardly be running legions of bloodhounds, not without making himself noticed at the office. If he was being followed it had to be by one, two or three persons at most, and they would need limpet-like skills to stay with him in this maze. It was well enough to be cautious – paranoid, even, but there was a point at which anxiety paralysed both legs and will.

He strode through the Gardens more quickly now, following the twisting routes but keeping his course generally southwards towards Unter den Eichen, and emerged at the main south gate. The arterial road was as busy as always, and he took time to check around and behind him before crossing. Again, he saw no-one who appeared to have Rolf Hoeschler remotely in mind. At the Botanical gardens bus-halt about a dozen people were waiting for the service into central Berlin; he joined the queue and remained there until the bus arrived, stepped on to it, gave the impression of a man who'd just recalled something and stepped off again smartly. None of the other passengers appeared to care; no-one made a sudden, frantic effort to join him on the pavement.

To his mind, that had to be it. Unless he'd somehow picked up the cream of CIA or KGB trackers he could assume that his visit to

Fischer's Time-pieces and Gramophones was not going to find its way into a report at Föhrenweg 19 or Karlshorst. He had about a further kilometre's walk in front of him, through a series of horticulturally-themed streets (the Second Empire types who'd colonized the then-village hadn't been too inventive when naming their new roads); he crossed Begonienplatz and turned on to Tulpenstrasse, no longer caring to check his wake. It was about 2pm now, almost three hours since he embarked upon a journey that might have taken a less wary commuter some forty minutes, and he stretched his legs to try to recapture lost time.

He was on the corner of Tietzenweg, waiting for the traffic to part, when his re-acquired calm was shattered by a loud, obnoxious voice, offering its opinion to half of that part of Berlin.

'But the sort I really detest are the rich Berliners who come south to poke sticks and make faces at us poor, rural folk.'

Dazed, he spun around. Otto Fischer's smirk was spread across both the right and wrong sides of his face. Standing next to him, young Jonas Kleiber seemed a less happy, though the prominent red stain on his white shirt that he was busily scratching with a fingernail might have something to do with his mood.

'Hello, Otto. I was coming to see you.'

'It's a pity you couldn't get here earlier, Rolf - we've just had an excellent lunch. Look - Jonas decided to bring some home with him.'

17

Lunch must have included wine, because Fischer's good mood seemed to survive most of what Hoeschler had to tell him. His lips pursed once or twice, and the frown (so habitual that the scar tissue had moulded itself to accommodate the furrows) hardly moved; but nothing else about him hinted that he found the revelations more than mildly disturbing. He picked up a watch and replaced it on his workbench several times while the tale was told, offered coffee, went into the shop briefly to advise a customer on a recording of the Nutcracker and generally gave the impression that he was taking the day's blows in his stride. Hoeschler felt half-reassured, half-insulted by this – so much so that he may have applied the darkest shades too liberally.

'I worry that he's suddenly going to demand a sum we can't pay, not without emptying Mila's Hamburg bank account.'

'I doubt that he'd do that.'

'Why?'

Fischer breathed on the Venus's glass face, rubbed it gently on his breast and peered closely for scratches. 'It's the amount he's asking – it's reasonable.'

'*Reasonable*? Eight hundred marks a month not to squeal to the KGB? It's fucking ...'

'I meant, reasonable for an extortionist. That he's doing it at all is criminal, obviously; but it seems to me that the sum isn't going to cover much more than his bar bill in the CIA's social club.'

Kleiber (who had rubbed the stain on his shirt until it was as snug as a trilobite in stone) perked up slightly. 'Do they have one?'

'I don't know.'

Hoeschler was unconvinced. 'Surely that reinforces the possibility that he'll suddenly ask for much more?'

'It more likely indicates that Mila's just one of several victims, who together make the squeeze worthwhile. It isn't as though there aren't plenty of Germans with bad history.'

'I thought of that too, but ...'

'Look, he's got you and Mila by the ... well, balls. Logic says that he can ask for money as long as he wants and you'll give it to him. I assume the other poor sods are in the same position. Why would he spoil that by getting greedy? If he decides to drop one or more of you in the shit, how can he be certain – really certain – that a counter-accusation against him won't stick? He'd need to be able to ensure that his all of his ex-donors became dead or Siberian simultaneously *and* before they could even squeak, and he can't do that.

'You think so?'

'No one who's exposing himself to a long prison sentence will do anything to increase the exposure unnecessarily. That doesn't solve your problem, of course – it just makes it bearable for longer.'

'Mila said I should cack him.'

Fischer smiled. 'She's an item, isn't she?'

'I couldn't do it, obviously; but we can't just throw up our hands, and she won't leave Berlin unless KGB are breaking down the apartment door. I need to put her somewhere safe while I think of an answer.'

'Wait a minute. Renate?'

Renate came into the repairs room. 'Yes, Herr Director?'

'Is your Mother's spare room still available.'

'Yes.'

'Ah. Thank you.'

When she returned to the shop, Fischer kept his voice low. 'It's going to be an ordeal, but Mila should be safe in deepest Dahlem. The rent's reasonable, the food's wonderful and the landlady's unbearable but discreet.'

'Otto, that's ...'

'She needs to do something for me in return.'

'Anything! What?'

'Put in a good word.'

'What sort of word?'

'I'll leave it to her. Something about me sleeping in my underpants and only changing them monthly. Or the digestive problem that earned me 'Corpse Arse' in the Regiment.'

'You're a marked man, then?'

'Tattooed, almost. She'd be doing me a great service.'

'How could she refuse? But you know she's viciously creative?'

'Any reputation I have is hers to ruin.'

Hoeschler's smile died quickly. The larger problem remained, even more starkly illuminated by the temporary easing of his fears for his wife. Between vengeful Ivans and a grasping American, what initiative did he have? A worm in the path of a *Jagdpanzer* had the same option as he – to watch it bear down and hope that the worst wasn't as bad as it promised to be. He wished to God now that he'd found her half-starved and homeless, grateful for his attentions but of no interest to anyone else. He could have been quite content with their living on next to nothing - it was much to be preferred to dying rich.

He looked at Fischer. His friend had done what he'd hoped he might, and far more easily than he could have expected. He couldn't ask for more, not from someone …

'It seems to me, Rolf, that there's a very necessary first step in putting this right.'

Hoeschler hadn't seen *any* steps, much less the one leading the parade. He opened his mouth but nothing emerged.

'This Smith fellow – you need to find out *who* he is. With a name, you have something. If you can point a finger, he isn't armour-plated.'

'Is it his real name, though? CIA's Berlin Station isn't going to hand out a personnel list to *anyone*, much less a German civilian.'

'Could you get him to meet you again? Jonas and I could follow with his newspaper's new camera. A likeness is as good as a name.' Fischer paused and shook his head. 'No, that won't do. He knows you have the money he's demanding, so claiming that you need to talk will trip a wire. He must know that he's only vulnerable if he's seen with you.'

Kleiber nodded. 'And I haven't finished paying yet for the old camera. The one that *you* broke.'

The conversation lagged. Fischer played with his broken Venus, Hoeschler stared into space and Kleiber tried hard to think of ways to seem more *au fait* than he was with their world. Eventually, all that came to mind was the inevitable.

'You should just sell up and get out. To South America – you, your wife *and* Otto. Think of the opportunities.'

Fischer sighed. 'Why is it *always* South America?'

'They say Buenos Aires is like any big European city. It isn't ever too hot or cold, the architecture's lovely, they've got a u-bahn and the politics aren't so democratic as to make Germans of a certain age feel uncomfortable.'

'Jonas ...'

'Rolf, you and Mila could buy up properties and spend your lives watching the world go by from a cafe terrace. Or dance! The Argentinians love ... '

'She wouldn't go. And we don't speak Spanish.'

'New Zealand, then. All of you have some English, don't you? Could either CIA or KGB even find it on a map? You'd be as safe as cash in a bank.'

Fischer halted the flow with a hand on Kleiber's arm. 'Abroad is just a different sort of problem. For the rest of our lives, everyone we met would assume we're Party types with ghosts in the closet, and we'd more or less prove them right by falling into the furtive habit. No-one with our accent gets the benefit of the doubt any more. Besides ...'

'What?'

Fischer waved a hand around the ailing mechanisms. 'I like Germany. It's home.'

Hoeschler nodded. 'Best place on Earth for Germans.'

Kleiber was tempted to argue further (perhaps for the Lancashire –
Yorkshire borderlands, another Great Beyond), but at least he'd
managed to put himself on the map, thinking-wise, and with what
was almost certainly their most sensible option. Surrendering, he
shrugged and nudged Fischer.

'Tell Rolf about *your* problem, Otto.'

Fischer winced. 'It may not be one. In any case, he's got enough in
his head right now.'

'What problem?'

'Otto's done something that might come back to bite him on the
arse.'

'We're not still talking about his landlady?'

'A bit of illegality.'

'This pillar of Lichterfelde's commercial community? What, tax
evasion?'

Fischer looked sourly at Hoeschler, whose spirits seemed to have
lifted slightly. 'A little favour, for a friend of Freddie's. It seems to
be more than it ... seemed.'

'But Otto got a fat bundle of cash for doing it. Enough to get to
Buenos Aires, easily.'

'Please shut up about Buenos Aires.'

Hoeschler shook his head. 'It's curious - all our troubles are to do with having too much money. You'd think that wealth would ease life's shittier passages, but it doesn't. Perhaps the *kozis* are right after all.'

Kleiber snorted. 'The Politburo's got enough palaces between them to make a Romanov blush.'

'I meant their principles, not what they do with them. *Everything* gets corrupted, once it stops being a theory.'

Fischer smiled. 'Are we being cynical?'

'We're Berliners – how else can we be? Anyway, tell me about your problem.'

Kleiber went into the shop to try another bout with Renate while the story was being related. Hoeschler listened, not interrupting, until they came to the moment at which the new Rudy Bandelin had departed the premises.

'Well, I can't say I'd have done anything differently. If Freddie recommended this Lamsdorf, I doubt that whatever his mysterious friend's involved in is anything too ugly. You may actually have saved him from some bad people.'

'Still, it was illegal. False papers are a big criminal industry in Germany.'

'Yes, but only for a certain kind of fugitive. A man missing a foreskin couldn't be further from *that* mainstream.'

Fischer picked up a screwdriver from a militarily-neat rank of similar, laid out in order of size. 'I doubt a judge will consider motivation, if it comes to that. Which it won't, probably. I just keep thinking about how little I wanted or needed the money. I did it as an exercise in cleverness, which just proves my idiocy if it goes wrong.'

'As you say, it probably won't.'

'Yes, but just saying that might ...'

Kleiber came – or rather fell – into the repairs room, almost bringing down the bead-curtain as he blundered through it. His usual cave-pallor had lightened by a shade or two.

'Otto, can you come into the shop, please?'

Requiring the proprietor's presence in the retail area was Renate's job, and Fischer assumed that Kleiber's persistent advances had driven her under a counter, or out into Curtius-Strasse. He put on his shop-coat, relieved to be distracted from an accretion of problems that wiser men might have avoided entirely.

Relief died before he reached the counter. A police *meister* and a civilian stood too far from the time-pieces or gramophones to be interested in either. The latter removed an *unterkriminalkommissar*'s warrant card from his pocket and waved it, revealing himself to be no sort of civilian.

'Herr Otto Fischer?'

At such moments, a man guilty of something might try desperately to search his memory for what had Gone Wrong, but Fischer had neither the inclination - nor, for the moment, the wit - to do anything other than present the blank face that perfectly mirrored his thoughts.

'That's me, yes.'

'Are you acquainted with a man named Rudolph Bandelin?'

'I ... am.'

'In what way?'

The strictly literal way, Fischer decided – the one that stretched the truth by the least distance.

'Professionally. He was a comrade in the last unit I fought with. In the East, in '42.'

'You've seen him more recently?'

'No. I assumed that he'd died about the time that I was injured. Most of the battalion was lost that day. May I ask what this is about?'

'You're assumption's half-correct. He's dead, but he died an hour ago - about a kilometre from here, on Schloss-Strasse, shot in the head from a passing car according to two witnesses. He had your name and telephone number in his pocket.'

18

The man had been sitting on the cafe terrace for almost an hour, slowly sipping coffee and reading the previous day's edition of *Oön* with what seemed to be close interest. He wore a slightly tired grey suit, well-made but well-travelled also, the sort that businessmen wear as much and for as long as won't disgrace their companies. Occasionally he checked his watch and glanced up and down the street (a pretty, tree-lined thoroughfare about a hundred metres from the River Traun), but there was nothing else in his manner to suggest that a schedule pressed too heavily that morning.

Just before eleven am another man, much more modestly dressed in a worker's collarless shirt and heavy twill jacket, approached the table and sat down in the second chair. The businessman said nothing to the newcomer but beckoned a waiter, from whom he ordered coffees and two slices of *linzertorte*. While they waited for these to be served they exchanged pleasantries about the weather and the second man's journey from Ansfelden that morning, and if anyone had overheard the conversation they may have noticed the respect with which the apparently wealthier man addressed the other.

When the waiter had retreated for the second time, the newcomer abruptly came to a point.

'Why am I here, Volker?'

The businessman smiled. 'Our issue is dealt with.'

'Properly? Carefully?'

'Both. We used comrades, good men who've done this sort of thing before. They'll be out of Germany by this evening.'

'Ah.' The other man relaxed visibly. 'And you're sure nothing was said beforehand?'

'We can never be certain, naturally, but I don't see how he could have had the opportunity. He's been a rat in a dark sewer for months now, not knowing who to trust. What might be known in the East, well, we can't say.'

'No, of course not. I have to admit, your idea was a sound one. I was worried that it would draw attention, but ...'

'*Something* was necessary, and we took care to cover ourselves beforehand with the right people.'

'Will it be enough?'

The businessman frowned. 'To take the obvious further step would be risky. We couldn't keep the thing quiet, and questions would be asked as to *why*. I'm not certain the link would ever be made, but even to risk it ...'

'No, you're right. In any case, a man treads more carefully when he has a stake in the world.'

'My thought, too. And the timing works very much in our favour – no-one will want this to be more than it is, so if he *does* try to make trouble he'll meet a wall that's moving the other way.'

The waiter returned with a coffee pot, and the conversation died. The businessman looked around as if he were seeing the town for the first time. 'How do you like these parts?'

'Very much. I grew up in them.'

'Yes, very pleasant. A world from ...'

The other man coughed, a hint that the waiter took promptly and retreated.

'It would be even more pleasant under different circumstances.'

'I imagine so. And the work?'

'Menial, but not degrading. It doesn't pay very well. Thankfully, the unofficial pension helps greatly, though I suppose it can't last forever.'

'People are very generous, but no. As time passes, commitment fades with memories - and comrades in the far abroad tend to requisition more of the shrinking pot.'

'Perhaps I should have joined them.'

The businessman laughed. 'No, you did the right thing. My occasional visit across the waters is always an ordeal. The nostalgia over there is quite suffocating – a foreign field forever 1938, somewhere near Berchtesgaden, the air shimmering softly with *ersatz* gentility, sighs and *what ifs.*'

His companion shuddered, picked up his cup, drained it and stood. 'I should get back to the factory.'

'Really? I was going to give us both lunch.'

'Thank you, Volker. My manager is very accommodating, but I shouldn't like to test his limits. Will you go back today?'

'This afternoon, yes. Are there any messages?'

The man in work-clothes considered this briefly. 'My compliments to whoever arranged the matter. To our friends in Bonn, please suggest that they continue to watch the other fellow carefully. I agree that he's probably not going to make trouble, but let's avoid any cause for regrets. Also ...'

'Yes, Anton?'

'Please, call me Wilhelm. Does anyone have a feel for ... the situation?'

'You mean 5 May, and after? I don't think so, not yet. Obviously, Adenauer isn't interested in opening wounds, but as to whether that might translate into a more amenable atmosphere, we can't say. The DDR would take great delight in flagging any obvious accommodations, the Soviets would do likewise and then the Americans and British would be forced to demonstrate that they aren't going to tolerate any sort of tacit amnesty. In any case, the

Czechs would hardly care to oblige Adenauer, even if he made the approach. This is regarding your own situation, I assume?'

'Naturally. You're saying my death sentence isn't going to be scratched from the books in the foreseeable future.'

'I doubt it greatly.'

The man in working clothes sighed. 'I suppose I should take some satisfaction from my notoriety.'

'Quite. I was speaking last year with a gentleman you've never met, who expressed his appreciation of your service. And he's considered an even greater prize than yourself, sadly.'

'This wasn't in Germany, presumably?'

'It was hardly anywhere, to be honest – a filthy, sodden wasteland, heavily populated with things that have either too many legs or none at all.' The businessman glanced around a final time. 'You should congratulate yourself, Ant … Wilhelm. Not many of us have managed to return home, much less to such an agreeable one.'

'Thank you, Volker. Had I been able to do it openly, without the shame of this Jew identity, it would be considerably more satisfying. Goodbye.'

19

Fischer insisted on making coffee for the two policemen, having persuaded them that he had been about to put a light under the kettle when they arrived. It gave him a few moments to think about the very many directions from which sewage might be arriving. In the meantime, Hoeschler stirred the fraternal bonds of law-enforcement with anecdotes of his time in East Berlin's *VolksPolizei*. If anything, it applied further mortar to the set expressions on their faces.

The *kripo* took his mug and went straight to it. 'The victim was moving north, away from here, when he was shot. You're saying you didn't meet?'

'No.' Fischer gestured at Kleiber, who was hovering, still white-faced, in the doorway. 'We've been at lunch for the past two hours – a restaurant, *Lorenzo's*, in Leyden-Allee. I'm sure the staff will recall us.'

The police *meister* sniffed. 'That's *very* close to Schloss-Strasse.'

'You can't think of any reason why he might want to speak with you?'

'As I say, it's been more than thirteen years. Unless he was seeking out an old comrade ...'

'Do you keep in touch with other former members of your unit?'

'Not for the sake of it.' Fischer gestured at Hoeschler. 'Rolf and I served together in *Fallschirmjäger* 1 Regiment – that was prior to my posting on the Eastern Front - yet we hardly ever talk about the fighting. It was another time, best left where it is.'

The *kripo* nodded and said nothing, waiting while the *meister* took personal details from both Hoeschler and Kleiber. It struck Fischer that at least one matter had been settled – Norbert Roth's work was good enough to pass close inspection, and there was no other physical evidence to tie the deceased man to …

Money. He had given the murdered man marks for dollars. During the several times he had handled the envelope containing Lamsdorf's down-payment he hadn't thought to check if the notes were numbered sequentially. Under normal circumstances it was hardly likely, but this was a substantial sum. If the businessman had drawn it from a bank, a teller's drawer could hardly have supplied it, in which case it may have been counted directly from a recent Länder Bank allocation. And what about the dollars that now sat in his safe? Were they clean, dirty, marked? All the *kripo* needed to do was to notice the Chubb to his left-hand side and ask to check the contents, and everything that Fischer had said so far might be presented as evidence at his trial. Who would need to find a motive, with a bag of lies to play with?

He was wondering what kind of half-confession would be necessary when Renate came into the repairs room. She looked worried.

I'm sorry, Herr Director. May I have a word? With the policemen?'

The *kripo*, taking in the view, almost smiled. 'What is it?'

She blushed. 'I overheard you. While Herr Fischer was out at lunch a gentleman came in and asked for him. He said he was an old friend. He wouldn't leave a name, but I gave him the shop's telephone number. I don't know if this was the same person who ...' she turned to her boss. 'I'm sorry, I should have mentioned him when you came back.'

Fischer, astonished, mumbled something to the effect that it didn't matter - though it did, tremendously. Not only was her testimony wonderfully absolving, it placed her firmly as an accessory to a capital crime should the lie be found out. It was something he might have thought of, given time, and would never have asked of anyone.

The *kripo* relaxed slightly, and tried to frown. 'It might have helped, yes. Can you describe this man, please?'

'He was dark, quite slim. About forty years old, and quite handsome.'

The *kripo*'s notebook closed. 'Well, it sounds like him, though he'll no longer tempt the ladies. The bullet did a lot of damage.'

Renate paled, and tears welled in her eyes - it must have broken Kleiber's heart, a performance that Lilli Palmer would have envied (it might not even have been an act). Fischer cleared his throat, and asked the innocent, stupid question.

'Do you think it was gangsters?'

'It was professional, that's all we can say. No-one kills with a shot from a moving vehicle if it's personal. Your old friend must have crossed some bad people. Did you know he was Jewish? I can't think how he kept that quiet, in the Army.'

Fischer thought quickly. A comrade would *know*, which is why he had to admit something.

'No, it was a medical thing. He was born with a defective glans. He had to explain that often, as you might imagine. I think he had a certificate from the hospital, to prove it.'

'Ah. One never thinks of the *necessary* circumcisions. It must have been difficult for men in that situation, back then.'

Not as much as for those who didn't have the paperwork. 'Yes, I believe it was. Will you let us know what happens? If poor Rudy has family, I'd like to write.'

The *kripo* nodded. 'Of course, though I doubt they'll be easy to find. His papers say he was a Danziger.'

Fischer suspected that no-one would bother to find them. Even ten years later, the *Volksdeutsche* were an embarrassment to the Republic – living (and usually impoverished) reminders of traditions and cultures that geopolitical realities had extinguished. A much different Germany was about to be reborn, one that looked firmly away from its antecedents. Perhaps a note would be placed on file, to signal that someone had thought of making the effort - it would be enough to cover arses, if the question was ever asked.

The uniformed policemen was already in the shop and halfway to the door, but the *kripo* took the trouble to shake everyone's hand before following (though it was probably only Renate's he really wanted to grasp). The gesture further eased Fischer's mind, and now he began to consider what real trouble he might have found. The policeman was right – this was an assassination, not a random killing. The perpetrators had known where to find their target, which meant they knew at least something of why he had been in Lichterfelde, and with whom he had business. Could he have been followed since he left his hiding place that morning? *No, of course not.* If they had known where to find him at the start of his journey, why not kill him there, in the dark, where no-one could witness it? Fischer applied a mental boot to his dullness, but then the logic of what he was telling himself raised another, altogether more frightening possibility.

When he heard the shop door close, he turned to Hoeschler. 'They flushed him out.'

'What do you mean?'

'It was Lamsdorf who was to have collected the papers and paid the balance owing. But he was arrested, in Munich, three days ago. They arranged it so that his friend would have no choice but to meet me himself. Who can do that?'

'Christ!'

'Probably not. I have to thank Renate for that wonderful, mad alibi she gave me, and then I need to think, hard.'

'About what?'

'About what I've stood in.'

It was hardly a moment for levity, but Hoeschler couldn't resist twisting the knife he'd recently been handed.

'We could all go to live at her mother's house in Dahlem. You said it was safe.'

Fischer pulled a face. 'Buenos Aires has first refusal, if it comes to *that* choice.'

20

At Munich's Main Station, Jens Lamsdorf resisted the strong urge to throw himself on the first available train to Nuremberg. He found a barber's shop, had his first paid-for shave in over thirty years and then ate a quick, standing breakfast at a platform coffee kiosk. He needed a shower badly (and preferably three), but had no intention of searching the city for a bath-house. He let his clothes wear him like an extra skin, and told himself that it felt far better than when he had done the same in coarse, grey Luftwaffe wool.

The service to Nuremberg was a fast one, but there the connecting Berlin train was delayed for an hour. He left the station, found an outfitter's, bought a new suit, shirt, socks and underwear, and made his ablutions in a small hotel. It cost him the price of a room for the night, a bargain by any measure.

The long journey from Nuremberg to West Berlin was a mixed treat. Until Halle, and on from there to the border, he had no complaints - the rolling stock was fairly modern and he felt much more comfortable in his clean skin; but at Ludwigsstadt they stopped for almost an hour while the locomotives and crew were changed, and thereafter the journey was speed limited to a maximum of 70kph on horribly under-maintained East German rails. It gave him all the time in the world to think.

His release had been as unexpected as the arrest, and almost as absurd. Apparently, the Italian Government had changed its mind, and no longer wished to hunt down the savage plunderer of a non-attributed altar diptych from a tiny church outside Udine, sometime in April 1945. He had readily admitted his crime, and even the name of the Bern art dealer to whom it had been sold; he said that he was happy to be extradited to answer for the offence, though he doubted that any restitution would be possible a decade later. The police who had interviewed him had tried their best to give the impression that they took the business seriously, and they hadn't begun to convince him. In fact, he got the sense that they were as puzzled by the charge as he.

As war-crimes went, the offence was pitiful. He had done far more that was wrong, and in a better organized manner, than that spur-of-the-moment misdemeanour. No doubt the good folk of the hamlet (whose name he could not recall and might never have known) had been mortified by their loss, but he doubted that anyone of greater rank than its mayor could even recall the incident. The vast part of Europe's heritage had been stripped out, misplaced, damaged or atomized; he was no more guilty than a million others, and considerably less so than Arthur Harris, or Jimmy Doolittle.

Three days in a prison cell, without even the courtesy of an arraignment to hear the charge and enter a plea - and then, this morning, he awoke to blank faces, shrugs, a large mug of foul coffee and no apologies for his incarceration (an admittedly comfortable stay, other than for the awful food and lack of sanitary facilities). He asked a single, futile question as to what circumstances had changed, and then declined to indulge the comedy further. He mind was already turning to what it meant.

Out in free and only slightly polluted air he went over the possibilities and returned, repeatedly, to the very worst of them. No Italians had been involved, no remorseless investigation undertaken, no purpose intended other than to keep him in a place for as long as it took to ...

By the time the train pulled into Zoo Station it was early evening, and he was certain of what he would discover in Berlin. He was almost calm, in the manner of someone who had come fully to terms with an unthinkable thing. A taxi took him to the address in Wilmersdorf, and he let himself into the basement apartment with one of the many keys on his pocket-ring. He didn't bother to announce himself.

It was a former cellar, two rooms given a minimum degree of improvement to make a dwelling for humans rather than coal. He went into the bedroom, found the book on the bed and opened it. In the frontispiece was a pencilled inscription: 'Plunder and Murder in Bohemia, p. 407'. Turning to the page, he went to the window. Angled against the light, faint marks could be seen down the right-hand margin. He glanced around for a pencil and paper, and then wondered what the hell he was doing. The book went under his arm, and he felt the first stirring of something he had known only once before in his life, when he had watched the box containing his mother lowered into the ground. It was not so sharp this time, but his anger was far greater.

The taxi driver was waiting for him, as requested. Lamsdorf asked his recommendation for a good, reasonably priced hotel near Tiergarten, had him drive there and then over-tipped him. A few days earlier, with a cooler head, he wouldn't have given such occasion for his face to be recalled; now, he was almost in the mood to be discovered. He had no weapon with which to fight off an attack, but if he could get close enough with his fists it would hardly matter. He doubted that the effort and will needed to kill a man that way would be beyond him.

In the small but neat hotel room he drew a sheet of paper from the complementary pad and wrote 'SDP' at its head. Beneath this, and after consulting the marks on page 407 of the tattered first edition of Gindeley's *History of the Thirty Years' War*, he wrote a series of numbers. Folded, the paper went into one of the hotel's envelopes, which he addressed from memory, placed upon the table in front of him and then sat back. He was raging still, his head bouncing between imagined, bloody tableaux, his various revenges upon men he had never met and wouldn't recognize if he did. The futility of it only fed the fire, and had a maid not knocked on his door he might have carried on until an artery burst.

When she had gone he drank the tea he had ordered slowly, deliberately, pretending to appreciate the taste of it, and collected himself. The envelope would soon be descending the stairs, on its way to the hotel's post-bag, and then his one possible revenge would be in the hands of God or blind luck. After that, he could do no more than to consider his own situation, yet he had very little idea of what that was, precisely. He had been released and the charge dropped, but he doubted very much that the *status quo ante* had retaken its cooling seat. He - they – had been betrayed, and he had no means of finding the precise culprit. There were too many parties, squirming to seize the fewer advantages that would remain when this nation could make its own choices; too many reasons to clear out a dirty, overcrowded cupboard while a very little time remained. This might have been the work of any of them, or perhaps it had been just a single vicious thrust, removing an old threat to older business.

So was it done, or did he need to learn the watching game? If it came at him from the front he could handle himself, probably, but a bullet in the back of the head couldn't be dodged. He had watched his friend live with hunched shoulders, permanently braced for the blow, and yet he had died anyway, probably without seeing his final moment arrive and pass. Lamsdorf doubted that he could live like that. He certainly didn't want it to end like that.

He hadn't yet sealed the envelope, because he still couldn't make up his mind about one other thing. It had been a safe recommendation, he had thought; but what if that was how they found Ruben? He told himself that a man's loyalties couldn't be measured or relied upon to remain unchanged, even by a friend. It seemed more likely than not, given what he knew – after all, they couldn't just have stumbled upon their prey, and he was as certain as he could be that he hadn't been followed on the one day he had risked discovery. And if he was wrong about that, the poison in his head told him that it didn't matter – someone had to pay.

He took the sheet of paper out of the envelope, opened it and picked up the pen. Below the last of the numbers he added a brief addendum, taking care not to think further about it as he wrote:

Otto Fischer, clock repairer, Lichterfelde.

21

Otto Fischer, idiot.

He'd ignored the *pings*, pretended the money was more necessary than it was, fooled himself that a routine needed to be broken occasionally, and now here he was. His entire adult life had been spent failing to dance successfully around the latrine's edge, and its lesson seemed to have been only that he found turds curiously palatable.

For once he could blame no-one but himself - not lying bastard generals commanding pretend-ordnance parks; nor method- or mass-murderers; nor black-marketeering Soviets; nor blind bad luck; nor even Freddie Holleman and his disaster-magnet family. The choice had been simple, and a regretful *no* would have made it go away entirely.

He was thumbing through the DG, Decca and RCA trade catalogues, vainly trying to bring his attention back to the available recordings of *Aida*. He didn't particularly like the work (too tiring, too much damn religion), but Lichterfelders couldn't get enough of it, apparently. If only they knew what sat almost on their doorsteps, Verdi wouldn't get a second thought. *Otto Fischer the Opera* would surely satisfy the neediest taste for over-heated drama – a blistering tale of love found and lost, conspiracies and bloody murder, with a hero whose serial blunderings would make Falstaff seem a model of understated writing. From oblivion to disaster in three acts, the climax an act of entirely predictable yet unintended self-immolation, no applause until the end, please.

The catalogues went into the bin with his self-pity. From the shop he could hear the muted rites of tidying and cleansing that Renate performed every time she found herself without a customer. Kleiber had gone back to his much-neglected trade, Hoeschler to fetch his wife to pained exile in Dahlem (no doubt taking a labyrinthine route both ways to throw off CIA or KGB pursuers who almost certainly weren't there), and two mantel clocks and that damn Venus awaited resurrection at the hands of a man whose mind couldn't come back from a death - one that couldn't have been prevented, yet needn't have been laid so close to the door of one Otto Fischer.

What had made the false Rudy Bandelin's murder necessary was a mystery, but that hardly mattered. Whoever killed the poor bastard couldn't know of his ignorance; they had to assume the victim had said something during the minutes he spent on the premises of *Fischer's Time-pieces and Gramophones*. Whether that *something* could incriminate someone, or provide a trail that the wrong sort of people didn't want trodden, or be of no importance whatsoever, Fischer couldn't say - because *something* hadn't been said, even obliquely. Clearly, that couldn't and didn't help, though he wanted it very much to do so. In fact, he found that his predicament, real or imagined, pressed very heavily, and he felt more exposed than he could ever recall. When he had been bothered by mere generals and mass murderers he had enjoyed the protection of the Luftwaffe, illusory thought that might have been. When he had searched the ruins of Stettin for those he had believed to be the murderers of his lover he had worn the shield of utter hopelessness and not cared for what further pain might come. When he fell into the hands of a murderous Soviet gangster he had actually hoped for death as the means of forgetting hers. And whenever he had pushed his head above the parapet for Freddie Holleman's sake it had been what a close friend did, and therefore not to be questioned or regretted until he had the leisure to consider things more or less calmly.

Now, he felt vulnerable, because in every sense his name was above the door. He was a tradesman, listed in the local business directory, a pillar of bourgeois staidness – an *employer*, for God's sake. The world had recalled its manners and extended a late invitation to the dance and he, damn fool, had accepted without checking the cost. He had acquired expectations - of nothing in particular but more than kept a man from anxiety about losing them.

If he was now a target, it was an easy one to hit. His routines were so set that a blind man wielding a stick could be led to a particular point and have a good chance of hitting him, and any competent assassin would be spoiled for choice. He might be found dead by Renate among his broken mechanisms, or slumped over a *Spezial* at his favourite bar, or face-down in his pasta at *Lorenzo's*, (he almost smiled at the last – it had such pleasing associations with bad gangster movies), or even in bed, his rest made far more eternal than he'd intended when he climbed into it. Against any or all of these possibilities, he could take no effective precautions.

So stop worrying, he told himself. Or call the police. Or go into hiding. Or take the Kleiber Express to Buenos Aires, second-class, single fare.

Or think.

He didn't even know the dead man's real name. Lamsdorf could enlighten him about that and more - given that he had organized and paid for the new identity, he must have known something of what had made it necessary. He was presently in a police cell somewhere in the Federal Republic, though, and the card he'd presented, giving a company name and an address that might be *postlagernde* (or even a fiction) but no other contact details, probably wasn't enough to allow Fischer to begin to close the gap between them.

There were only two obvious options that he could see – to go on as before, hoping that whatever business he had stumbled into had been settled by a bullet on Schloss-Strasse, or to make a quick and remorseful retraction of the statement he had made an hour earlier, admit to everything, hand over the money in his safe and take the punishment. If he was very fortunate, the assistance this gave to the murder enquiry would stand for something at his sentencing.

Both had their disadvantages. The first might lead nowhere or to an early, surprise execution. The second – other than reintroduce him to prison rations and lose him his home and business - would implicate

Renate and betray Lamsdorf. He didn't particularly care to revisit the days when even a bowel movement had to be authorised, but the other was unthinkable.

It was horribly ironic that an otherwise feasible third option was both entirely denied to him and precisely the cause of his needing options at all – that of going to ground elsewhere in Germany with a new identity. No matter how good the paperwork or deep the hole into which he put himself with it, his half-face would draw attention more effectively than the Kolberg lighthouse.

By closing time he had neither advanced his thinking nor made a start on any of his patients. As the clocks chimed six, Renate closed the metal shutters in the front window, handed him the keys and cash from the till, put on her coat and paused.

'Herr Director?'

He suppressed the wince. 'Yes, Renate?'

'The lady who's going to be Mother's new tenant – do you know her well?'

'Not very well, no. I was Rolf's best man at their wedding. She owns quite a number of properties, so the rent won't be an issue.'

She flushed. 'I wasn't thinking that. Why is she coming to us?'

'I understand that someone's trying to extort money from her. She wants not to be bothered – for the present, at least.'

Renate considered this. 'She has secrets, then?'

'Who doesn't? For our generation it was belonging to the Party, or having history in the War, or needing to pretend that an old photograph of a rigid, outstretched arm and gleaming eye was of someone else entirely. Rolf's wife isn't guilty of any of that.'

As he finished speaking he looked up from the money he was counting. There was a slight frown on the girl's face that didn't seem like disapproval. If forced to give an opinion, he would have called it wistful. She sighed.

'It must have been ... interesting, then. Nothing happens these days. I get up, make breakfast, come to work, go home, eat dinner, listen to the radio and go to bed. Between Saturday lunchtime and Monday morning my time is my own, and I hardly know how to fill it except with boring things. One day I expect I'll be married, and then nothing will happen to me, ever. I wish I could have lived in consequential times.'

Renate had never before spoken of how she felt - about anything. Astonished, he forgot the day's takings and wondered how he might explain the profound disadvantages of *consequential*. It came to him suddenly that it was really very simple. He pointed to his face.

'This is what consequential does. There are millions of half-families in Germany who've had their fill of it. They wish sincerely that life had kept on being boring - and I'm talking about for most of this century, not just since 1933. We took a bad path, started running and went off a cliff.'

She nodded absently, the way people do when they can't contradict a thing but can't believe it either. He knew that she had lost her father before the war, to cancer or some such foul luck, so the personal impact of the century's greatest fuck-fall would have been limited to hard rations and evening rushes to the shelters. Doubtless she had plenty of school friends whose fathers and brothers had gone to war and never came home, but the pain of that would have been blunted both by her youth and the foul prevalence of similar tragedies that marched through it. If his face couldn't paint a convincing argument, words would hardly do the job.

He could see now that her providing him with an alibi hadn't just been about loyalty. She had committed a criminal offence - her first, presumably - and made life more interesting by any measure she recognized. A less circumspect man would have felt privileged to have been able to offer the opportunity, but he feared what her mother might say or do if it all came back to bite them. He wanted the woman to lose interest in him, not have him pushed under a tram.

The money went back into the till tray, and that into the safe. The fat envelope keeping it company there was emitting invisible but malevolent waves, inviting him to recall that what had previously been an unanticipated windfall was now unadulterated blood money. He tried to ignore it, but Hoeschler's comment on the curse of wealth kept returning to him. Perhaps he'd find a worthy cause and donate it all, paying for his redemption as rich medieval sinners did on their deathbeds – *The Otto Fischer Lazar House and Soup Kitchen* (prayers for the patron's soul welcomed but not obligatory), or a small research institute devoted to studying the correlation between luck and the random movements of atoms.

Or a stray dogs' home. He heard the front door close behind Renate. She should have a pay-rise, at least. The alibi aside, a girl whose industry would shame a dray-horse deserved to own more than two dresses, both of which she was obliged to wear (and wear out) for work. The trouble was, the gesture would be entirely misinterpreted by her Frau Knipper, a woman who could detect an amorous advance in a weather-front. Again, he had to blame his face for not doing the one job that aviation fuel had so ably fitted it for.

A solution occurred as he locked the front door, and he found it difficult not to laugh aloud. He could reward Renate suitably and forestall any further interest from her mother, and all it would cost him was at least one friendship and any reputation he might have in the district. A candle-lit Italian dinner, during which he would lay out his earthly estate and lack of need for any form of physical intimacy, should do it. She wasn't interested in men particularly (as Jonas Kleiber could attest), so the peculiarity of the relationship wouldn't itch too much, and thenceforth all her industry would be devoted to her own advancement rather than that of her employer. In twenty years at most she would reap the harvest, for the very modest outlay of a half-decent funeral and reception afterwards.

Renate Fischer. They'd call him a goat, a pervert, and Kleiber would never say another word to him. The only man who might understand would be another goat, the proprietor of the *Süd-west Berliner Zeitung*, who had similarly taken a child-bride and repented at leisure thereafter as she worked her way through the junior officers' list at Camp Andrews. In time, they might even become fast friends, bonded by their outcasts' status and shared taste for young flesh.

Half an hour later he was upstairs in his apartment, finishing the last of his supper, and despite the sombre background noise of Bach's B minor *Mass* on the (repaired but unclaimed) Dansette Plus-A-Gram, the thought of Frau Knipper as a mother-in-law set him off again whenever the tickle threatened to subside. He could never do it, of course - it would require far greater courage and less moral core than he possessed; but even a ridiculous stratagem was one more than he'd previously stumbled upon, and his mood was raised considerably. It took a sudden, loud rap upon the door at the top of the fire-escape to drop it with the plate that fell out of his startled hands.

22

On a cold stone bench in the Altes Nationalgalerie, Ernst Beltze stared into Friedrich's *Moonrise at the Ocean*, letting its dark vista ease his eyes. It reminded him a little of a pleasant wartime evening on the shoreline of a lake near Magnitnyy, a *KdF Truppenbetreuung* sing-along to raise the soldiers' morale a few days before their unit commenced its valuable work of misidentifying local Russian civilians as partisans and shooting them. The air had that same heaviness to it, though necessarily missing the slight chill and spring odours he recalled.

He sensed rather than felt his friend Melchior's arrival, the bench being dense enough not to transmit the vibration of a rump landing upon it. For a few moments neither man spoke; Beltze, having come by invitation, waited to be enlightened as to why their tactical estrangement had been interrupted so soon after its commencement.

By way of explanation, the *kripo* passed a piece of paper to him. It required no great study, being a short list of numbers and a name, but he gave it some attention. Their meeting had inconvenienced his work schedule, and he wanted it to be worthwhile.

'What am I looking at?'

'I'm not sure.'

'I don't do puzzles.'

'Of course you do, Ernst - you're a Corpse Examiner. What fun would it be, if bodies didn't tease?'

'Alright then, I don't care for opaque scribbles. I assume there's no provenance?'

'No. The envelope it came in had a West Berlin postmark.'

'Ah, well, you've narrowed it down to about three million suspects. If they're suspected of anything, that is. But we don't know, do we, because this might not *be* anything.'

'Five numbers. Five bodies ...'

'*Seven* bodies.'

'Well, let's pretend five for the moment, because that's what we were left with.'

'I thought we were going to let the business die gracefully? For our health's sake?'

'We were, certainly. This arrived in the morning's post, though. I didn't say I wouldn't consider new evidence.'

'But is it?'

Look at it. What does 'SDP' mean?'

'I have no idea. Perhaps the author meant to write SPD?'

'Then I assume he would have done so. You're thinking that these might be Party membership numbers?'

Beltze sighed. 'It crossed my mind.'

'They're all of three or four-digits. When was the SPD founded - the 1860s? To have Party numbers this low would require that our victims be centenarians. I don't recall that they were.'

'So, a bad idea. I shouldn't have ambitions to be a policeman. Who's this fellow, by the way? The Lichterfelde clock-repairer?'

'Forget him for the moment. If the numbers *are* to do with our bodies, then the poor bastards are linked by more than their fates. What organizations assign numbers to their membership?'

'Just about every one of them, everywhere. How else are subscriptions collected, or postal lists compiled? But might they be case numbers?'

'The men have criminal records? That's ...' Fux frowned; '... a good idea, Ernst. But again, the identifiers would contain far more digits – and letters, of course.'

'Medical cases? A particular, uncommon disease?'

'Mm. But why were they killed for that?'

Beltze smiled. 'They were contagious?'

'And so the killer, or killers, used the most intimate, self-infecting method of killing them – all but the last one, that is.'

'Do you know what I think, Melchior?'

'What?'

'That your piece of paper has nothing to do with what we shouldn't be talking about anyway. And even if it has, haven't we had enough hints about what should be done with it?'

Fux stared at 'his' piece of paper. For as long as his name had been on the investigation he hadn't wanted it, but since he'd been relieved (in every sense), the thing had been biting him like a rabid dachshund. It was a heroically pointless pastime, and part of his frustration derived from knowing that.

'You're probably right, Ernst.'

'You're not going to throw it in a bin, are you?'

'Not just yet.'

'How is your new assignment? The burglaries in Neukölln?'

'It couldn't be better. We made two arrests, extracted two confessions, the gang splintered and now we have commendations from the top floor and a new outbreak in Tempelhof that should keep us busy for the next six months.'

'Yet you need the extra grief of a case that's been officially designated a non-event?'

'Put that way, of course not.'

'Perhaps you feel that you're the only good police in a rotten department, and this is a personal crusade to put things right – the bright steel of justice wielded by a latter-day *Parsifal*?'

'Fuck off, Ernst.'

Beltze shrugged. 'It's what it smells like. I assume you haven't mentioned any of this to your wife?'

'No – neither having the case killed, nor me not letting it go. If I did, she'd wait until I slept and then put the flat iron up me.'

'Wise girl. It should tell you something.'

'It does. You're right, naturally. I'll move just a little further, and if it comes to nothing, the paper and everything else goes into that bin.'

'What's the *further*?'

The *kripo* tapped the paper. 'This name. I asked around the Pen, whether anyone had heard of the fellow. Do you know an *unterkommissar*, Robert Holzmann?'

'Vaguely. I think his name was on an initial report that was pinned to a body I examined last year.'

'Well, he looked surprised – said he'd spoken to the man only two days ago, about another killing, in Steglitz.'

'Shit!'

'Holzmann doesn't think he's involved. He just knew the victim, an old comrade from the war that he hadn't seen since. He's a wounded veteran, apparently - has a face like two shot badgers.'

'Still, a coincidence like that - I can see now why you're being idiotic about that piece of paper. I'd probably be the same.'

'I've asked to have him brought in, to Friesenstrasse.'

'Was that clever? If anyone gets even a hint that you haven't let go ...'

'It's a risk, but people tend to talk more readily in an interview room than their parlour. Or shop. I'll be careful – oblique, that is.'

'You won't mention the killings? How would that help?'

'I'll try to bring him to it around the houses. We'll talk about his dead friend first, then I'll suggest there might be a connection with ... *recent* killings elsewhere. If I'm lucky, and he wants to chat, something could come of it. Even a twitch could tell me that what's on the paper might be worth following. If I get nothing, nothing's been lost.'

Beltze scratched his chin and gave the painting in front of him some more attention. The wall behind it had been repaired since the war but hadn't yet been plastered or painted, so *Moonrise at the Ocean* had to compete strenuously with an anything-but-reticent background. He wasn't unduly bothered by that; its potential to raise memories apart, art had never really interested him other than as an investment. His parents' house had been a dark, dour place, made more so by a surplus of heavy Second Empire portraits and mountain views on its walls, and to his mind an art gallery was merely an industrial-scaled version of the same. He preferred libraries, both for their odours and their capacity to help a man lose unwanted hours.

Fux was looking at the painting as if for the first time, and seemed unimpressed.

'Are those two women conjoined?'

'No, it's the perspective - and the lighting, I expect.'

'Very poor. I prefer a still-life.'

Over-stuffed depictions of flowers, pewter flagons and dead animals awaiting skinning, were, to Beltze, as ghastly as they were inexplicable either as art or decor, but knowing little of the subject he decided not to argue the point.

'Ah.'

The *kripo* stood. 'I have to get back. Do you want me to let you know how it falls out?'

To his surprise, the Corpse Examiner found that his interest in the business had been rekindled, despite his head telling him to run and hide.

'Please, Melchior. Though I don't know what's to be done about it, whatever you find.'

'Neither do I. But to *know* would be better than having to pretend that nothing happened.'

'I suppose it would. At least all those reports wouldn't be ...'

'Be what?'

Beltze paused for a moment, surprised that a very obvious point hadn't impressed itself before now.

'Ernst?'

'For every victim – every one that wasn't snatched from us, I mean – I prepared an Examiner's report.'

'Of course.'

'Each of them copied to the British.'

'Well, they like their paperwork, don't ...'

Belatedly, Fux got the point. Word had come down that the investigation was to be wound down – or rather, disappeared into a dark hole. Until now, both men had assumed that the decision had been made in Friesenstrasse, or possibly Bonn. But no such German-sourced order could possibly affect what the British would or wouldn't do with what they had been given. So, either the business might still be very much alive (unlike its subject matter), or the two of them were defying not only their superiors but one of their Occupiers also.

Beltze stared at his friend. 'Shit! You don't think the killers are Tommies?'

'Let's not – think it, I mean.'

'It would explain why everything's been filed under Oblivion.'

'It might. So might other possibilities.'

'Melchior, you can't go against the British.'

'No, and I can't go against my own bosses, either. I'm not trying to reopen the cases; just to understand what it is about them that's poison.'

'Write to Winston Churchill. Tell him you'd very much like to have your mind put at rest, and that it's worth a cigar.'

The *kripo* tried to smile, but his heart wasn't in it. He tapped the paper. 'No, I'll speak to the gentleman with the two-shot-badgers face. And if he can't help me it's finished, I promise.'

'Then I pray for his ignorance on all matters of murder.'

23

Hoeschler considered several routes by which he and Mila might get from their Schöneberg home to Dahlem without being followed. All were tortuous, involving several stages – a taxi from *here* to *here*; then the s-bahn, two stops to *here*; then the u-bahn to *here*; perhaps a short back-step to *here*; finally, his wife would go on ahead by foot while he followed to ensure that the final few hundred metres to Frau Knipper's home remained unpopulated by rogue CIA hirelings. He mentioned a few of the shrewder potential detours to her, and took her silence for agreement, or at least acquiescence. It was only when she waved from their apartment window to a car parked in the street below that he realised he had been wasting both his head and breath.

'It's Walter. He does plastering work for us.'

Clearly, plastering was a second career-choice for Walter. Hoeschler helped his wife into the rear seat with her bag and then opened the front passenger door to take his place next to the driver, but a grey-ghost Walther P38 had got there first. Its owner tossed his head.

'In the back, please. Keep the rear window clear for me.'

That was all Walter had to say about anything. The journey (as convoluted as anything Hoeschler might have conceived) took only fifteen minutes, and the man's eyes seemed to be on the road ahead for very few of them. The rear-view and wing mirrors held all of the rest of his attention, yet the drive was as smooth and safe as if an ambassador's personal chauffeur were at the wheel. Mila spent the time staring out of her side-window with no more apparent interest than if she had been coming home from the market on a bus, while Hoeschler devoted considerable will-power to not turning every ten seconds to act as Walter's second pair of eyes.

The car parked at the end of a short street, and remained there while Hoeschler and his wife walked to the address Renate had provided. The house was small, old but beautifully maintained, the short path from iron gate to front door flanked by two mature magnolia trees. At the stoop, Mila paused and turned to her husband.

'This really is necessary?'

'I don't know. That's the point.'

He was about to rehearse once more the reasons with which he'd worn her down when the front door opened.

'Ah, the Hoeschlers! Welcome!'

The dreaded Frau Knipper was hardly the miscegenation of witch and vampire that they had been led to expect. Her face was creased by a smile that seemed to live easily on it, and the source of her daughter's considerable beauty was immediately apparent. Hoeschler judged her to be in her late '40s, but only from the colour of her untreated hair; otherwise, her features encouraged a man not to consider age an issue. Mila, here only by the grace of remorseless pestering, made up her mind immediately. She stepped forward and embraced the other woman, an impulsive display of affection that was wholly out of character. Hoeschler held out his hand, and felt almost churlish about it.

'Come in, please. I'm making tea.'

They followed her into a house that was equally unexpected. The over-stuffed pre-war style had been banished (if ever it had been present) in favour of a Scandinavian sparseness that made the most of the small rooms. On the (plainly painted) walls hung a small number of artworks that the previous regime would have declared *entartete* in a moment, and the furniture had enough Moravian simplicity to turn any Kaiser's stomach. Everything was so much of the style that Otto Fischer favoured that he must have sensed a trap the moment he crossed the threshold for the first time.

She's a siren, and he has no main-mast.

Frau Knipper waved them to a sofa and went into her kitchen. As they sat, Mila glanced at her husband, her look saying much of what he was thinking. Hoeschler was afraid that she might start giggling – it happened too rarely to be called a habit, but invariably it struck at the least appropriate moments, and once started it had to run its course. Even he had to fight down a delightful image of Otto Fischer unmanned by the advances of a warm, attractive widow; he put his hand on his wife's knee and squeezed, hoping that the gesture wouldn't set them both off.

The knee began to tremble badly when Frau Knipper returned, pushing a tea-trolley. Hastily, Hoeschler jumped up and took over for the final half-metre to the occasional table that was clearly her goal, a pointless effort that nevertheless diverted his attention. He could hardly believe how overladen the thing was; rationing had ended in Germany over five years earlier, but the amount of butter and sugar required for the profusion of small tarts and cakes on offer must have emptied half the shops in that part of Dahlem.

Frau Knipper looked down sadly. 'I'm sorry, it isn't much, but I was going to bake again tomorrow.'

Mila bit her lip and moaned softly. Without thinking about what he was going to say precisely, Hoeschler tried to cover the noise.

'Otto mentioned to your daughter that we're not quite sure how long my wife will need the room. That isn't inconvenient, I hope?'

Frau Knipper's bosom (ample but not heavy, he decided - in every way suitable to its distracting purpose) heaved perceptibly at the name.

'Of course not. You can let me know when your arrangements are settled. How *is* dear Herr Fischer? We saw him last Sunday for lunch, and I thought he seemed a little tired.'

'He's fine, I think. He's doesn't sleep much.'

'You've known him long?'

'We served in the same unit for almost two years, though I only came to know him briefly before he transferred out.'

The bosom rose considerably. 'You were with the *Fallschirmjäger*, too?'

'I was, yes. Though very few of us were airborne after Crete.'

'You weren't at Gran Sasso with Skorzeny?'

'I never met the man. He was SS of course – that was his only time with our lads.'

'It was such a daring raid, to snatch *Il Duce* from his betrayers!'

And a big, fucking show-off Waste of time, too. 'Yes, we all admired him for that.'

Frau Knipper's gaze moved slightly from his face, and he wondered if it was lingering on the strapping heroes of Operation *Oak*. Goebbels hadn't begrudged the newsreels their share of footage in the weeks that followed that mini-triumph (God knew, there was precious little else that was good to report), so she probably recalled more of its details than he.

She sighed. 'If only Herr Fischer had remained with you in Italy. He might have been spared all that suffering.'

It had long been Hoeschler's belief that a single bullet, fired randomly into a vast and otherwise untouched landscape, would somehow have found the poor bastard, but he sipped his tea and said nothing. Mila, whose colour had come down by now, cleared her throat.

'Do you take in guests regularly, Frau Knipper?'

For some minutes, the two women delicately disassembled the reputation of the modern travelling salesman while Hoeschler ate a slice of *zwetschgendatschi* (the best he'd ever tasted) and brooded about their Smith problem. He didn't want to be separated from his wife but needed to be out of Frau Knipper's house as soon as possible, so that he could ...

What? The previous day, he had made their first payment of eight hundred Deutsche Marks into the account of Martin Ruprecht Janssen, and it had hurt like a blade being removed from his abdomen. He didn't really care if he and Mila were rich or poor, but begrudged every pfennig they had been cowed into paying. He *was* ex-*Fallschirmjäger*, and yet he was colluding in a shameful arrangement with no greater show of resistance than if he were a pig in a slaughterhouse.

It had been said only half seriously, but he was beginning to think she had the right idea. He should hunt down an FG-42 with scope, suppressor and at least one full magazine, fill a rucksack with food and water, find a room that overlooked the main gate of Föhrenweg 19 and wait. Eventually, Smith would show his face, and have it shot off.

The assassin would almost certainly be caught and hanged for it, but was a quick death worse than living timidly? Wouldn't it be better than Mila mourn a loving and loved husband rather than let months or years of impotence kill any affection she felt for him? Christ, he should be dead by now as it was; most of the men who had dropped with him onto the Aalborg airfields hadn't survived until the surrender four years later, so the further decade he'd been given was time owed.

Plotting a path to the gallows must have brought on the frowns, because the conversation had paused and both women were looking curiously at him. He coughed.

'Could we see the room please?'

The 'room' was a suite, the bedroom opening onto a small sitting area, with a lavatory beyond. It was all as pristine as if the builders and decorators had just packed their vans and driven away, and had it been a hotel Hoeschler would have expected the tariff to have been ten times what Frau Knipper was asking. If a certain time-piece and gramophone repairer could have borne this luxury for two months and then fled back to Curtius-Strasse, his fear of entrapment had to have approached phobic dimensions.

Mila managed to keep her voice steady. 'Yes, this will be quite suitable.'

Her new landlady and best friend beamed. 'I'm so glad! Supper is at seven, when Renate returns. We can have a lovely chat then about our heroes, without making them blush!'

Hoeschler looked helplessly at his wife. Clearly, her secret mission of character assassination was doomed before it ran out of runway.

He doubted that Frau Knipper could conceive of sunlight radiating from anywhere other than Otto Fischer's fundament, so hints that he might possess a darker side would break against her laws of physics. It might be all that Mila could do to bring down expectations to merely mortal levels.

He held out his hand to the prospective bride. 'I'll go, then.'

She ignored it, stepped forward, grasped his forearm and kissed him on the cheek. 'I'll look after her', she whispered huskily, squeezing, and for a moment he too felt something of the torments of both Odysseus and Otto.

A bird in a cat's mouth would stand a better chance.

Mila came to the front door with him, and applied her own hand to the arm.

'Do nothing stupid, alright? Like you keep saying, we have time now.'

He nodded. 'I'll speak to Otto again. We'll think of something.'

Her smile almost cheered the last of the death-wish from him.

'You'd better do it quickly, before another problem crowds out everything else in his head.'

24

At Friesenstrasse Police Praesidium's reception desk, Fischer presented the card that *Unterkommissar* Holzmann had given to him the previous evening. The *wachtmeister* examined it briefly and waved vaguely. Assuming the gesture had intended to indicate a selection of stand-chairs against the wall, Fischer chose one, sat down and picked up an abandoned copy of the *Morgenpost* from its neighbour.

He had managed to read it from front to back and then commit the wall opposite to memory before a finger beckoned him back to the desk, where his card was returned.

'Third floor. Ask for *Kriminalkommissar* Fux.'

As the name was written clearly on the card, Fischer assumed that the *wachtmeister*'s efforts over the past hour had been devoted to excavating a nostril and locating the gentleman on a staff list. He nodded his profound thanks and took the stairs.

A man in a dark, well-worn suit was waiting for him on the third floor landing. He held out his hand.

'Fux.'

'Fischer.'

'Yes, *Unterkommissar* Holzmann gave me an adequate description. Please ...'

They entered a small office with two desks. Fux waved him to a seat. 'Thank you for coming.'

'Had I a choice?'

The policeman smiled. 'Well, you might have made me come to you - which wouldn't have been a great imposition, I suppose. I was last in Lichterfelde in '38 - the Gardens, with my then-fiancée.'

'It's a nice place for courting. The other gentleman didn't say what this was about.'

'No, I wasn't very precise. Would you like coffee?'

Old memories of police coffee being (perversely) fresh still, Fischer was about to refuse, but anything that stretched the pre-interrogation bonhomie was to be welcomed.

'Please.'

Fux left the office to get them himself, a venerable tactic to stretch a suspect's nerves. Fischer used the time to get a sense of the man's workload. His desk was tidy, the only hint of 'load' nestling in a wire tray – four files and a small pile of individual papers, most of them probably internal circulars generated by the sort of police who tried to avoid fresh air and criminals. He noticed that the rest of the desk (unlike its opposite number) bore few personal items – no photograph of the family, no police sports' medals set in wooden shields, not even the framed graduation certificate that had pulled him out of uniform and into the *kriminalkommissar*'s plain clothes.

Either the gentleman was supremely uninterested in marking his territory or he had yet to make a start on it.

A new man, or just newly arrived in the room? Fischer was considering this when his beverage arrived, its odour dredging up wretched memories. Fux sat down and lifted a thin sheath of stapled papers from the tray.

'Unterkommissar Holzmann told me about your old comrade … Rudolph Bandelin. He was killed before you spoke with him, yes?'

'Before I even knew that he was looking to speak with me.'

'Were you close friends in the Service?'

'Not really. He was one of the Regiment's clowns, a popular man, but I hadn't been with them for very long when I was injured. I didn't see him again after that.'

'Yet he seeks you out, years later. That's odd, isn't it?'

'Yes, very. I can't say why.'

'He didn't write you or call beforehand?'

'No. I have no idea what he wanted, though ...'

'What?'

Fischer shrugged. 'I suppose it isn't unusual for men who've fallen on hard ground to try to tap old comrades. If he had, I would probably have helped – a little, at least.'

Fux frowned at the paper. 'He was reasonably well dressed, and had money in his pocket. I doubt that he needed it. You aren't close to other former comrades?'

You want to know if I've worked on the South American u-bahn, but you aren't so stupid as to ask.

'Just two ex-Luftwaffe men – Rolf Hoeschler, whom your colleague met, and Friedrich Holleman, a former pilot. He's a career policeman – in Trier, these days.'

Fux made a note of this and looked up. 'May I ask about your war service?'

'Certainly. *Fallschirmjäger* I regiment, from the outbreak until late 1941, then artillery units on the Eastern Front until early 1942 and this …' he waved at the ruined half of his face '… then I wore a mattress for the best part of nine months before transferring to the Luftwaffe War Reporters' Unit at the Air Ministry. It was dissolved in mid-1944 and the personnel were re-assigned to Luftwaffe Intelligence East. And then ...'

'Then?'

'I surrendered. With everyone else.'

Fux had scribbled diligently as he spoke. It was nothing so much as a twitch, but Fischer was almost certain that he had reacted to mention of the Intelligence unit, and braced himself for what came next.

'Now, you repair time-pieces?'

'And gramophones, yes.'

'Have you always done this? I mean, outside of war?'

'No, I used to do your job.'

'Really?'

'In Stettin, until 1937. It wasn't … *rewarding* work, back then.'

'I imagine not.' Fux's face was carefully neutral when he said it. 'But since the end of the war, this repair work is what you've done?'

Yes. Except for a brief period.'

'When …?'

What could he say? One didn't admit to having been employed by the Org, even if it and he had parted on unfriendly terms; but he didn't know how much information Fux's piece of paper was showing him, and no lies were inconsequential.

'I worked for the anti-communist Front. I can't really say more than that.'

The paper received more attention. 'This *brief* period seems to have lasted for almost four years. Am I correct?'

'I was caught and imprisoned by the Soviets. At Sachsenhausen.'

'For …?'

'Again, I can't say. You understand?'

Fischer had more or less painted a picture, framed it and stood it on the desk. He only hoped that Fux's eyesight was up to seeing it.

The *kriminalkommissar* pursed his lips and gave some attention to his paper, forgetting himself so much as to take a sip from the mug in front of him. He winced.

'Herr Fischer, I won't ask you the name of this anti-communist front, or if it had a name at all; but can you tell me if its work was sanctioned by the Western Allies?'

'It was, by one of them.'

There had been plenty of such 'fronts', most of them amateurish, ad hoc associations of Eastern veterans, usually under the leadership-in-name-only of some forgotten general officer; but few had been recognized by the Allies. By now, though, Fux could choose from a short-list of just two organizations. The largest, the Gehlen Org, was the CIA's pet and Adenauer's preferred candidate to become the official foreign intelligence service of the Republic. Then, there was – perhaps had been – Otto John's Domestic Security Agency, BfV; but John had made the mistake of trying to encroach on Gehlen's territory by planting agents across the line. The General, playing his usual long game, had retaliated - harrying his rival ruthlessly, insinuating and blocking, deflecting and planting false information until John, seeing which way the wind blowed, had suddenly, and very publicly, defected to the East. That had been late in July the previous year, since when BfV had been almost picked apart in the search for further hints of treachery.

Fux knew all this, of course, and asked the intelligent question.

'Not that I will, of course; but if I were to approach this *front* for confirmation of your past association, they would provide it?'

'I'm sure they would.' Actually, Fischer doubted very much that Gehlen's people would so much as fart if they thought that it might help him; but that wasn't the point. They were the only people whom Fux *could* approach anymore in expectation of a response, so he had his answer by default. He looked quite pleased about it, for about three seconds. Then the frown returned.

'Obviously, *political* matters require a certain degree of discretion. I wouldn't want to embarrass or compromise you.'

'That very kind.'

'And I'd like to ask the same of you.'

Here it comes. Fischer returned the frown as a concerned, dutiful citizen would. 'I assume that everything I hear today is confidential, naturally.'

'You've heard of the recent … incidents, in Spandau?'

'The murders? Yes.'

'Five of them, over a space of three months.'

'I heard … seven.'

Fux seemed surprised. 'You heard that? From whom?'

'A neighbour, a journalist. I think he put a few drinks down a policemen.'

'Is he printing it?'

'No. He hasn't been able to confirm anything, and now no-one's talking to him.'

The policemen relaxed slightly. 'What else did he say about it?'

'That the two extra bodies were claimed by civilians before police could investigate. That's all.'

'Did you speculate?'

'Idly. It seemed to me that it was a clean-up by interested parties. Obviously, to overrule police procedures they'd have to be … connected. As to why, I assume that the corpses were in danger of being identified. Obviously, it might all be nonsense.'

'Very possibly; but, from your own experience, would a German anti-communist organization be prepared to carry out political assassinations?'

Fischer pretended to consider this. He knew little enough about the subject and would have preferred to tell Fux precisely that, but he also wanted to know why he was on the gentleman's list of interesting people.

'In extreme circumstances, possibly. I worked with them at a time when it was a desperate business – a lot of their agents across the line were being caught and retired, so there was a sense that we were all at war still. Now, I don't know. It seems to me that the dance has more rules these days, and that permission probably has to be obtained beforehand. Also, killings would earn reprisals, so if this *is* political business, there must be a strong reason for it. Of course, if it was the work of the other side, who can guess why?'

Fux nodded and examined his fingernails, and Fischer began to give some attention to the peculiarities of the interview. Why was a middle-ranking Criminal Investigations officer still holding onto a case or cases that should have been whipped out of his hands by now? Whichever side had killed the men – if this *was* political business – the whole thing should have been placed beneath several camouflaged tarpaulins and every policemen involved told to put his thoughts elsewhere. He recalled enough about Gehlen's operation to know that its territory was defended as robustly as any forward trench – as Otto John could attest. So, the chances of it allowing an official investigation to proceed unhindered was as likely as *Stasi* hosting a defectors' symposium. It didn't make any sense, unless both he and Fux were entirely wrong about what this was.

'May I ask …?'

Fux looked up from his manicure. 'What?'

'Why am I of interest? It's been a long time since I did anything other than repair things. It can't have been about poor Rudy Bandelin, can it?'

The policemen detached a small piece of paper from his sheath and pushed it across the desk. Fischer picked it up and read it.

SDP

0835

1423

2414

2786

3417

Otto Fischer, clock repairer, Lichterfelde.

Belatedly, his stomach decided that it would have preferred Fux's explanation to be a shade more ambiguous. He looked up.

'What is this?'

'It was sent here, anonymously, two days ago.'

'And why do you think it involves me in anything you're investigating?'

Fux took his time to answer, and for the first time Fischer sensed that the man was moving around rather than *through* something.

'I … have no opinion, one way or the other. But the envelope this came in was addressed to me personally. I want to know *why*, and you're the only thing on it that might tell me.'

'I have no idea what it means, or why my name's on it.'

'It's possible the five numbers refer to the five bodies we were allowed to examine.'

'That's a bit thin. What's SDP?'

Fux smiled again. 'I hoped you might tell me. A colleague suggested the author might have meant to write SPD.'

'Because this business *might* be political?'

'I know, it isn't likely.'

Fischer pushed the paper back towards the policeman. 'It doesn't amount to much. Murder investigations suck in a great deal of useless so-called information, I recall.'

'They do, certainly. Do you have enemies? A business rival, perhaps?'

Fischer almost laughed. 'The clock repair trade isn't too cut-throat, though customers can be difficult. About a year ago I mended a Haller that gave up the ghost a few weeks later. I wouldn't refund the cost because the cause of death was unrelated. The gentleman blustered a bit but went away eventually. You think this might be his cold-tasted dish?'

'Probably not.'

'I can think of a few people who might want to do me a disservice for older offences, but putting my name – literally - on several killings would be peevish.'

Fux pushed back his chair. 'You aren't a suspect, just a potential material witness.' He reattached the paper to the sheath. 'If I need to speak to you again I'll call first - and perhaps come to pretty Lichterfelde. If anything occurs to you …?'

'You'll hear the same hour as it strikes me.'

At the stair-well they shook hands. Fischer's descent to the ground floor began at his usual pace but slowed considerably as something tried and failed to rise from long-interred memory. It hadn't struck him when first he saw it but now, like a quiet echo becoming audible only when more immediate noises fade, it returned, frustratingly indistinct. For entirely selfish reasons he sincerely wanted to help *Kriminalkommissar* Fux. He had no idea why his name should be on that paper (other than as an unrelated jotting of someone who needed a clock fixed), and his ignorance made him nervous – particularly, about how far and how deeply it ran. Doodles didn't signify much until they became something else, and if they did it would be best if Otto Fischer were to provide at least a little of the enlightenment.

This prudent conclusion endured until he reached the main reception hall of the Praesidium, and then memory took another lunge at the echo, this time catching and making it distinct.

Shit.

It told him only one thing – that his name really should have had more sense than to get itself onto that paper. *Enlightenment* could only be the worse for him now, though he was innocent of anything it might drag out into the light. He would be judged with the rest, or at least stained indelibly by association. It took a rare kind of luck or fate, to be required to pay for a small crime with a far greater infamy.

Out in Friesenstrasse he forgot about the s-bahn ticket in his pocket, waved down a taxi and promised the driver a hefty tip if he could get to Curtius-Strasse in half an hour. It took ten minutes longer that that but he paid extra anyway, not wanting to waste further time arguing the point at the roadside. He rushed into and through the shop, ignoring the half-question with which Renate commenced her interrogation and had the telephone receiver in hand before she could regroup.

Freddie Holleman was giving a lecture on investigations protocols in the *VolksPolizei*, apparently, and wouldn't be available for more useful matters until lunchtime. With an effort, Fischer kept his voice steady and asked that a note of his call be put into the *Oberrat*'s hand as soon as he came off the podium. When he replaced the receiver Renate was waiting; he told her as much as had scribbled on the back of a till receipt earlier that morning before leaving, though its repetition seemed to satisfy her without further details being necessary. Then he made (bearable) coffee, paced the shop, rearranged some timepieces in the window and all the while turned it over in his mind, trying to find some angle from which it looked less ugly than it was.

SDP. Would it have been better or worse if his memory had done its job while he was still facing Fux - if he'd just blurted out what he knew before thinking it through? To have stated it freely, openly, might have taken the edge off its implications for him – after all, would anyone other than an innocent man have spoken of it?

He could think the thing to death, but no other interpretation was feasible. Five men – at *least* five men - had died for a reason, and he feared that he understood part of what it was. If it came out, what would be done? A decision like that would be have to be argued and made far from the third floor at Friesenstrasse Police Praesidium. It wasn't just about the crimes; the timing was exquisitely bad, the potential for embarrassment colossal, the repercussions potentially immense.

And Otto Fischer was on the paper.

He had the receiver to his ear before the telephone rang for the second time.

'Freddie?'

'Christ, Otto, who's dying? They're going to give us a decent lunch today ...'

'Never mind lunch. Do you believe in coincidence?'

'Oh, wonderful, a riddle. No, I don't.'

'Why not?'

'Because in an infinity of random events, some are bound to collide eventually. When people talk about coincidences, they usually mean something more than that - like Karma, which is donkey balls. If things that fall into each other seem to be related, there's a reason for it.'

'I agree. It's your fault, then.'

'What is?'

'Never mind. You're forgiven, if you do just one small thing.'

'Fuck your Mother! *What?*'

'Find Jens Lamsdorf for me. Today, if possible. Tomorrow, if not.'

25

Jonas Kleiber had three hundred words of copy to write on Paul Busch of Stirnerstrasse, Steglitz, and his decade-long matchstick construction of a 1/175th scale model of the Oberbaum Bridge. As fearless reportage went this was not an onerous task, but his distracted mind was making heavy work of it. It was not that the gentleman had been taciturn about his achievement – quite the opposite – but rather the weight of guilt that pressed upon the young man's conscience.

He had wished harm upon a man who had died less than an hour later, shot in broad daylight as he strolled down a road in a respectable neighbourhood. It shouldn't have happened to anyone, naturally, yet for Kleiber the horror was magnified considerably by the very real sense that he had abetted the crime by hexing the poor bastard, and all because Renate had gushed a little - really, no more than expressed a momentary hormonal appreciation of features that turned to have had only minutes remaining in their traditional order.

He possessed no great spiritual convictions, but even a lazy agnostic (that is, someone who couldn't be arsed to even think about what he believed in, if anything) acknowledged the iron inevitability of evil being repaid with evil. At that precise moment, someone with spite in his heart at some story written by Jonas Kleiber might be wishing damnation, ruin or aggravated syphilis upon him, and he would deserve every last bitter part of whichever it was. He was convinced that Renate herself would now spurn him, having some intuitive ability to look into a suitor's eyes and spot the rotten heart beneath, and he would deserve that, too.

Poor Rudy - or whatever his name had been. He shouldn't have died just for being prettier, better built and more charming than the romantic competition he hadn't even known he'd had (the small, rational voice that suggested these were probably not the principal reasons why cold-souled assassins had opened fire on Schloss-Strasse made little way against this prevailing surge tide of remorse). It was a tragedy, despite the victim's now-theoretical potential for disrupting a difficult courtship.

Kleiber sighed and managed to bang out a couple of sentences on Herr Busch's damascene conversion from hide-based glue to a synthetic polymer, but his attention wouldn't synchronise with his fingers. It wandered back to an irritatingly persistent image of a weeping Renate, devastatingly gorgeous in black, tending the grave of her never-to-be lover, husband and soulmate while an ageing, love-lorn hack went the way of most of his profession, gradually wearing an elbow-shaped depression in the counter of his favourite bar and pretending to prefer the unencumbered, uncooked-for life. It persisted because he had been nurturing it for some hours now, feeding it with the mulch of having no idea what Renate had been thinking since they last spoke, the previous day.

Naturally, he wanted to sprint the three doors down to *Fischer's Time-pieces and Gramophones* to set his mind at rest, but he had no way of knowing that the effort would meet that happy end. She might look at him with disgust, or disdain, or (worst of all) with no feeling whatsoever. She might have concluded already that Kleiber was culpable (the fact that they agreed on very little else usually was a small comfort), or even that he possessed some dark, diseased faculty that no Christian woman should tolerate, much less marry into. He doubted that he was up to taking that sort of rejection.

He glanced at the colour photograph of the Oberbaum that he had pulled from the Paper's images library. Herr Busch's effort looked like its distant, dwarf cousin at best, but part of the job of a local reporter was to make interesting what otherwise would find fully-deserved oblivion. Is this what his life was worth - its uttermost achievement? He was almost twenty-six, an age at which most men had at least pointed themselves in the direction of building a posterity, and his best chance to date was probably thinking of him as a succubus, a golem or moral emptiness, while Otto the Half-Face was presently having to fight off her quite lovely mother with a bayonet. What was equitable about that?

He sighed more deeply, and felt a little better for it. What was needed was a turn-around event, something that would lift the reputation of Jonas Kleiber from fissure to peak in the eyes of at least one young lady, and preferably in every eye from Schöneberg to the Schönwald (or at least Schönefeld). In his experience, however, a man's name was lifted suddenly only by some heroic deed, and heroism involved danger. He had confronted death only once, and that had been in the form of a Lee Enfield no. 4, wielded by a Tommy who hadn't cared to shoot a uniformed fifteen-year-old trying frantically to touch sky with both hands. To seek out new perils on the back of that apprenticeship, even for the good opinion of a modern-day Sheba, seemed unwise.

What else could he do? His only real skill was dry-stone walling, a POW pastime at which he'd become quite adept (two farmers for whom he'd worked in his final weeks in England had offered him a paid job on their bleak, blasted, over-grazed moor and been surprised at his refusal), but Berlin had a degenerate fondness for mortar – in any case, the raising of walls was not considered particularly heroic other than during military reversals. He could also whistle piercingly (as enemy sheep had discovered much to their discomfort), speak a strange kind of English fluently, juggle three balls indefinitely, recite Goethe's *Auf dem See* so beautifully it made people (well, his late Mother) cry, and …

Write. Even four years into the job he had to remind himself still that he *was* a journalist, (mainly because he trod water in the profession's lesser pond). He had never regarded it as a calling, but why not? Look at Hemingway, and Murrow, and Dimbleby – and people did, often, with admiration. All they'd needed was the opportunity, the story that had to be told. Get it right just once, and success brought more success, and standing, and reputation …

He sat up, and his chair complained loudly. This was Berlin, in 1955 - if he couldn't put those two together and make something interesting from it he wasn't fit to be called a journalist. Fuck matchstick Oberbaum Bridges, and flower shows, and centenaries of local folk who'd be dead next week anyway; this was a city – *the* city – in which the world's two atomic Superpowers squared off against each other, and while he was writing shit about shit, other men were chronicling the looming Fatal Moment. It was no wonder that Renate's underwear had persistently failed to slip off at the prospect of Jonas Kleiber.

The thought of her (she had been straying from his attention for almost half a minute by now) shorted some synaptic space, and two things came together beautifully. His paper's reports on the Spandau murders had been no more than verbatim reproductions of other journalists' stories, and though he had taken the trouble to quiz one of his pet policemen about them, Herr Grabner had decided that western Berlin's travails weren't the core concern of the *Süd-west Berliner Zeitung*. Now, though, they had a murder of their own, committed hardly a half-kilometre from the office. The *Zeitung* would run a piece on it, of course, but Grabner always preferred to see what *news* newspapers were saying before he let his reporter loose on a serious story. Their next edition wasn't published for two days yet, so Kleiber would follow form and put together something that differed very little from what was appearing in the Dailies that very day. After that, though, he might persist – might actually investigate the crime as a *real* reporter might, and in doing so go far to redeeming his unfortunate part in it.

And - who was to say that the Spandau crimes and this one weren't related? Not Jonas Kleiber, certainly. The peculiar nature of the latest slaying, its blatant, professional execution (in every sense), almost begged comparison with the five - or seven – earlier incidents. At least, *he* was going to beg it, repeatedly, until it was picked up by newspapers that actually mattered. Hard facts and verifiable connections would be useful, but for a story to become a great story the only vital ingredient was momentum, and he would push it harder than a bailiff did an evicted *zigi*.

It would all need to be cleared with Herr Grabner, of course, but the man wasn't the editorial cliff-face he used to be. His refusal to chase the Spandau murders had come during one of his brief, lucid spells, when one bottle had gone in the bin and another couldn't yet be found. Since offering Kleiber a fifteen percent shareholding in the business (the capital to be collected by way of deductions from salary until more or less the end of time), the editor-proprietor had devoted more of his waking hours to mourning the departure of his young wife to America, a vigil he undertook in the company of Herr Johnny Walker, most days. His only full-time reporter had taken up much of the editorial slack and supervised the print-room also, though luckily they had long employed the services of an excellent compositor whose career had begun under Gutenberg. All it would require was for Kleiber to make the case earnestly at a moment when Herr Grabner had taken a few sips and started to get teary, and that sort of moment had become hard to avoid recently. It might even give the old man's morale a lift, to know that his newspaper was chasing the heavy stuff for once.

And, for the moment, only Grabner would hear of it. Kleiber knew his own abilities well enough not to claim the prize until he could measure the distance. He would let his copy speak for itself, and then Renate would see that he was a serious man - and so too would Otto, who had never said a poor word to or about him, but who always looked as if he was choking back a smile when they spoke. It was weak to want the good opinion of others, obviously, but any man who didn't care about his reputation was either oblivious, rich or so bloody good at everything that praise didn't matter more than a fart.

He tore the few lines he'd devoted to immortalising Herr Busch's Oberbaum from the typewriter, screwed them into a ball and threw it in the waste basket. For the moment at least, he was done with local colour unless it was arterial red. He laughed aloud at the sanguinary thought, pleased that he was already hardening his heart for the brutal yet brilliant exposé with which he would astound and horrify the public, torment indolent police and politicians and win the plaudits of friends and colleagues. Germany didn't have an equivalent of the Pulitzer Prize for journalism, but breathless admiration would fill that space very adequately.

The Spandau Killings file was on Herr Grabner's desk, placed there by the proprietor on the day he'd declared them to be Done business. Kleiber retrieved it and put on his glasses to indicate both to himself and the world at large that he was serious about this (he avoided them usually because they gave him the appearance of a teenage Himmler with learning difficulties). There was a great deal to read, the police having offered an unusual degree of information to the Press in the hope of teasing out new evidence, and he needed to know it all. Somewhere among the detail was a mistake, an unasked question or overlooked piece of eye-witness testimony - he told himself - that would give him his first article and the investigating officers acute indigestion. After that, a weekly dose of fearless, shameless *why oh whys*, spiced with probing. non sequitur'ish observations that went straight to his readers' anxieties about crime, the times and the price of cheese even, and Jonas Kleiber would be out of journalists' base camp and onto the steepening slopes.

It was possibly his imagination, but he felt a little tougher, more world-weary and cynical as he trawled previous reports on the murders. It was a novel, pleasant feeling, and he decided both to nurture and try to reflect it in his manner. Renate could hardly fail to notice (though she was very good at not noticing), and once his pieces began to appear in the Syndicated Press, even Otto would have to admit that he had undervalued his friend.

Syndication. Even the word thrilled, but he suppressed the shivers and frowned at the cuttings in front of him. As far as he knew, no other Berlin newspaper was following the murders too closely any more (their interest waning for want of new details to dangle before the public), and he had to get his name on the business before the false Rudy Bandelin's execution shook someone else into noticing the present vacuum. It would be entirely in keeping with his habitual shitty fortune if …

He repeated it to himself: no one was following them anymore. It hadn't been his business until now so he hadn't noticed, but why were five – or seven – murders not occupying more attention? So the investigation had hit a wall – wasn't that more a matter of acute public concern than indifference? When did the Third Estate lose interest, just because a culprit hadn't been found? Was Jack the Ripper less or more fascinating for having got away with it?

Christ. If he couldn't make a conspiracy from this he deserved to cover the Lichterfelde Flower Show until the End of Days. *Whose is the Unseen Hand that Halts the Chase? What Dark Secrets are being kept from Berliners?* Kleiber shivered again, involuntarily. Fuck insinuation – why not: *Police helpless – is the Killer being protected by the State?* Push a uniform onto the podium to laugh at the question and they'd be pouring petrol on what he'd lit; threaten him with an action for slander and even other journalists would think there was something in it. Either way, the floodlight would rest squarely on Jonas Kleiber.

He put a sheet of paper in his typewriter. It needed to be kicked off gently, the public led to understand that they had cause to be worried without Herr Grabner being coaxed into an aneurism. Something suggestive yet vague - a finger waved, though not yet pointed too precisely; the tragic story told of a man killed on Schloss-Strasse that hinted at much more than a single, brutal slaying. Really, the first step wasn't going to be too difficult. He typed quickly, briefly, and then sat back, admiring what would need only the slightest tweak to inaugurate his campaign

What the Hell is Going On?

26

What are we supposed to think about it?

It hadn't occurred to Hoeschler until he was dressed, breakfasted, out of doors and confronted by the first *Bundesflagge* fluttering gently where, usually, it shouldn't have been. Today was the day: Germans rejoice - partly! Three of their Occupiers were now officially allies of the Federal Republic; the fourth, its existential enemy. From today, his homeland was permitted a standing army, navy and air-force, despite the very real pressure (from France, usually) to keep the Teuton hordes defenceless forevermore. Could he be proud of that, he wondered, or was it just that the West needed a nation-sized punishment battalion to absorb a future Soviet offensive long enough to scrape together a response?

As he walked he examined the faces of his newly-liberated fellow citizens, and saw few signs of trepidation. It was early, so the faint glow of inebriation was missing yet; but quite a few of them had a quaint look about them, of folk privy to some pleasant secret that couldn't yet be shared. He wondered how memory could sift out past horrors so quickly.

His mood wasn't allowing him any bright sides this morning. Mila had been exiled to Dahlem and he had no good idea how to end it other than by a spectacular act of suicide. He missed her already, he wasn't eating properly, the house was getting untidy and now he was on his way to work, and though it was Thursday he suspected he had a full week's grafting ahead of him before the weekend. BVG was negotiating with its tram drivers over present pay and future prospects (trams were to be phased out entirely in West Berlin over the next decade, to be replaced by buses), and Potsdammerstrasse's meeting rooms had resembled angry beehives for days now. He found it hard to care much either way (having unexpectedly married into money), but the shouting and posturing was beginning to give his rear end a headache.

And he was being pestered about subsidence in a u-bahn tunnel. As his specific role was infrastructure maintenance it was his duty to be pestered, but he felt pestered just the same. It was probably due to war damage, something that was going to be a problem for years – possibly decades – to come, even after the last of hundreds of unexploded bombs had been dug from their unintended graves (his department held a curious sub-species of Berliner, who ardently wished that Allied ordnance had been better armed and primed). He had put in a request for a works unit to investigate, but BVG bureaucracy tended to move about as quickly as the subsidence itself. No doubt minds and attention would be focused when the tunnel collapsed.

The problem of Smith eclipsed any work matter, of course, but he had worried about it so much that the same sort of numbness had crept upon him as that which once had allowed him to jump out of aircraft without dwelling upon what a damned stupid idea it was.

Perhaps if the threat was more urgent, Mila's discovery by KGB more obviously imminent, his mind might sharpen considerably. As it was his thoughts ran in circles, re-treading old ground like a tethered horse's hooves.

On the bus to Potsdamerstrasse he idly checked and ticked off the driver's correctly-buttoned uniform, the cleanliness of the windows and absence of litter on the floor (though none of these were his responsibility) and then watched the passing commuter foot-traffic. It was as any other work-day - shifts needed to be endured, bills paid, errands run and preoccupations borne until alcohol or a deep armchair could ease them, and most heads were bowed by the weight of one or more of these. When he'd first come to West Berlin and joined BVG it had surprised him that swapping a career in criminal investigations, communist-style for the comforts of a capitalist desk-job wasn't an entirely advantageous move, despite the better money and lack of corpses. Boredom was an unexpectedly bleak sensation to absorb, the more so for its promise of being a career-long companion. Now, he heartily wished for it, even to excess.

He got off the bus a halt early to stretch his legs. At a kiosk he bought some cigarettes and glanced at the papers. The *Morgenpost* was running a shouting headline: *Federal Republic Today Sovereign*, with a photograph of a smug Adenauer beneath it (as if he *was* the Republic), and a mug-full of toy black, red and golds had been stood on the pile of *Der Spiegel*s for those passing commuters who wished to flag-wave their way to work. Hoeschler didn't avail himself of the offer, excusing himself on the basis that Berliners hadn't yet been invited to the party.

He worked in an open office that was already populated sparsely by the long-term inmates (as he thought of them), men who had served in the same jobs and knitwear since before the mergers of ABO, GEHU and BSB in 1928. He didn't ever work late enough to confirm the theory, but he suspected that members of this venerable group had to be whipped or bribed out of the office and the doors locked behind them. He told himself that if he ever began to wear sleeve bands, to frown at every scraped chair or to put down his pen precisely ten seconds before the designated tea-break he would know that he had joined their blighted company.

He nodded at the only one of them who looked up when he entered and went to his desk. Usually, it was clear when he arrived (he made a point of dealing with every pending matter before leaving), but today an internal envelope, already heavily-marked by the scored-through names of past recipients, sat precisely centred upon it. He undid the string binder and removed a single sheet of paper. It was plain, unstamped, and upon it a single, short, hand-written sentence made Hoeschler's blood freeze.

Don't be too clever.

Had it arrived in the post it would have been in its external envelope still, unopened, so it must have been brought into the building by a

member of staff who had at least some idea of what he was
delivering, and why.

Involuntarily, Hoeschler glanced around the room. Every head was
inclined downward, attending to its own business, oblivious to the
startled, stupid expression on his face. He could hardly suspect his
immediate workmates of being CIA lackeys (it was more likely that
they had evening jobs as show-girls in a Burlesque), but one of them
might have noticed the fellow who brought this little bomb to his
desk. How could he ask, without giving off at least a whiff of panic?

He tried to calm himself. Smith couldn't know where Mila was, only
that she wasn't where she should be. It would be strange if he wasn't
having their home watched, given his 'investment', and anything
that wasn't usual would be reported to him. That was alright,
Hoeschler told himself, the man was just reacting to a slight prod. If
it were more than that, wouldn't the warning have been more
salutary? How difficult would it be, to have someone fling a
Molotov Cocktail through their apartment window – they lived on
the first floor – or send a message via a short but energetic kicking in
an alleyway? It wasn't as if he couldn't be got at, day or night, even
by much lesser players than the Central Intelligence Agency.

His heartbeat began to slow, to a point at which he could take in air
once more. *Christ.* This was worse than being the General's prisoner
– at least then he'd only had his own skin to consider (much as its
slow removal would have irritated). Family made a man weak, prone
to sidelong glances and twitching expectations of the sort of trouble

that a reasoned argument and two fists couldn't deal with. Why the hell couldn't she fall in love with a city other than Berlin? It wasn't as though another twenty years could make it pretty once more, even if anyone was building prettily (they weren't). Why not Paris, or Lisbon - or even Worms, if she couldn't be bothered to learn another language?

'You seem angry, Herr Hoeschler. Is it the strikers?'

He hadn't noticed Baldwin Mohr creep up on him, which was strange, because the scent of mothballs preceded him like incense, usually. The old man stood over him, scratching a cheek that hadn't been shaved for several days and wouldn't be until it was time once more for Sunday Service, probably. He was an oddity in an office of oddities, someone who had not only avoided two world wars – a slight deformation of the spine had exempted him from military service - but most of the shit that came with them. Unmarried, he lived with his sister in a house in Zehlendorf that hadn't seen so much as a chip of plaster displaced either by the RAF, USAAF or Red Army, yet over the years he had managed to build such a store of grievances against fate and its excretions that the first admonishment given to every new recruit to BVG was *For Christ's sake, don't get Mohr Going.* Despite this, Hoeschler (distracted during his first week on the job) had committed the tactical error of not walking away when offered an introductory survey of the present age's injustices. He had then compounded it by making vaguely sympathetic noises while not listening, and ever since Mohr had regarded him as a sure harbour for his ship of grief. It was a measure of the tenderness and gratitude this had earned that the man was asking a question at all, rather than launching straight into some new complaint.

'No, Herr Mohr, it's just … a headache.'

'Ah, migraine. I used to suffer terribly from them, but liquorice tea helps wonderfully. You might wish to try it.'

'Thank you, I shall. Is there …?'

'They say they've come to terms with the Union, and that the settlement means they can't afford increases for office staff over the next three years.' Mohr sniffed. 'It's disgraceful.'

'Aren't you retiring next year?'

'Yes, but it means my pension will be calculated according to a lower final salary. I don't know what Gelda will say.'

Hoeschler imagined that a lifetime's cohabitation with Mohr would have rendered speech a redundant faculty, but he didn't say so. He made a throat-noise instead, to convey a degree of sympathy without encouraging further discussion - a futile tactic.

'I should think we'll starve, eventually. At the least, there'll be no more holidays to Bad Tölz.'

'You take the waters?'

'They ease wind considerably. Have I told you I suffer from it? What is it that you shouldn't *be too clever* about?'

Hoeschler hadn't realised that Mohr could see the note. He resisted the urge to slam his hand over it and shrugged. 'I don't know. I think it's a practical joke.'

Mohr sighed contentedly. 'It wouldn't surprise me. That stupid boy Janssen hasn't a serious bone in his head.'

'Janssen?' Hoeschler knew him by sight – a loud, cocky young man who needed attention like wiser men did oxygen. He worked in the timetabling office, though (perhaps fortunately for travelling Berliners) he was more often to be found holding court among the trainee mechanics, who seemed to find his boorishness fashionably irreverent.

'It was him who put it on your desk. About two hours ago, as I arrived.'

Mohr was always at his own desk as soon as the first bus service could deliver him from Zehlendorf, which meant that Janssen had planned not to be seen – an admission of some sort of guilt. Hoeschler glanced at his wristwatch. A monolithic structure, BVG processed its workforce accordingly; there was a canteen tea-break in two shifts, the first at ten o'clock, the second twenty minutes later. From the timetabling office to the nearest canteen was a brisk three-minute walk, requiring a brief detour outdoors through the senior managers' car park. It was a good place to make polite enquiries.

He excused himself to Mohr and was in the car park two minutes later, taking a blank section of wall in front of emergency vehicle spaces that were hardly ever occupied. He expected to need both canteen-breaks and had begun to test excuses in his head, but Janssen obliged him by claiming pole position on the first. He emerged from the building flanked by a pair of admirers, fellow shirkers barely out of their teens whose careers with BVG probably had months to run. They wouldn't amount to much of a potential bodyguard.

Hoeschler waited until Janssen was passing directly in front of him and then stepped out.

'Hey.'

The younger man gave him an up-and-down and a smirk and kept going, so he took a further step and talked to the receding backs.

'Are your ears full of shit, boy?'

That worked very well. Janssen stopped on a coin then moved in reverse, turning as he did so. His mates – his audience – stood and waited for the show. Hoeschler moved back to the wall, brace himself against it and kicked hard when the other man's fists came up. A knee cracked impressively.

He glanced around, but no-one else was in the carpark yet and the anguished *fuck!* wasn't loud enough to carry through glass. He knelt beside Janssen and put a hand on his shoulder.

'Who told you to deliver the message?'

'The fucking fairies.'

Hoeschler slapped his head without putting any real effort into it. 'No, really. Who was it?'

The bodyguard hadn't moved a centimetre to interfere. He looked up, staring at them until they got the message and moved backwards, towards their tea-break. Anyone else coming into the carpark now would see a man helping a friend who had taken ill, and no-one with just twenty minutes' leisure time was going to linger for curiosity's sake. The hand, back on the shoulder, squeezed hard.

'Janssen, I'll ask again, and then I'll stamp on an ankle. If you're lucky you'll pass out; if not, you'll feel the second one go. I don't care either way. At some point you'll tell me who.'

For a few moments it seemed as if pain in the knee might be crowding out consideration of ankles, but eventually Janssen looked up at the bricks in front of him and spat it out.

'Some guy in a bar, last night. I don't know him.'

Hoeschler slapped a little harder this time. 'And you just said yes?'

'He gave me a hundred DMs.'

'To post a note? Hell, that was generous.'

'He … he told me it was serious, that you owed him money. You broke my fucking knee.'

'I know. Describe him. Do it very well.'

It was a brief effort, but adequate. Hoeschler had thought Herr Smith's command of German excellent, and the fact that Janssen didn't mention it confirmed that judgement. For the first time in days, he felt a degree of relief. If the American was risking his own arse to communicate a message he couldn't have a large staff of abettors.

He patted the shoulder he'd squeezed. 'Now tell me where he really met you, and don't say a bar or one of your ankles gets broken. I know this man. He wouldn't risk being seen in a public place, arranging something. Nor would he know that you worked in my building unless he'd done the research first.'

Janssen groaned, trying to ease the pain by shifting his leg – a mistake. 'He came to my house. I mean, my mother's house.'

'Were you to contact him when it was done?'

'Yeah. He gave me a 'phone number.'

'Show me.'

It was written on a cigarette pack - the same number Smith had given to Hoeschler in Thielpark. Again, he was pleased by that. If the man could rely upon more than a single secure line he would have spread his risk. Hoeschler stood.

'By all means, let him know that you've delivered the message, but nothing else. And get that knee looked at. It was a shame you slipped and fell. They really should lay a more regular surface over these cobbles.'

'Bastard.'

'I know. You probably should have asked about that before you took the money.'

When Hoeschler returned to his desk Mohr was stooped over a small pile of works invoices, committing them carefully to his day ledger. Two minutes later, at precisely ten seconds to 10.20, he looked up, nodded to Herr Lemmel (an equally vintage specimen, similarly knitwear'd), and both men rose for their tea-break. Despite the company's meticulous planning, the first shift-break had a habit of lingering slightly over its collective beverage, which opened a gap in the flow - perhaps a couple of minutes - during which Hoeschler would be alone in the office. He intended to use that time wisely.

He made two telephone calls to the same number – too few to make it seem deliberate. Neither he nor the person who picked up the receiver spoke. He had expected it, and was more interested in any ambient sounds he could make out in the moments they were connected. He heard nothing, nothing at all, which was as much as he'd hoped for.

He had no idea how the CIA worked. Like BVG, it was a large company, but its peculiar function may have required a less rigid command structure. He could well imagine that a resourceful, intelligent man wouldn't have to serve a certain number of years before being considered for advancement; but Herr Gregory Smith was a very young man, and he didn't believe that he could have risen too far, so soon. As rich and status-conscious as the Americans were, they didn't hand out executive suites to junior staff. When Hoeschler called the number on the cigarette packet he had expected to hear the bustle of an open office, but there had been only silence, which meant one of two things. Either he had called Smith's home on what should have been a workday, or …

Don't leave a message if I'm not available.

Why? Because a message either might, or would, be written down and thereby become evidence – *might*, if he worked in a busy office; *would*, if the gentleman's post was at one of the outlying, one- or two-man operations – a listening station, perhaps - that CIA had established across West Berlin, their most sensitive front line. So, Herr Smith was reachable. All that was necessary was for Hoeschler to gain access to the Company's most confidential files, somehow discern the correct location from the many alternatives and devise a means of excising his tormentor without drawing attention either to the fact or himself.

It was a measure of his previous dolour that these unthinkable tasks, having been conceived at least, cheered him considerably - so much so that at lunchtime, when the office manager demanded from his troops a round of hurrahs for their now-fully sovereign Republic, he joined in enthusiastically.

27

'I've found him.'

'Where is he?'

'I don't know.'

Fischer closed his eyes and breathed deeply. He knew that Freddie was making perfect sense to himself, but enlightenment always came in dribbles when a whimsical mood took him. The trick was to control the conversation.

'Where *did* you find him?'

'He'd been detained at Bonn's Praesidium, but the arrest only appeared on the books forty-eight hours after he was brought in. I made sure that someone's going to pay for that.'

'I assume he's not there now.'

'He was released two days ago, at dawn. No charge, obviously.'

'What about his company's registered address? The filed accounts?'

'I checked that already. It's a notary's office. The fellow I spoke to there said he didn't have addresses for the directors.'

'Is that legal?'

'I have no idea, though I doubt he'd have admitted it if it weren't.'

'The business must be operating from *somewhere*.'

'If it's operating at all. From what the accounts said, it looks more or less moribund. That's a word, isn't it? Moribund?'

'So Lamsdorf could be anywhere?'

'Yep.'

Fischer rubbed his head. He was beginning to feel like a worm impaled on a fish-hook, waiting for a large mouth to emerge through the gloom.

'You have no other ideas about where he could be? What about his Luftwaffe cronies?'

He could almost hear the shrug. 'I was carried out of Luftflotte 2 in 1940. He stayed there and in 3 'til the bitter end. He could have made an army of new friends I don't know about - in fact, given his dodgy evening work he probably needed to. Maybe Albert Kesselring's given him a bunk.'

'Don't be facetious ...'

'What?'

'Kesselring.'

'Alright, it was a poor joke.'

'No. He's President – or whatever it is – of the veteran's association, isn't he?'

'The *Luftwaffenring*? He's their *honorary* President. Men like him don't actually do stuff.'

'I wasn't thinking of approaching Kesselring himself. But the membership – they must provide addresses when they join, surely?'

'I suppose so. But what makes you think Jens belongs to it? *I* don't, and I'm damn sure you don't, either.'

'No, but we're not in the military supplies business. Lamsdorf's company accounts mentioned a provisional contract for uniforms, didn't they?'

'Yeah.'

'Well, half the senior officers in the Wehrmacht and Luftwaffe who aren't in prison are elbow-deep in our infant defence industry, and surely a shrewd businessman would keep well-connected? Look at the men who've been associated with *Amt Blank* - it's like a roster of … *shit!*'

'Harsh, but fair.'

'No, I mean, forget the *Luftwaffenring*. What about *Amt Blank*?'

'What about them?

'They *are* the Ministry of Defence – from today, in fact! I read last week that Adenauer's decided to appoint Theodor Blank as his first Defence Minister.'

'And?'

'Who else would Lamsdorf be intending to make uniforms for? The girl guides?'

'You're going to ask *Amt Blank* – or whatever they're going to be called - for an address?'

'No. I'm a clock and gramophone repairer, living in a place that isn't even the Federal Republic. *You're* going to ask.'

'Why? I mean, I know why you want me to, and why I should; but what reason would possibly convince them not to tell me to fuck off?'

'You need to find an old comrade, because ...'

'That's the bit I bounce off, too. If I mention what happened to Jens' friend they'll ask things, and then you'll be dropped in it.'

'You don't need to. For once, you can tell the truth – the partial truth, that is. You had a tip-off that Lamsdorf – an old friend and comrade - had been arrested on what now appears to have been a trumped-up charge. When you approached Bonn Praesidium you found that he'd already been released, but that for at least two of the three days he was detained there wasn't a booking. If he has a business relationship with *Amt Blank* they'll be worried or angry enough about it to give you – a policeman - what they have, which can't be more than a contact number or address. If he isn't, they'll hang up the 'phone and we'll need to think again.'

'What if *they* decide to do something about it?'

'In their first week as the Federal Ministry of Defence, and him just a contractor? You don't think they might be busy with - oh, let's say, getting an army off the drawing board?'

'I hate sarcasm.'

'Then don't be a cock.'

Holleman sighed. 'Who will I speak to?'

'They must have some sort of procurements office – it's they who'll know Lamsdorf, if anyone does. It doesn't matter if you're passed around a little before you find the right person. It'll make the enquiry seem all the more innocent.'

'Alright. This is still urgent?'

'Until I know more about the poor bastard I arranged papers for, it's damned urgent.'

'But he's dead, and you didn't do it. What can they put on you?'

'I don't know, but it isn't just about Rudy Bandelin mark II. My name's on a paper, and it shouldn't be.'

'What sort of paper?'

'The sort that might connect me to five dead men.'

'What, the Spandau business?'

'You know about that?'

'Even Trier gets copied in on the serious crimes' circular. How the hell can you be tied to *that*?'

'Freddie, I have no idea.'

'Well, why do you think that knowing more about Jens' friend can help with it?'

'Because ...' Fischer took the receiver from his ear. What could he say, when he might be wrong about everything? He knew – he *believed* he knew – something about the dead men, and his name on that paper placed him with them, but only if he was right about what he knew. It was thin, relying upon one indisputable fact, and that was all he could or wanted to speak to, for the moment.

'Have you ever read Dickens' ghost story?'

'*Weihnachtsabend*? What German hasn't? It's my favourite book.'

'Really?'

'Yeah, it's very short. Why?'

'Scrooge's friend, the dead one who visits him, dragging chains?'

'Jacob.'

'Him, yes. That's what this is about, I think - dragged chains.'

28

On Mila's second morning as paying guest of Frau Knipper, she was offered a glimpse of the lady's opinions on the nation's political life. Many folk approach this delicate subject laterally, perhaps with a comment on some issue or policy that hints at their broader sympathies, but clearly, Frau Knipper regarded such subtlety as lacking integrity.

Mila had been reading a newspaper article on Adenauer's proposed official visit to the Soviet Union, to beg the case for the poor wretches, Germans taken on the Eastern Front, who languished still in the gulags and quarry camps a decade after the Surrender. She offered a comment on the matter, too anodyne to be recollected fully by the time it was out, expecting at most a noise-in-the-throat response from her preoccupied landlady. Instead, Frau Knipper placed her wooden mixing spoon on the kitchen table and regarded the wall opposite for a few moments. When she spoke, her face was almost as white as the flour that spattered the apron beneath it.

'That thin-lipped ogre! A traitor to his own kind! My God, they used to know what to do with his sort!'

Mila, confused, made what she usually would have regarded as a cardinal error by saying more.

'But … hasn't he got us free from the Allies?'

'What, by agreeing to fight for them in the next war? The Führer would have died rather than submit to such humiliation!'

Actually, I think he did was the first response that occurred to Mila, but she strangled it. 'And he got them to agree to stop the denazifications.'

'By promising to pay Israel compensation! To give money to the Jews!

'He got von Neurath released from Spandau last year. And Raeder.'

'And he sacrificed Dönitz to please the British! Schumacher may have been a stinking communist, but he was right about Adenauer – he's the Allies' Chancellor. Gestapo Müller should have put piano-wire around his neck, when he had the chance!'

Mila decided that to offer further examples of Adenauer's better qualities would not be constructive. In any case, she was momentarily disoriented by this nostalgic glimpse into the heart and soul of the *Frauenschaft*. It was as if she was hearing an astral echo of her own mother, a woman who hadn't so much lived through the National Socialist era as marched in step with it.

A memory of *Mutti*, prostrated before the family radio to catch every nuance of Goebbels' rants (*there* was a man who appreciated a woman on her knees), faded only slowly, and by the time it had gone her landlady's sunny disposition had returned. She was stirring her cake mixture, humming *Guten Abend, gut' Nacht* softly, a half-smile on her pretty, kind face, and Mila had another recollection, of an

English article she had read some years earlier, on how and why a cultured, sophisticated race like Germany could accept so wantonly the precepts of their deranged Austrian demi-god. It had offered no great insights – merely raised further questions about the power of conviction to undermine former certainties. At the time – and now – it struck her that the authors should have spent more time with the womenfolk, not the ex-soldiers.

She returned to her newspaper, though it was hard to concentrate on its contents. Most of the stories were re-hashed, speculative meanderings about What Now for Germany, a question that might have one or many answers, as any fool knew. A few of them burbled at some length about *the Community of Nations* and whether they were all to be welcomed back into it; others were a little lighter on that mythical beast, confining themselves to hopeful noises on the progress of the pan-European coal and steel arrangements and customs union. After several minutes of trying to absorb this anthology of flipped coins, Mila turned to the local news page, to find something she might comment upon without scattering dragons' teeth once more.

'They don't seem to be closer to solving the Spandau murders yet.'

'Oh, no, dear.' Frau Knipper dribbled water into her bowl and set to once more. 'These gangster feuds persist until everyone's dead or a truce is called. It's another world, even to the Police. As long as they're not killing decent folk we shouldn't care.'

'I thought Spandau was a … respectable place.'

'It was, certainly. My sister married a Spandau man, God bless her – a *very* respectable man, in banking. But it's the way of the world, that places rise and fall. Look at poor Charlottenburg - until the end of the First War it was a lovely place, but then the Republic let the queers, the lady-men and other degenerates out of their holes, and suddenly decent folk couldn't walk across Nollendorfplatz without being accosted by filthy, squealing perverts.'

Christ. 'Well, Hitler did for them, didn't he?'

'He tried, dear, but even the Führer couldn't look under every rock. And now, of course, it's as bad as ever.' Frau Knipper smiled and leaned a little closer. 'Why do you imagine the English demanded that part of Berlin? They're *all* of them homosexuals, apparently.'

Mila folded the newspaper and placed it on the crockery sideboard, fearing that some comment on the previous day's racing at the Trabrennbahn would drag out a rant about International Jewry's manipulation of the Race, Betting and Lottery Act. Appalled as she was, the task of representing Otto Fischer as something less than the ideal husband-to-be was looking less difficult than formerly. Perhaps she might mention his former association with the Soviets, or hint at some symptom of what Frau Knipper would consider turpitude – a tattoo, or predilection for the Roman Rite. Then again, Rolf had mentioned that Fischer had worked personally on some secret matter for Hermann Göring a matter of weeks before Hitler sacked him and ordered his arrest. Surely that was evidence of treason by association? The more Mila considered things, the less likely it seemed that the man's perverse inability to conform to National Socialism's finer precepts would impress her landlady, were she only to be fully enlightened.

And what better time to make a start on it, than when some steam had already been vented?

She cleared her throat. 'He seems a gentleman, Herr Fischer.'

Frau Knipper regarded the wall with much more affection than earlier. 'I don't believe I've ever had a finer one. Staying with us, I mean.'

Was that innuendo? The face gave away nothing, but Mila pressed on.

'I understand his wife died a few years ago, quite tragically?'

A sigh, almost convincing. 'Yes. She was a businesswoman – in the laundry trade. An American GI drove his truck over her, in Bremen. Quite typical.'

'That's so sad. And then he came to Berlin, and made a success.'

'Yes.'

The word dragged itself out, and it was as much a Mila could do to let it ripen in silence.

Frau Knipper paused her dough-strangling. 'I just wish he was a little more ...'

'More?'

'Renate says he doesn't charge enough, either for repairs or the pieces he sells. He doesn't seem to be interested in more money than it takes to keep the bills paid. He's good at what he does, obviously, but perhaps he needs a little push.'

'My husband's like that.'

Frau Knipper smiled. 'You're quite wealthy, so it doesn't matter.'

'I suppose not. It may be something to do with the war. Rolf told me that what he saw and did back then makes a normal life seem strange sometimes, as if he hasn't quite rejoined the stream. I imagine Herr Fischer feels something similar'

'Well, it's been ten years since all of that. He should think to the future more than he does.'

Mila could well imagine the sort of *future* she meant – one in which the poor man would have his slightly inconvenient edges taken off with a carpenter's plane. Was it that he had sensed when he stayed here, or had she given him a glimpse of her inner Eva Braun – a casually-dropped comment on the persistence of the gypsy problem as she ladled her excellent *hochzeitssuppe* into his bowl one evening?

Either way, Mila now had a better understanding of his problem. The woman was an attractive ogre, a mantis who would consume the last of her groom before the wedding cake was distributed. It was hardly surprising that the intended prey wanted to be made less palatable.

She tried to keep her tone casual. 'He was in the east for a while after the war – Stettin, wasn't it?'

'So Renate tells me. A desperate place, full of Polish gangsters. He was lucky to escape alive.'

'Rolf told me he owned a lot to a Russian officer there – one of their intelligence men.'

Frau Knipper's lips pursed slightly, but she shrugged it off. 'It was a difficult time. We all did what was necessary to survive.'

'My husband knew him, too - a Major Zarubin, of MGB. He defected to the West.'

'Ah, a good Russian. There are some, at least.'

'And then he defected back again.'

The lips pushed out further, unrelieved by a shrug this time. Mila pressed on, and down.

'That was two years ago. A few months later, Herr Fischer received a photocard, a view of the Kremlin. There was no message, only a Moscow postal-frank; but he took it to mean that the Major's change of heart hadn't been fatal. Rolf told me that Otto had had something to do with getting him out of Berlin safely, and that he seemed pleased how things had turned out. It's funny, isn't it ...' her voice rose innocently, '... how the unlikeliest friendships can bloom?'

It occurred to her suddenly that perhaps she was over-selling Fischer's Red connection – that Frau Knipper might well move from adoration of the object to denunciation; but the habitual serenity of her landlady's mood appeared to have reasserted itself.

'I'm afraid you don't understand how things are in their world, dear. Renate told me that she'd overheard Herr Fischer telling young Kleiber about some service he'd done for the Gehlen people – obviously, this was it. I expect that this Major has gone back East as an American or German spy, and that Herr Fischer was the means by which he survived the experience. It would be so like him. A man doesn't stop being a hero when the fighting ends.'

Mila, on the ropes, decided to stop swinging blindly. She was going to need more, and more damning, history to breach the edifice of Frau Knipper's regard for Otto Fischer. It was going to be difficult. Rolf had told her that the day he and Fischer first met, the two men had spent hours pressing their faces into dry earth, desperately willing the New Zealanders' highly accurate fire to find some other target. No doubt that somewhat craven (if sensible) tactic would be interpreted by her landlady as a *stand* – an indomitable resistance to overwhelming odds. If they'd raped Greek peasant girls by way of unwinding that same evening, the lady would parse it as a noble attempt to improve the wretched local gene-pool. If they'd put civilians against a wall and …

They *had* put civilians against a wall, and shot them. Rolf had confessed it, with a shrug that hadn't come close to hiding his shame. Fisher had been part of the same squad, given orders that allowed no distinction between partisans and farmers who'd always owned bird-guns. It was a stain, a war crime that wouldn't ever be punished in peace-time, and Mila had no intention of mentioning it to Frau Knipper. The last thing the edifice needed was to be shored by buttresses of concrete.

29

'Are you sure about this, Jonas?'

Herr Grabner was scratching his belly (clear evidence of his disquiet), but he hadn't pressed Kleiber on the evidence, and that was a good sign. Despite his natural caution when it came to reporting anything that happened more than a kilometre from the offices of the *Süd-west Berliner Zeitung*, he'd been impressed by the article. It was the kind of thing he might have written once, years ago, before prudence applied the brakes to his sense of what could or should be risked.

His star reporter wasn't stupid enough to answer the question directly (which, of course, hadn't been asked with that end in mind).

'It'll rattle the cages at City Hall and Friesenstrasse, I promise.'

'Oh, it'll do that, all right. What I meant was, can you *defend* it?'

'Yes, definitely. It's another murder, after all.'

'But not like the other five.'

Seven. 'Well, the fifth one wasn't like the first four, was it? *That* was a bullet to the head, too.'

'Hmm.'

'The thing is, this happened on our doorstep, in Schloss-Strasse, in front of witnesses. It's what the English call *taking the piss.*'

'What has murder to do with bowels?'

'It means cheeky, beyond what's decent, a slap in the face.'

'So?'

'So, it's time to point out to the long-suffering citizens of this city that our police force has been sat on its collective fucking arse for too long while murderers promenade at will through our streets, offing decent men without fear of discovery.'

'How do you know they're decent? They might all be criminals.'

'We don't know that they're *not* decent. It seems to me that it's not Christian to assume the worst in folk, especially when they've been cacked and can't defend themselves.'

'Alright, so they're angels. What if the police put out a statement that this latest one – what's his name?'

'Rudolph Bandelin.'

'Him, yes. What if they say that it has nothing to do with the others, and that the *Zeitung*'s just being sensationalist and provocative?'

'Then we ask: *What Aren't the Police Telling Us? Berliners Demand the Facts!*'

'Oh, that's not bad! They'd have to say how they *know* there's no connection, or admit that there might be.'

The snare sprung, Kleiber pressed on. 'Depending on how they react, we can make a start on *'Who are these Victims? Why isn't More Being Done? Are the Killers Being Protected?'*

Grabner shook his head. 'I don't like that last bit. You've got to be careful, throwing sticks at big dogs.'

'It's an *inference*, Boss. That's why it's put as a question that can't be answered. What can they do about it – prosecute us for *taking the piss*?'

Grabner smiled – a rare event, these days, given that his soul's aching for a young, fled spouse had grown legs that might have shamed Orpheus, or Queen Victoria.

'It's baseless, blatantly disingenuous and titillating – you may have invented a new form of journalism, Jonas.'

'No, the Anglo-Saxons were there first, but there's no reason we can't join them in the cellar. The more we're attacked for it, the greater the exposure - eventually, the bigger papers are going to have to stand by us or condemn what we're doing. Either way, they'll have to mention us.'

The smile was wistful this time. 'The *Morgenpost*!'

'*Morgenpost*, hell! What about the *Frankfurter Allgemeine*? The *Süddeutsche*? *Die Welt*?'

'Really? Do you think ...?'

'Why wouldn't they? The very week that Germany becomes a self-respecting nation once more – well, half of it, anyway – we expose the darkness in the very soul of the body politic - or something like that. How could they not pick it up?'

Grabner looked down at the article once more. It was fairly brief, a poisoned taster laden with innuendo and half-lies masquerading as half-truths, punctuated with more question-marks than could be found on a philosophy exam paper. As a piece of investigative journalism it couldn't have stood with the help of crutches; as a salacious hors d'oeuvre it could hardly be bettered.

He shook his head regretfully. 'It's a pleasant thought, Jonas, but ...'

'Boss?'

'You may as well hear it now. I've been thinking of giving up the *Zeitung*.'

'I know. You've said it about once a month for years now. It's too expensive; it's too time-consuming; you're too old to wade through shit; life's too short; what's the point of ...'

'No, I've *really* been thinking. I'm sixty-four and I look at least seventy-five, I drink and smoke far too much, I get as much sleep as a scared fawn and my heart's got a rhythm like one of the clocks that Otto Fischer takes in. It's time to let it go, to sell up and buy some walking boots before the worms get me.'

'But ... what about my fifteen percent?'

'Don't worry, Jonas. For a local paper we've got a reasonable circulation and hardly any debt, so it wouldn't be too hard to get a good price for the old girl - unless, of course, she was mired in a scandal of her own making. Who'd want to buy a business that might be dragged into court at any moment?'

Really, Kleiber wasn't worried about his stake in the Grabner news empire. He'd been pleased to have it offered – a modest incursion into capitalist conformity did no harm to a man's eligibility, and the monthly deductions from his salary to pay for it hardly affected his extremely modest lifestyle. But he had a plan now, a strategy to raise the Kleiber reputation that would be killed in the cradle by any commitment to probity, integrity and the avoidance of groundless accusations. Even a fifteen percent slice of the cake gave him some rights at the shareholders' meeting (which this was in a way, because one hundred percent of them were gathered at the moment, speaking of the *Zeitung*'s future), and he searched desperately for an argument that would appeal to more than protecting the business's goodwill.

'You've been at this a long time, Boss.'

'I have, Jonas. And please, call me Ferdinand. We're friends, I hope.'

'We are.' Kleiber shook his head. 'I'm worried.'

'What about?'

'Your legacy. Nearly forty years in newspapers – a man should be recalled for it.'

'It's just a local rag. I don't expect the National Press Club will hear about my going.'

'What if they did?'

'Americans don't pay much attention to things that aren't America.'

'Who's to say that they won't, if the story's big enough?'

Grabner sighed. 'Half a dozen murders in Berlin is big news, in Berlin. They wouldn't make page eight of the New York Times.'

'They would if the State was trying to smother an investigation into them, and we broke the scandal.'

'But they're not. Smothering, I mean.'

'They might be. Do you know how the investigation's going?'

'No.'

'Neither do I, and I've asked. If it's just lack of interest, or incompetence, they've become very good at it.'

'We can't just say that there's a conspiracy. They'd climb the walls, and drop on us.'

'Of course we can't. We hint at it, but not as subtly as hints go, usually. If there's some sort of official response, we attack it as deflection, a cover-up; if they say nothing, we go at it again from a different direction.'

'What direction?'

'*Were these Men Executed ex-judicially for Crimes against the State? Were they Soviet Spies?*'

'I thought they were angels?'

'They *are*, until they're not. Eventually, we're going to irritate someone enough to get a reaction.'

'Yes, but *what* reaction? It's very dangerous game, Jonas.'

'*And* we'll be making a name for the *Zeitung*. It has to be better than sticking with local colour - which is grey, always. If – when – the nationals pick it up, your shares are going to be worth a lot more than they are now. Notoriety never hurt a newspaper.'

'Legal actions did and do.'

'So we make sure we say nothing actionable. The question mark is our shield.'

For the first time in years, Grabner laughed aloud. 'I've raised a monster. Why don't you get a job with *Bild*?'

'Because I want to scare people, not tell them what they want to hear in pictures.'

Around the *Zeitung*'s tiny Press Room, pages from previous editions, recalling some of their most popular stories, adorned the wooden walls. The editor-proprietor had put them up to bump his own morale as much as his subordinate's, and he scanned them now, the manifest of his four decades' service to the community – his first entertainments review (of Anita Berber's scandalous four-week residency at the Titania-Palast in summer, 1922); the bland, matter-of-fact report that Herr Hitler had been invited by Hindenburg to assume the Chancellorship; local celebrity Else Eckmann's 110th birthday party (attended briefly by Goebbels himself, who presented her with the *Mutterkreuz* even though it wasn't 12 August and she was a spinster); the near-legendary rose display at Lichterfelde's 1947 Flower Show (legendary, because of its revelation that roses existed still in the world); the dozens, perhaps hundreds, of arcane, inexplicable hobbies fiercely pursued by men - always men - through years of war, peace, bereavement, separation and destitution – and sighed deeply.

'It's all crap, isn't it?'

'Not crap, Boss. Just not as ... *remarkable* as it might have been.'

'Alright!' Grabner stood up, more quickly than his paunch should have allowed. 'We'll run this one and see what happens. I'll find the cash to put a few hundred extra copies out to kiosks in Schöneberg and Mitte to get it noticed. If Authority comes back with something we'll think about what to write next.'

'Front page?'

'Where else? If you build a bomb there's no point sticking it in the outhouse.'

30

'I'm sorry, Otto. I don't know where Jens is.'

'Freddie, it's only been a day. You can't give up yet.'

'I didn't give up. I had my arse handed to me. I called the Ministry, found the right department and told them about his arrest and release. All I asked for was an address or telephone number, if they had it. A fellow took my number and said he'd call back. He did, but not me. I've just been upstairs with my Boss, trying to explain it away, and he told me not to bother them again, ever, on pain of traffic duty.'

Fischer had been about to deploy his special reserve of curses, but held fire. 'That's odd.'

'Yeah, I thought so too.'

'Why would they object to you doing your job?'

'And so quickly, as if someone had been waiting for it.'

'Perhaps someone *had* been waiting for it.'

'Yeah, I thought that, too.'

'So, was this someone involved in his arrest?'

'Or are they trying to protect him from more of the same?'

'And, in either case, why?'

'We'll know that when we find out why Jens' friend was shot in the street.'

'And we won't know that until we find Jens.'

'Fuck.'

'As you say. I'll have to think again.'

'Otto, I'm ...'

'What?'

'Sorry, about recommending you to Jens. I just thought you may as well have the money as anyone else.'

'It's alright, Freddie. All you did was point him in my direction. I could have told him no.'

'So we're both cocks, then?'

'We are. And it may be that this will come to nothing.'

'What is *this*, exactly? You've only hinted at it.'

Fischer had a strong urge to think and speak of anything other than his idiotic decision and its consequences. 'I'll tell you if I ever need to. How's Kristin? The boys? My god-son?'

'Everyone's good. Little Otto said his first word last week.'

'What was it?'

'Adolf.'

'That's unfortunate.'

'It's our neighbour's dog.'

'Ah. And your liberation?

'From the fucking Luxies? We had a leaving parade, to make it look like something other than comedy. They put on their fancy braid and we police formed an honour guard for them, with strict orders not to laugh. Then, they all got on a train and we ran up the Black, Red and Gold. It wasn't much.'

'Still, freedom ...'

'I know, it's good. What are you going to do, Otto? About this business?'

'As I say, think some more. And do some digging.'

'Regarding what?'

'Historical matters.'

'If we weren't Germans that would sound a lot less worrying.'

'It's nothing that I was ever involved with. Though it turns out I might have been, apparently.'

'Eh?'

'Never mind. We'll speak again soon.'

Fischer replaced the receiver and looked up. Renate was in the doorway, her tender frown far too reminiscent of the one her mother bestowed upon him whenever she spoke of his diet, or dress-sense, or the pity of living alone. He shuddered involuntarily.

'Is it about that poor man, Herr Director?'

'In a way, Renate. Don't worry, I have two alibis, remember? Yours, and your young man's.'

'He's not my young man. He just wants to be.'

Poor Jonas would be sorry to hear it, but that particular crisis stood well down the queue in Fischer's preoccupations. The *digging* he'd mentioned to Holleman was both necessary and extremely problematic, as there was no readily available data upon which to draw. He had an obvious starting place, but he couldn't go there; there was a probable rationale, but he couldn't explore it. So, it all came back to Jens Lamsdorf - the necessary starting point, the only gate out of which he could proceed.

'Renate, would you be a sweetheart and get me some lunch? I didn't have breakfast. Your choice.'

When she had gone he picked up the receiver and dialled.

'That was *quick* thinking!'

'Freddie, before *Amt Blank* was that it was something else, for about eight months at the turn of the decade.'

'Was it? I didn't follow Wessie politics too closely back then.'

'It was run by General Schwerin.'

'The saviour of Aachen?'

'That's him.'

'And?'

'You have a police database – you're going to find him for me.'

'Oh, hell. Why do you think he'll want to speak to me? Or you?'

'He probably won't. But Blank replaced him because he talked too much - and to the newspapers, no less. If I'm lucky, he hasn't grown reticent.'

'Alright. Goodbye.'

'No, wait. There's something else you can do.'

'Wonderful.'

'I just need information. You were a good *kozi* once, weren't you?'

'I wouldn't say *good*.'

'I want to find one – a *kozi*, I mean. Of a very special and probably rare species.'

'Go on.'

When Fischer explained, Holleman laughed. 'Rare like unicorn turds, you mean? Obviously, if there *are* any above ground still, they'll be in the DDR. I can only recall a single mention of their community, and that was for the trouble they caused. In Brandenburg, I think.'

'Trouble?'

'Yeah – religious trouble, believe it or not.'

'I thought *kozis* were atheists?'

'A common error. Even Trotsky was married by a Rabbi.'

'What trouble, then?'

'Despite official discouragement, Brandenburg's still as Protestant as Luther's cat, and most of the new arrivals of the particular sort you're looking for were Catholics – or at least, they'd been dipped that way. It didn't make for fraternal bonds.'

'And that was ten years ago.'

'Yeah.'

Fischer sighed. 'It was a thin hope. Presumably the local authorities wouldn't go out of their way to assist an enquiry on the topic.'

'They'd tell you to fuck your fist. Anyway, how would it help you find Jens?'

'It wouldn't. I was trying to come at my problem from another direction. All you've told me is that there isn't one. See if you can find Schwerin. He's probably never heard of Lamsdorf, but for the moment I can't think of anything or anyone else.'

31

Renate had been about to buy some pea soup for Herr Fischer when she thought about how his shirts had been hanging from his frame even more loosely lately than usual. Being practically minded, it occurred to her that his health was important to her continuing employment. Though she was not well-paid (and knew it perfectly well), the job was a good one, involving as it did every aspect of running a small business except the repair work itself. She intended to have her own enterprise someday, and appreciated the informal university of commerce at which she presently studied.

So at the kiosk she decided against pea soup, and bought instead some sliced pork knuckle doused in chillup sauce, with a side-portion of *kartoffelpuffer*. Herr Fischer preferred not to dine heavily at midday, but he had offered her the choice, and this was it – food fit for a working man, not a costive sparrow.

Being served in a cardboard carton the dish required some care in transit, and she became aware that she was being followed only when she turning back into Curtius-Strasse and took the opportunity, passing a dress-shop window, to check her reflection. He was directly across the street, moving in the same direction as her, and she wouldn't have noticed him had it not been for his pantomime-obvious reaction (he stopped, turned his head swiftly away, and pretended to find something interesting in a fishmonger's display).

She didn't like the look of him, and not just because he appeared to be stalking her. His clothes were smart enough for the office, but he slouched, and walked with his hands in his pockets, and well-brought-up young men didn't do either (nor, of course, did they follow women to whom they hadn't been introduced formally). She assumed that he was yet another admirer; but when she walked on he waited a while before following, and when she entered *Fischer's Time-piece and Gramophone Repairs* he took up position at the bus-halt across the street and pretended to read a newspaper.

Herr Fischer gave his lunch an eyebrow but didn't complain, and while he was eating it she returned to the counter to surveil her surveiller. Her suspicions about him sharpened when a bus came and went and he stood there still, lighting a cigarette, looking as if he was going to make an afternoon of his visit to Curtius-Strasse.

Renate was quite aware of her effect upon most men, but she doubted that her beauty was such that one of them would waste hours in contemplation of it. Either she was being mistaken for someone else or the vigil was upon some other matter, almost certainly involving her employer, whose colourful life – so piteously worn on his face – doubtless had acquired many regrettable accretions. He had been a Luftwaffe officer of course, but also a policeman, a spy and not only a bereaved husband but – something she hadn't yet told her mother – of a once-prostitute (she had Jonas Kleiber to thank for that morsel), and any one of those careers might have brought him into the company of bad characters. She also knew of the desperate business two years earlier, on these very premises, when he had killed a would-be assassin and almost died himself, and while she didn't quite believe all of the story (particularly not the heroic part that Kleiber claimed for himself), it was obvious that the unassuming, modest gentleman with whom she spent much of every workday had deep, spreading roots.

She had to tell him, naturally. If this was another plot against him he needed time to devise some cunning strategy, or to run, or to call the police. In films, a heroine would stab a finger dramatically at the looming danger and then swoon, but she had a horror of appearing ridiculous. On the other hand, to casually mention that a moment of danger might be upon them would make her seem like she was trying too hard to be Susan Hayward, and that was worse.

The wisest option, of course, would be to appeal to Herr Fischer's male vanity and let him take the initiative. She went into the workshop.

'Herr Director?'

Fischer was wiping pork grease from his hands. He looked up.

'There's a man across the street. He's been there a while, waiting for a bus but not getting on any of them. I thought you might want to know.'

He nodded. 'Thank you, Renate.' He dropped his towel, went into the shop and returned moments later, whistling softly. Renate was surprised that he wasn't more concerned, and only partly reassured when he went to the desk, removed his pistol and loaded its magazine.

'Should I call the police, Her Director?'

'No. I doubt that the gentleman's business is with either of us.' He lifted the pistol slightly. 'But it doesn't hurt to be sensible. We'll put this in the drawer under the shop counter.'

'Are you *pleased* about this?'

'Pleased? No, I'm … hopeful.'

'Why?'

'Why do you think we're being watched?'

Renate could think of only one reason. 'It must be about that poor young man who was shot.'

'We haven't seen any other excitement recently, have we? But now he's dead, so how can we be of interest?'

'I don't know.'

'Well, I mend broken things. There's nothing about it that should attract the wrong sort of attention.'

'Could it be about the poor young man's friend, Herr Lamsdorf?'

'I think it probably could, yes.'

'So he might come back?'

Fischer shrugged. 'I don't know. If we're being watched, someone thinks it's possible, at least.'

'Is that why you're hopeful?'

'Yes. I'd very much like to speak to him.'

Renate considered this. Herr Fischer wasn't one for gabbling much – a quality she prized greatly – but the disadvantage of a quiet boss was that the staff didn't get to know much.

'Are you in trouble?'

'I might be, though I'm not sure *how*. If I knew more ...' he smiled '... I'd know more.'

She tossed a thumb. 'And *him*?'

'We ignore him, very watchfully.'

'But what if he killed the young man?'

'Oh, I doubt that he did. It was a professional execution, and men who can do that are valuable - they wouldn't be wasted on a routine watch. The fact that you spotted this one suggests that he's not very good. He probably has one job, and that's to report when Lamsdorf shows his face.'

'Can't we find a way to warn him?'

Fischer groaned. 'Another circular problem labelled *Jens Lamsdorf*. I'm beginning to think he's some sort of test.'

'I'm sorry?'

'It doesn't matter. You did well to notice the man, Renate.'

'Thank you. Herr Director.'

'But that lunch – what was the sauce?'

'It's chillup – a new thing, with Indian spices.'

'No more of it, please. I'm almost certain it's that, not Herr Lamsdorf, that's giving me heartburn.'

32

'Why are we here again, Volker?'

It was a rule, unwritten but almost universally obeyed, that the same meeting place was not to be used consecutively, yet the two men sat once more at a table on the café terrace in the pretty town by the River Traun.

Volker was wearing the same well-silvered suit as previously, but the other man had abandoned his factory worker's clothes for slacks and a short-sleeved shirt (it being an unseasonably warm Saturday morning). He was irritated and slightly anxious – aware of every movement around him, his eyes flitting constantly from his companion's face to survey the immediate terrain with the distracted air of a platoon commander expecting an enemy battalion. For Volker this was familiar behaviour, observed in dozens of men who shared a peculiar situation, and it was part of his job to ease their ignited nerve-endings to the point at which they did or said nothing that was hasty, or unwise, or just stupid. He had an easy manner and a way with sensible advice that served the task well, usually.

'When we spoke last, there was an outstanding matter, about which something might or might not be done.'

The other man nodded. 'You were going to watch him, closely.'

'We were. But we can't find him.'

'He's been released?'

'Of course. There was nothing to put on him that could have kept him where he was.'

'He hasn't gone home?'

'He hasn't gone anywhere we know of – his home, workplace or points between. We've put men where he might show his face, but that's in hope, not expectation.'

'Has he any family?'

'None. Worse, he's very resourceful – he has to be, to have done what he's done and left almost nothing we could use against him.'

'So, he's scared. What does that mean?'

'It's hard to say, because we don't know what he knows. He might have been told everything or nothing.'

'They were close friends – surely, he must know?'

Volker shook his head at an approaching waiter. 'Would a friend willingly share dangerous knowledge, unless it was necessary? And even if he *does* have the information, what motive would he have for using it now? He'd understand the risk.'

'Revenge? For what happened to the other one?'

'It's a possibility, certainly. It's equally likely that he knows just enough to be what you say he is – scared.'

'Can we take the risk?'

'The last time we spoke you said we couldn't.'

'That was before he disappeared.'

'Hm.' The two men considered their empty coffee cups. Both knew themselves to be on the same side, both knew that their priorities diverged widely, and both knew what was coming next.

Volker cleared his throat. 'Given the recent situation, it's clear that care needs to be taken.'

The other man nodded but said nothing.

'The general opinion – I should say consensus – is that we proceed as if the worst is most likely. Therefore, the priority is to ensure that connections can't be made between those already at risk and the rest.'

Another nod. 'I'm not to expect further assistance.'

'No – at least, not until things are settled. Of course, it's the same for the others.'

'How many are there?'

Volker's eyebrows rose. 'We can't say for certain. We don't know what the exiled Jew said, and of course we can't question the one he spoke to. The information exists but it can't be quantified, so we have to assume that everyone who *might* be implicated is. I can tell you, it's taking time and a lot of money to cover all the potential exposures, and we've lost considerable goodwill among those we rely upon to keep official heads turned away.'

'Can't we get at the Jew himself?'

'Absolutely not. He's been spurned yet they watch him closely, hoping that we'd be stupid enough to try. We'd risk everything by attempting it.'

'I should have killed him when he was of no consequence to anyone.'

'Ah, Anton. If we could read the runes we'd all be somewhere else.'

Call me Wilhelm. The other man almost corrected him, but it occurred that such caution was no longer necessary. They were about to become strangers to each other, and a sense of loss pressed hard. He had never been sentimental, but when all of one's natural society has been taken away what remains is more precious. And now he was about to be cast out by the very people who cared for the outcasts. It was both logical and necessary, and if he had been in Volker's place he would have insisted on precisely this – and, probably, less gently than he was hearing it. It hurt no less for all of that.

He stood. 'When will I know, one way or the other?'

Volker stood also, and held out his hand. 'If it's *one* way you'll hear nothing, ever. If we manage to find our elusive friend and deal with him I'll contact you the usual way, but only after we've made absolutely certain that every piece of shrapnel's been accounted for. Either way, you should proceed on the assumption that you're on your own.'

'I will. It seems that I should have chosen the far-abroad after all.'

'No, you did the right thing, believe me. I rarely meet with smiling faces over there. The past hangs heavier the further one travels from the *heimat* - everything that's different over there is just another reminder of what might have been but wasn't. I've seen it in all their eyes, even when they're slapping me on the back, speaking too loudly and showing me around their big houses. It's never more than a minute before they get wistful and start to ask the questions – what's it like now; has anyone asked after them; is that old bar still there on the corner of this or that street in the old town? At least you have your family with you, and a familiar view from your window, and you can speak your own language still. *They* have only the reassurance of an ocean's width, and even that might not be enough.'

'What do you mean?'

Volker shrugged. 'I hear the Israelis are learning to swim.'

33

By temperament, *Polizeioberrat* Friedrich Melancthon Holleman
was not the man to let a job oppress his spirit. His head clocked in
and out at the prescribed times, and was sufficiently flexible to add
or subtract a few hours as necessary; but when a shift ended he
placed all matters pertaining to his employment into a mental
pending tray, awaiting further consideration when next he graced his
office. Family time was just that, and not to be shaded, soured or
consumed by what more committed (or less sensible) toilers
regarded as the pressures of work.

Recently, however, thoughts of work left the building with him and
kept him company through Trier's pretty streets and alleys, not
minding at all the increasingly circuitous route he adopted (on his
new, far more comfortable capitalist prosthetic leg) between the
Police Praesidium and his home in East Trier. For a native Berliner
these detours were novel, taking in as they did true antiquities (the
Roman Baths, Porta Nigra and the poor, half-ruined Cathedral); but
the mosquito-buzzing in his head often distracted him from their
glories, to the point at which he often arrived home unrefreshed and
peevish.

His wife Kristin had begun to notice his uncharacteristic moodiness,
and, being both loving and plain-spoken, was torn between tender
concern and an urge to apply a shapely foot to her soulmate's arse.
She knew that he felt out of his depth in the extremely shallow pool

of law enforcement in this beautiful, tranquil region (having been breeched as an *Orpo* on the violent pre-war streets of Berlin and then raised to high police and political office in the Red City), and that he regarded his present job as an advanced notice of retirement. He was homesick for the East more days than he wasn't, complained constantly of office politics (at once so pervading and trivial that only heavy ordnance might effect a cure) and for the first time in his life was taking off the occasional day to pamper a migraine. Being now a grandmother – one who helped lift the burden of early parenthood by having little Otto during weekday work-hours – Kristin had enough wailing, incoherent tantrums to deal with without wishing further weight upon her shoulder, and said so.

Consequently, there had grown between them a slight but palpable frisson that made them very much like other couples of their age, and in recent evenings it had been fed by the further matter of the favour that Holleman had imagined he had pushed Otto Fischer's way.

He couldn't tell Kristin about it - she'd kill him, disinter the remains and kill them, too. She was heavily burdened still by the memory of their clumsy defection from the East and her part in almost putting Fischer into an early grave. Even two years on, she never passed by her church without going in to light a candle for his continuing health and happiness (though a very poor sort of Catholic himself, her husband was fairly sure that this wasn't what votive candles were for, but sensibly he hesitated to say so), so the revelation that a member – the chief, sinning member – of the Holleman family had once more dropped the poor man into a pile would have sent her on a long, steep trajectory. Holleman knew and respected her temper, and took great pains not to goad in unnecessarily.

He wished sincerely now that he had told Jens Lamsdorf that he had no idea how a man could be disappeared, and left it at that. He been an acquaintance at most (though an agreeable one), with a reputation that wiser men would have considered carefully before pointing him in the direction of a closest friend; yet Holleman too had a keen sense of the large debt the family owed to Otto Fischer. He had wanted very much to repay it, and a fat pile of cash hadn't seemed the worst means to that end. If only he had shared something of his friend's instinctive caution he might at least have paused, and thought deeply about it.

But deep thinking was not one of his natural virtues. His jump-first instincts had made him a good fighter pilot, a decent police officer and a bad friend, and once more he had all the time in the world to reflect upon the last. He was determined to do what Otto asked of him, naturally; but he had caught the deflated note in his friend's voice, the more-than-hint that this was his final, forlorn idea. General Schwerin might be found and might even be willing to talk; but how likely was it that he knew the present whereabouts of Jens Lamsdorf?

Bloody Jens. What the hell was the man involved in? Holleman had wondered at first if he was some sort of spy, but if that was the case his arrest would certainly have been followed by a swift removal of the body, not by its release three days later. If this was some sort of organized criminal business then Bonn's Police Praesidium was rotten to its foundations, and even a former *VolksPolizei* man couldn't believe that was possible. But what options remained? That Lamsdorf himself was – or had been - a thief was indisputable. Apart from the aircraft parts he conjured from nowhere and for which he always took a finder's commission, his march through Belgian had been much like Attila's, and Christ and Jens alone knew what further riches he'd acquired in that plunderer's department store, Italy. He'd probably come out of the war with a larger Swiss bank balance than Göring's art agent, and no-one got that rich, that quickly, without attracting enemies.

Otto should have heard all of this before having to make a decision, and had Holleman's new leg not cost an arm and a leg he might have removed it and used it on his own arse. Everything had been quiet, mundanely proceeding without strife, bloodshed or a threat of rain, and he had stirred it all with his size twelve boot. Wasn't it just like …

He stopped in the street. He was almost home, halfway along the stretch of Mustorstrasse between Ostallee and Güterstrasse, and two things occurred to him almost simultaneously. Of these the most disturbing was that he had assumed his recent mood to be upon several points of dissatisfaction with his new life, when it was probably more to do with the loss of all the shit that had soiled the old. If trouble had followed him throughout his adult life, it was probably because he had welcomed its attentions, and now he was missing it so terribly that he had flung a little in his best friend's direction, probably to savour it by proxy.

And that was the second thing – being followed. He had been distracted by his thoughts ever since hobbling past St Peter's, but at about that point his subconscious must have filed a slight disturbance, a peripheral shadow, and then allowed his head to go its own, preoccupied way. It might have nudged him gently a few times since then but he hadn't noticed until his pause brought the world back into near-view. He half-turned, giving the western stretch of Mustorstrasse a single glance, and then stooped as if to adjust his leg. The shape was with him still, hovering at the corner of Ostallee – a big man (if the woman presently passing by him was of normal proportions), and curiously interested in the cleared space of a former bomb-site between a chemist's and real-estate agent's premises.

In a moment, Holleman's wind-break of guilt had been swept away by the prospect of slapping someone, questioning him roughly as to what he was about and then slapping him again. He walked on slowly to Große Eulenpfütz, stepped to the left and left again, putting himself behind the small corner tower of the *faux* medieval building on the corner. Less than a minute later, approaching footsteps gave him momentary warning; he sprang out as the big fellow rushed by and from behind wrapped an arm around his neck.

For a moment, inertia was with him and he dragged his pursuer halfway to the ground, but the man was strong - as much so as Holleman himself - and the descent slowed to a clumsy, crab-like wrestle that was neither upright nor prone, as if two normally-staid neighbours were having their first-ever brawl over the matter of a garden boundary.

In that standoff, two legs had the advantage over one, and Holleman began to feel his grip open. He shifted, risking his balance, and punched upwards into a jaw. The other man staggered but kept his own grip, and the second punch did nothing useful, so Holleman deployed a thumb instead and went after an eye. That brought a muffled curse and a kick that sent the artificial leg sideways and its owner crashing to the pavement.

'You silly bastard! You almost blinded me!'

On the ground, Holleman rubbed the nose that had broken his fall and looked up.

'Let me get up and I'll finish the job. Who the hell are you?'

His adversary, hand clasped over one eye and tie wrapped twice around his neck, groaned and reached for a handkerchief.

'I was told to say a friend, but that would be a fucking lie.'

It was the faithful, remorseless Renate who brought the bad news with two slices of her mother's bee-sting cake, as if one unfortunate association might sweeten the pain of the other.

Fischer rarely took a heavier breakfast than two black coffees, but he had eaten his share before his mind registered the fact or his stomach complained, such was the force with which both were reeling already.

Neither he nor his assistant habitually read the local newspaper. Fischer had bought a copy fifteen months earlier when first he had placed a small advertisement for clock and time-piece repairs, and only then to check that the details were correct. Being a relatively recent immigrant to the area, the minutiae of Lichterfelde life neither raised pleasant memories nor stirred nostalgia, and while in principle he wished its centenarians as much of a happy life to come as they might reasonably expect, he felt little loss at not knowing when the milestones came and went. Renate, of course, had the iron indifference of youth to which elderly locals were doing what, with whom and why, so when she placed that morning's edition in front of her proprietor he was mildly surprised - for as long as it took him to read the uncharacteristically large headline.

Schloss-Strasse Slaying – Have the Horrors of Spandau come to Lichterfelde?

The stretch of Schloss-Strasse upon which the false Rudy Bandelin had been brutally murdered lay just over the border, in Steglitz, but

Fischer didn't care to notice this sleight of journalism. He was thinking about Jonas Kleiber's thin neck, and how conveniently his hands might fit around it.

Christ.

'Renate, would you watch the shop for a few minutes?'

She nodded, having entirely expected the question, and took her slice of cake to the front counter. Halfway into his jacket, Fischer paused, took it off again and forced himself to read the entire story. If he was about to commit murder, he wanted to be sure it was amply deserved.

The 'story' was a masterpiece of supposition, inference and no hard fact, and its utter lack of meat confirmed his suspicion that the author hadn't been Herr Grabner (whose taste for dangerous journalism extended to predicting winners at the Flower Show). Had it carried the proud by-line *Inspiration, Property and Entire Fault of Jonas Kleiber* he couldn't have been more certain of its genesis. The jacket went on again, and with both hands he rolled the paper tightly, to better fit its intended destination.

The edition had come out that morning, so the print room was empty other than for the compositor's apprentice, who was sweeping the floor with a painful lack of enthusiasm. Fischer looked up and saw a shadow-movement in the journalists' den. For once, the deadly state of the staircase didn't put him on his toes; he took the entire flight in just four strides and burst through the glass and wood door. Jonas, at his desk, levitated visibly.

'Otto! I almost shat myself!'

'Don't unclench yet. What's this?'

Fischer dropped the rolled *Zeitung* onto the desk. Kleiber beamed. 'Have you read it? There'll be a few red faces in Friesenstrasse this morning - *and* the Senate, if we're lucky. What? I mean, what's wrong?'

'Why did you do it? There's no connection between the Spandau business and that poor bastard I helped - you *know* that.'

'I do – I think. But what better way to put a foot up Authority's arse? If one of those dead men had been a banker or a politician they'd have drained the Spree to find the culprits. As it is, the only things being emptied are coffee mugs and fat, idle bladders.'

Fischer sat down in Herr Grabner's chair, put his elbows on the desk and head in his hands. Kleiber frowned solicitously.

'Are you alright, Otto? You look pale.'

'That would be the blood following my stomach to the floor, you silly bastard!'

'Me? What have I done?'

Fischer looked up. 'I was interviewed about the false Rudy Bandelin's murder, wasn't I?'

'Yes, but you're clear. You were having lunch with me. And then Renate ...'

'No, I'm not. Three days later I was summoned to Friesenstrasse in connection with the Spandau business. The *kripo* running the investigation heard about the Schloss-Strasse thing and wondered if they might be related.'

'You didn't tell me! Why would he do that?'

'Because he was out of ideas, and because someone - in a very oblique way – implicated me in the earlier murders.'

'How?'

My name's on a piece of paper he has, keeping company with a little puzzle. The *kripo* hasn't solved it yet, so he isn't too excited about me. But if or when he does, I'm going to need damned good alibis for every one of the five or seven killings in Spandau. He might not work it out, but you've just pushed a *schlagstock* up his arse as an incentive to try harder.'

'Oh, shit. I didn't know.'

'Which is why I didn't bring my gun. At the least, this *kripo* is going to be looking a lot more closely at that piece of paper and wondering what it is that seems familiar about what he's seeing. He might very well pass it around his Bull's Pen, and in someone's head, however empty otherwise, a distant peal will ring. After that ...'

'Are you sure this puzzle's got a bad solution? Bad for you, I mean.'

'It's bad for anyone whose name's sat next to it.'

'What is it, then?'

'You really want to know – you, the man who told the *kripo*'s colleague that he was sitting opposite me in a restaurant when Lamsdorf's friend got shot? Once they work out the puzzle you'll be dragged straight back to Friesenstrasse as a potential accomplice. They'll question you, hard, and if you even drop a hint that you know what's on that paper, it's all to fuck for both of us.'

'Jesus!' Horrified, Kleiber stared at the wall behind Fischer's head. Being a fearless journalist required a degree of, well, fearlessness, and those episodes of his life to date which had placed danger front and centre did not entirely shine in memory. He was fairly sure – he was absolutely, money-on-it certain – that he would resist a rigorous interrogation for some minutes before telling them everything they wanted to know and more. Yet he had, in effect, just implicated himself and then distributed the confession via the *Zeitung*'s largest ever print-run.

'I'll write a retraction!'

'Put the gas back into the cylinder? That would be clever. Presumably, the police will shrug and say fair enough - or, they'll assume that the fellow who's just publicly taunted them with their failure to solve the case is having a further laugh at their expense.'

'What can we do?'

'I have no idea. None of the vague plans I've entertained involved a public declaration of guilt, carried across eight columns. All I – *we* – have is the alibi; reinforced, of course, by the lie that Renate told.'

Kleiber brightened a little. 'Did you keep the receipt? For that lunch?'

'No, because there wasn't one. Lorenzo has an Italian's love of taxes, so he shaves five percent from a bill for cash. In any case, the restaurant is so close to the spot where the shooting took place that either of us could have driven around the corner, done the business and been back at the table before anyone noticed. The only solid part of our alibi was that which Renate volunteered.' Fischer smiled. 'The one you've now called into question. If the police return, they'll be a lot less trusting of her pretty face.'

Kleiber closed his eyes. With a single, deft stroke of the quill he had cast both his friend and himself into the Proverbial, invited his intended *innamorata* to separate him from the means of extending the Kleiber bloodline and probably killed Herr Grabner's chances of retiring before the mid-70s. Compared to *Barbarossa* it was a relatively minor error of judgment, but only because he hadn't had the wit or resources to make it more epic.

'Otto, I wish you'd told me about that piece of paper.'

'I wish you'd asked before chaining the Spandau business to Rudy Bandelin.'

'Um.'

Fischer rubbed his face, picked up the newspaper with which he'd intended to violate Kleiber and read the offending article once more. As a piece of trying-it-on hackery it was really quite good, casting wide, indiscriminate aspersions that didn't quite solidify into anything actionable. No-one in West Berlin's law-enforcement community could imagine that he had been spared the lash, yet no one man or department was explicitly accused of ignoring or abetting the killings. Had Fischer himself - a one-time *kriminalkommissar* - been painted with such a broad, damning brush, it would have done the job. He would have fretted about it, been goaded either into kicking the author or going back over the ground to find what had been missed the first time. Either way, trouble had been poked with a stick. Even if a link couldn't be made between the Spandau and Schloss-Strasse slayings, *Kripo* Fux would be looking far more closely at Rudy Bandelin. The dead man's papers might stand up to close scrutiny but the word would be put out - and, if any of the real, long-dead Bandelin's relatives had managed to survive the death-marches westwards, they would come forward. The corpse wouldn't be nearly sufficiently decomposed to make an identification difficult, and after that Otto Fischer would be a primary suspect in at least one murder case.

He couldn't really blame Kleiber. He *should* have told him about the piece of paper, if only to cover his own rear end; but a damned Möbius predicament had wound him up, around and sideways until he was ready to disappear up the same feature. The fact was, he had nowhere to go and there were no signposts in sight. In any of his previous collisions with bad luck he'd been able to draw upon something – Luftwaffe resources, witnesses, the chaotic camouflage of a failing war or the mood-swings of an idiosyncratic Soviet Intelligencer; now, he had his deadly skills as a mender of clocks and musical boxes and an address that anyone could find in the local South Berlin Business Directory. He had felt slightly less vulnerable on his only Cretan holiday, lying face down in a ditch with his rifle almost close to hand, the bullets buzzing like a stirred hive above him.

'What are we going to do, Otto?'

Kleiber was waiting patiently, an affecting, gun-dog cast to his face. It was almost a pity to disappoint him, but Fischer had no gift for raising moods and in any case preferred to ease the pain by sharing it.

'As I said, I have no idea. I'm waiting for the light, and don't know if it's coming. Tell me more about Buenos Aires.'

'Oh, don't say that ...'

'Otto!'

The noise came from below. Both Fischer and Kleiber leaned towards window and peered down. Rolf Hoeschler was stood in the middle of the now-deserted Print Room, glancing around.

'Up here, Rolf. Mind the stairs.'

Hoeschler's ascent tore groans of anguish from the ancient woodwork, and his head appeared only slowly as he traversed the deadly flight.

'Jesus! Can't you get them fixed?'

Kleiber seemed mildly surprised by the question. 'Yeah, probably. Coffee?'

A pot of the beverage, well-stewed, sat on an electric plate in the corner of the Press Room. While Kleiber was pouring into three mugs, Fischer regarded his former comrade curiously.

'Is Mila alright?'

'Hm? Oh, yes. She's deadly impatient to come home, though.'

'You're not at work, Rolf.'

'No, I'm not ...'

'Is something wrong?'

'Sort of wrong. I've been suspended, pending a disciplinary hearing.'

'Did you send the trams the wrong way?'

'Ha. No, I was seen beating up a co-worker, and ratted on.'

'Oh.' Fischer shrugged. 'I suppose they have rules about that sort of thing.'

'Apparently. It was an over-cocky little shit, bribed to deliver a threatening message from Herr Smith. I answered it.'

'You're not worried he'll react?'

'How? By killing the goose before it's fattened? I doubt it. Anyway, I had time on my hands and no wife to go home to, so I thought I'd bother you.'

'You're very welcome. What else is news?'

'Nothing worth reporting. I've had no good ideas about what to do.'

'I know the feeling very well.'

For a few moments the three men sipped their coffee, each examining the pit of a personal conundrum. Then Hoeschler cleared his throat and looked up.

'So, Frau Knipper's a Nazi, then?'

Kleiber coughed out a quantity of coffee. Fischer pulled a face.

'Mila told you?'

'She did. Is that why you're avoiding the woman like a dose?'

'Not really. She had to be *something*, and it's not as if she's going to open a new Front. The problem's her other Führer urges. She has a way with her, the gentle criticisms, that tell me the only thing she won't be working on – given the chance - is this bloody face. Everything else is to be moulded to the lady's requirements.'

Fischer turned to Kleiber.

'Renate's a wonderful girl, but she's her mother's daughter, too. You might want to think about that.'

'What about *me* needs any moulding?'

'You'll find out. Here … ' Fischer pushed his copy of that morning's *Zeitung* towards Hoeschler. 'Jonas has had a sharp idea.'

Hoeschler took the newspaper. His eyebrows rose when he saw the headline, and he took his time reading what lay beneath it. Belatedly, Kleiber made a start on his rehabilitation, lifting a bottle of Bärenjäger from his desk drawer and pouring a liberal measure into each mug.

'Fuck your mother!'

'You don't know the worst of it. There's a piece of paper at the Police Praesidium containing a veiled reference to the men who died in Spandau. My name's sitting next to them.'

Hoeschler shook his head. 'You're sure? That it's about them?'

'I'm almost certain. The *kripo* who's working the case hasn't made the connection yet, which is why I'm not presently warming a cell at Friesenstrasse. I can't hope that he'll continue not to get it – particularly now that Jonas has stuck a boot up his fundament.'

Kleiber winced. Hoeschler glared sternly at him but asked only one of the many things that came to mind.

'Why?'

'I wanted to *do* something. Before I get too old.'

'Well, it's *done* alright. Otto, I take it you're trying to find this fellow who hired you to arrange papers?'

'Not with any real hope. He's gone to ground, and I've no means of flushing him.'

'Herr Director!'

'Christ.' Fischer stood and went to the door. 'What is it, Renate?'

'Don't worry, I've locked up the shop. Someone named Freddie telephoned. I'm to say that he's sending a package that may or may not help. He wouldn't tell me with what.'

'A package? He didn't mention what was in it?'

'Not *in*. He said it would be large, and that you'd recognize it by its very red eye.'

35

'Look at that.'

Fux picked up the newspaper and read the only story that could possibly have moved *Oberrat* Genschler to send for him (though *moved* didn't quite do justice to his puce complexion and inability to light a cigarette at the third time of trying).

He read it slowly, trying to make time to think about what it meant – to him, that is. It didn't add up to much. Certainly, there wasn't anything so solid as to suggest that someone had been talking to the Press - it was more a grope in several darknesses, asking the reader to use his or her imagination to devise their own opinion. The trouble was, people always tended to come to the least sensible conclusions - which, in this case, would be to assume that the Spandau and Schloss-Strasse killings were not only linked but a direct stab at every single West Berliner.

He looked up at Genschler. 'It's nonsense.'

'Is it?'

'Of course. There isn't the slightest evidence to suggest that the latest killing is linked to the others.'

That wasn't true, obviously; but Fux wasn't going to admit that he had ignored very clear orders and chased a piece of paper he should have burned the moment he received it. There was one link, a name, of one Otto Fischer, and unless or until he had strong evidence to put the man over several bodies he wasn't going to put his own arse in the firing line.

Genschler, the puce darkening a shade, waved a hand. 'That isn't the point. The Spandau business is dead, by order of Upstairs. It should have remained that way. And now ...'

Fux might have kept his mouth closed that point, but the matter raised had been on his mind for days now.

'How far upstairs? Here? Friesenstrasse?'

The *Oberrat* shook his head.

'City Hall?'

The head began to move once more, but Genschler paused and looked hard at his subordinate. 'Don't keep thinking Berlin.'

Hell. If it wasn't Berlin, then it had to be Bonn - there was nothing in between, upstairs-wise. Why would the Federal Government want a Berlin murder investigation stopped? The city wasn't even *in* the Republic, officially.

A small, sensibly voice told him *don't ask*, and he heeded it. The newspaper report was nothing to do with him, whatever his boss suspected or feared. Unless Ernst Beltze decided to open his mouth about what they'd discussed recently, his only offence was not to have forgotten the cases that no-one wanted solved anyway. He relaxed slightly, and tapped the newspaper.

'What do we do about this?'

'Nothing.'

'They might follow it up.'

'Let them. All they have is supposition. The public will either believe the nonsense they read or they won't, and nothing we say will persuade the convinced or sway the doubters. If a question's put directly, we tell them the obvious – that on-going investigations aren't commented upon. Eventually it'll die, like even real stories do.'

Genschler was correct, of course. The public's attention was easily distracted even in unremarkable times, and right now the matter of Germany's partial rebirth was sucking the oxygen from all other news. A panicked response from Friesenstrasse was exactly what had been intended by the article's author in the hope of keeping it alive beyond midweek. The idiot was a puppy snapping at big ankles, and best ignored.

Fux had the clearest path imaginable laid out before him. Upon the very - the *very* - highest authority, an investigation with no apparent leads had been lifted from his hands and put in a dark, secret place. No discredit was laid upon him, no obligation other than to acquiesce to a collective amnesia. A man with a sharp sense of self-preservation would glance upwards and thank his guiding angel for having come through a heavy cross-fire unscathed.

So it was intensely frustrating that he didn't feel relieved (in every sense), or exonerated, or particularly fortunate. Against all reason the five – or seven - corpses spoke to him still, making their case that they had not ceased to represent an injustice merely for having been scratched out of the records. They were no longer his responsibility – hell, they had never been, other than by reason of an administrative roll of the die – yet he felt a runaway father's weight of guilt for having abandoned them. Why?

Parsifal. Ernst Beltze had mocked him, but there was a case to answer. What grail was he seeking, to wilfully ignore the easy, correct option and continue upon a course that had little chance of success and could bring him no advantage? If the murderer or murderers were protected, what could he do that would mean anything other than disgrace and penury – for his wife as well as himself? His arrogance appalled him, yet he couldn't stamp it into submission.

'Are you alright, Melchior? You look like you ate a green mussel.'

Genschler actually seemed concerned, and it struck Fux that he hadn't been invited to the *Oberrat*'s office under any hint of suspicion – his boss had simply wanted to ease the pressure a little by sharing his outrage. He shook his head, and went with the game.

'It's an outrageous slur on the Force.'

Genschler sighed. 'It is, and the bastards deserve a kicking; but that wouldn't help anything other than our moods.' He picked up the newspaper, folded it and dropped it into his waste bin. 'For whatever reason we can't know, this is all about nothing.'

'Right.' Fux waited until the hand rose to dismiss him and then returned to his new desk in the Bull's Pen. He kept the word *nothing* in mind, repeating it to himself as he made a show of re-reading informers' reports on the breakaway Tempelhof gang. Around him, his colleagues got on with the serious business of investigating other crimes that were *something* still, working for a safer city, a decent wage and comfortable pension. He could have all of that too, at no cost to anything other than a tender conscience. All that was required was that he remove the piece of paper from his drawer, tear it into tiny pieces and get on with what everyone expected of him. That wasn't so much a challenge as an imperative, and for a few moments he felt himself surrendering to common sense.

Afterwards, he decided that it was Ernst Beltze's fault. The Examiner had called and left a message while he'd been in Genschler's office, and this was brought to him by a *watchmeister* as he struggled with his inner fool. It was innocent enough – an invitation to an Examiners' Society Dinner in Friedrichshain in five days' time – but it brought him back to the pained rationale (if that's what it was) he had rehearsed previously with his friend. This wasn't about why some corpses should or shouldn't be forgotten, but what he wanted to see when he looked in a mirror. He wasn't proud of much in his life – his marriage was probably its high-point, his war-record (though unstained by any personal crime) its lowest. Around and in between those extremities lay nothing much of note. He had never excelled at anything, nor worked at a job harder than it took to stay in post, and he had been content enough with that. It had taken the prospect of another sort of extremity to make him ask the question – what *would* move him to do more than just enough, if not this?

He had a few numbers, an acronym and a name, and they might mean everything or nothing. Weighing against them was every sensible option, every correct course, and until he knew exactly what he had in his desk drawer, he was going to ignore them. Even if he could do nothing with the knowledge, the dead deserved at least that much of a vigil.

36

Fischer couldn't recall ever having visited Zoo Station, though its homely, barn-like roof was (too) visible from much of the rest of central West Berlin. It had recently been repaired and re-clad, and though not a fan of bare concrete facades his professional interest was stirred briefly by the Bauhaus-style clock clinging to a bald stretch surrounding the main entrance. The effect was austere but modestly monumental – something that Speer might have conceived had he been able to break free from his neo-classical obsessions. Of course, it was in entirely the wrong position – out here, it could only tell the arriving travellers how late they were for their trains, whereas indoors it would have told them how late their trains were for them.

Instead of entering the station he crossed the tram lines to his left, found the cafe amid a row of businesses built under the elevated tracks, and entered. At eleven-thirty it was already busy with lunching citizens, though only one of them was either sufficiently hungover or fashion-conscious to be wearing sunglasses indoors. Fischer went straight to his table and sat.

The gentleman removed the glasses to reveal the damage. It seemed more the fault of a thumb than a knuckle, the area around the eye being unbruised. The rest of the face was unmarked and cleanly-shaven, and the clothes were a well-matched, expensive looking ensemble that Fischer might have envied, had he more – that is, any – interest in his own appearance.

They shook hands. The other man waved at a passing waitress and looked expectantly at his guest.

'Nothing, thank you, Herr …?'

'No names, if you don't mind. I'm not in Berlin, nor probably ever will be.'

'And I haven't seen you. You have information for me?'

'I have an apology. From Jens Lamsdorf.'

'Ah. He put me on that piece of paper?'

'Yes.'

'Because he thinks that I betrayed his friend to the killers?'

'He thought it, briefly. He was very moved by the man's death, and probably wasn't himself.'

'He didn't think it more likely that he'd been followed to my shop?'

'Obviously he should have, but he rather overrated his ability *not* to be followed. You were unknown to him other than by recommendation, and from a man he hadn't seen for years. Also, given his … situation, a degree of paranoia is unavoidable.'

'Still, he might have spoken to me about it before pushing in the knife.'

'He was – he *is* – looking over at least one more shoulder than he owns. I doubt he can take the risk of being seen.'

'Where is he?'

'I don't know, truly. The telephone conversation we had felt like a farewell.'

'Can he run for long?'

The other man laughed. 'He's got money enough to run forever – or settle where God Himself can't find follow. The work was only ever a hobby for him.'

'The work? What is it he does, or did? We found his company's accounts, but ...'

'Call it the supply chain. It's how I know him.'

'You're from *Amt Blank*?'

Astonished, the other man paused, his coffee cup half-raised. 'Why do you say that?'

'A guess. Lamsdorf's company has a provisional contract to supply uniforms. Who else would want them?'

'Oh, yes. Well, I'm involved with the Federal Ministry of Defence.'

'Which was *Amt Blank*, until last week.'

'As you say.'

The man would be covered by official restrictions on what he could say, but that didn't necessarily mean he couldn't be of use. It depended upon how close he was, or had been, to Lamsdorf. Fischer side-stepped a little, trying to find the gap.

'I have to call you something. Will Hans do?'

'Of course.'

'Did Lamsdorf say what you could tell me?'

'No. He said that we should speak, and that I should give you his apology. He didn't go into details.'

'Alright. Let me talk for a while, and you can tell me if I'm close or not, or if you can't say. Is that reasonable?'

'It is.'

'The five numbers on the piece of paper that he sent to the police – they refer to the men killed in Spandau?'

'I believe so.'

'As far as you're aware, none of these men were under investigation by the Federal Government?'

'Not as far as I'm aware. Obviously, that isn't a no.'

'I assume that Lamsdorf's friend – the dead man – was ...'

'His name was Ruben.'

'I assume that he had information on these men that made him dangerous to someone?'

'Yes. He'd been gathering it for a number of years.'

'May I ask why?

'I'm not sure. But he was Jewish, so it isn't hard to conclude that he had some strong motivation.'

'And you don't know his sources?'

'I know a very little about one source. Jens met Ruben at about the turn of the decade, just after *Dienststelle Schwerin* - that was the precursor of *Amt Blank* ...'

'Yes, I know. Its purpose was to prepare the ground to re-establish domestic military resources, if and when the Allies permitted it.'

'That's right. I met them both at that time, and I know that Ruben was busy with something other than work. He disappeared on several occasions, sometimes for days at a time. When I asked about it, Jens told me that he was *on his little crusade*, and that he'd found help from someone now living in Rome. A survivor, he called him'

'A survivor?'

'It wasn't a secret what Ruben was – how could it be, with a name like that? I took Jens to mean a camp survivor, a fellow Jew. He more or less confirmed it when he joked about the man. He said he'd be grateful that Ruben had visited, because none of the rest of his people would even speak to him.'

'An outcast?'

Hans shrugged. 'Shunned, I think they call it. Perhaps he was a collaborator, I don't know. Anyway, this fellow gave Ruben some names and a particular context that was important, though he never told me what it was.'

'Does Lamsdorf know the details?'

'I couldn't say. I doubt it, otherwise he probably would have given more specific information on that paper he sent to the police. I don't believe Ruben would have wanted to put him in that much danger.'

'How close were they?'

The other man glanced around and then regarded Fischer carefully, as if weighing things.

'They were lovers, for a while.'

'Oh. Freddie Holleman didn't tell me ...'

'I doubt that he knew. The old Regime wasn't very forgiving of that sort of sentimental feeling.'

'He told *you*, though?'

'No, but it was fairly obvious, seeing them together. Men don't tend to hold each others' gaze unless it means something'

'I suppose not. Do you know anything else that might hint at what Ruben was looking for? Something that might link these corpses?'

'Something, yes.'

That was it. Hans picked up his coffee, sipped it, kept his eyes steady on the half-ruined face and said nothing more. If this was merely restricted information the man would say so – which meant that he knew something he wasn't supposed to know. As tempting as it was to fill the silence between them, Fischer kept his lips together. To ask the man if he might tell what he knew was almost to invite a refusal, while an appeal to his better nature would just raise a laugh. Reeling in the information was a matter of nerve, and holding it.

Eventually, the room got another comprehensive examination before Hans spoke.

'What's been the biggest domestic news of the past year?'

Fischer needed to give that one very little thought. 'Otto John.'

'It was sensational, wasn't it? The head of an Intelligence Service, walking across the line and declare for communism like that?'

'There was nothing else in the papers for weeks.'

'Everyone had a theory about it – that he'd been a deep-cover counter-agent for years, that he'd been caught in a sex-trap, alcoholism, drug-addiction, money … what did you think of it?'

Fischer pulled a face. 'Not much. We've had floods of defectors from the East for years; there had to be some going the other way. Perhaps his job prospects were better over there.'

The other man pointed a finger at the table. 'They couldn't have been worse *here*.'

'Why not?'

'Jens told me that you once worked for the Gehlen Org?'

'Briefly, and a long time ago. We didn't part on the best terms.'

'Gehlen hates John – *hates* him. He still thinks of the July plotters as traitors, and John compounded his crime by fleeing to England and helping the British to identify war criminals after the Surrender. It was John, you'll recall, who was instrumental in getting Manstein imprisoned, and Gehlen worshipped the General. Well, from the moment word went around that John was to be head of the new *BfV*, Gehlen worked to prevent it. He failed, of course, and John immediately began to move into Gehlen's counter-intelligence kingdom, appointing former Abwehr men to set up new Intelligence stations around the Federal Republic – you can imagine how a good ex-Nazi like Gehlen regarded *them*. Still, both Gehlen and John realised that they needed to maintain an appearance of being able to work with each other, and for a while a sort of truce held.'

Hans turned and waved to a waitress. When she had refilled his cup and retreated, he continued.

'So, we had the Gehlen Org and John's *BfV*, dancing around each other like boxers. Then things became more complicated, with the setting up of *Dienststelle Schwerin*. Gehlen had wanted the job of creating such a department, and he was the Americans' favourite for the task; but the British and French have never trusted him, and they vetoed it. Once Schwerin was in the post he was given the task, among others, of setting up a purely Military Intelligence agency. This was a considerable shock to Gehlen, whose ambition was and is to rule all matters of Intelligence in the Republic. Schwerin himself had no prior experience in the field, so he gave the job to Joachim Oster, son of poor General Oster who fell in the bloodletting after July 1944. Oster, in turn, recruited Friedrich Wilhelm Heinz. Have you heard of him?'

'Vaguely. I can't recall the context.'

'Together, Oster and Heinz got to work. Soon afterwards, *Dienststelle Schwerin* became *Amt Blank*, whose new Intelligence arm was named the *Friedrich-Wilhelm-Heinz Amt*, and Gehlen began to feel himself surrounded by the ghosts of Abwehr. He was soon on Heinz's tail, trying to discredit him, and this turned out to be an easy task. Heinz was a bluffer, who bribed Germans working for the CIA to pass information to him also, which he presented as his own Intelligence. In fact, he had no real network of his own. Gehlen gathered evidence of this and then – what?'

Fischer shrugged.

'He was too clever to go after Heinz publicly. Everyone knew how ambitious he was, and a denunciation might have been seen merely as one player assassinating a rival. So, he gave it all to Otto John, and furthermore insinuated that Heinz was plotting to become head of *BfV* in his place, bringing both Domestic and Military Intelligence into his own hands.'

'Christ. And I thought the Reich had been a rats' nest of Intelligencers.'

Hans laughed. 'It must be something very German, to duplicate endlessly the means of accomplishing a single task. Anyway, John moved quickly and got Heinz booted in September 1953; Oster resigned in protest and suddenly *Amt Blank*'s Military Intelligence Agency was a fading wraith. Heinz's last word was to warn John that this had all been a plot, and that Gehlen would be after him next. John didn't listen of course, but something must have got under his collar sufficiently to make him defect last year. At a stroke, Gehlen was rid of the last obstacle.'

'To what?'

'To his Org becoming the only candidate for the vacancy of our newly-sovereign Republic's principal – perhaps only - Intelligence Agency.'

'The British and French will allow that?'

'They have little choice, with John gone and *BfV* discredited. Theodor Blank's been fighting a rear-guard action against it, but Adenauer has always preferred Gehlen to any alternative, despite the very obvious fact that the Org is infested with ex-SD and other unpleasantries. It will happen, believe me.'

'So, what has this to do with Lamsdorf's friend?'

'Ruben had known Joachim Oster from childhood, and obtained a position in Heinz's group through him. It was Ruben who liaised with many of the CIA's German people and brought them in, and it was he who warned Heinz that if he didn't start paying them they'd turn on him.'

'He didn't *pay* his agents?'

'A little, to begin with; but he was a fool, and thought that what the CIA was giving them was adequate. No doubt it was one or more of them who went to Gehlen and told him that all of Heinz's information was in CIA hands already. So, Heinz fell, Oster resigned and Ruben ...'

'Ruben what?'

'Ruben found that he had become vulnerable. While he was in Heinz's *Amt* he took all opportunities to remind everyone's bosses that Gehlen had hired some pretty bad people, and that it wouldn't look well if they became part of the new German Intelligence Service. Once Heinz had been kicked out he was exposed, and the bad people came looking for him.'

'Gehlen authorized that?'

'I don't think so. He's a bastard, but a clever one - he wouldn't risk hurting his dream of the past decade to squash a fly. For the ones who were after Ruben, it was more personal. *How* it was more personal, I can't say, though Ruben mentioned something to me a few years ago that must have been significant.'

'What was it?'

'He said it was ironic that it wasn't the Germans he needed to watch out for – not *real* ones, at least.'

Fischer sat back. He'd just been told that his theory about the five numbers on the fatal piece of paper was correct. On a shallow, vain level he was pleased with his cleverness; for the sake of his arse, less so. His name really didn't need to be on the same piece of paper as cholera.

He looked up. 'You said you might know how the Spandau corpses were linked.'

'Towards the end of last year, Ruben noticed that he was being followed, and fairly constantly. It seemed to him that things were coming to a head, and that he needed to do something. He was still in touch with Heinz, and persuaded him that he could do several disservices simultaneously to those who had brought him down. In December, Heinz went to KGB Headquarters at Karlshorst, a flying visit. I can't say exactly what he gave them, but the following month bodies began to appear in Spandau. I assume that at least some of the victims were of the same breed as Ruben's shadows.'

'Then the dead men were employed in some capacity by Gehlen?'

Hans nodded. 'I assume this also. And, given that Otto John had defected a year earlier, blame for these betrayals could very well be put at his door, rather than Heinz's. Three birds, one stone.'

'But someone worked out that it had been Ruben's work.'

'Obviously, both he and his killers had something – a *context* - that we don't.'

No wonder the man had needed new papers. Whoever his enemies were, they had enough pull politically to disappear Lamsdorf for three days and flush out his lover, and both the resources and nerve to carry out a daylight assassination. Fischer now had some idea of who and what they might be, but not nearly enough to make a start on saving himself from the taint of association.

It was something at least, and he was grateful for it. Hans - whoever he was – had done him a considerable service. Fischer cleared his throat. 'Let me pay for your rail ticket. And coffee, of course.'

The other man extended his hand graciously. 'The coffee, perhaps. My fare goes on expenses.'

'May I ask why you came today? You were under no obligation.'

Hans smiled, but only with his mouth. 'Because I was Abwehr also, once. Many of my comrades were murdered by filth now living the lives of forgiven men. I find that very painful.'

'But inevitable.'

'Of course. I have no illusions – nor the sort of persistence that made Ruben so dangerous to them. That doesn't mean I won't cause damage when offered the opportunity. What will you do with this?'

'At the moment, I don't know. None of it *was* my business, but Lamsdorf attached me to it.'

'You have a problem.'

'I do. I don't know how bad it is or might get, but waiting and hoping isn't sensible. I have one last question?'

'Ask it.'

'How many men have died in Spandau?'

Hans looked blankly at Fischer. 'Five, you said. That's right, isn't it?'

'I did, yes.' Fischer stood.' Well, thank you for coming to speak with me. How are things in our new Defence Ministry?'

Hans shook his hand. 'As busy as everywhere else in Government. It's been an interesting week. A few days ago we came into existence; today, we join NATO. Perhaps next week we'll declare war on someone.'

Fischer laughed. 'Try to apply the brakes on that one, if you have any say.'

37

Afterwards, Fischer wandered for almost an hour through the Zoological Garden, trying to pin his options. That he had to do *something* was all too obvious - a man with a gun to his head didn't reassure himself with *well, nothing's gone wrong so far.* The readiest solution would be to return to Friesenstrasse, ask to see Fux and make a full, open and frank confession of his crime. It would mean another visit to prison, of course, but he doubted that it would be either as long or as onerous as his previous incarceration. On the other hand, a man's remaining mortal years became more precious to him as their ranks thinned, and the prospect of starting from yet another scratch thereafter didn't appeal.

Or, he might take Kleiber's half-facetious advice and test the quality of life in Buenos Aires or somewhere equally welcoming. German law enforcement didn't follow *anyone* to Latin America, and he doubted the Israelis would care to notice a man who'd tried to assist a Jew, however unsuccessfully. Even with Lamsdorf's generous deposit he couldn't afford to live the idle life there, but it was enough to buy time to look around and finance some future venture. The Argentinians liked to dance, after all - gramophones had to be as ubiquitous there as here, and given the number of homesick German expatriates among them he would never need to search for customers for the old, sentimental songs.

He smiled at a chimpanzee that was regarding him through bars, chin on fist, with a serious, dignified gaze. Otto Fischer Abroad didn't look right from any angle. No doubt he would enjoy the exotic novelty for a year and perhaps two; but then the same pathetic longing would seize him as it had his putative *schicksalmusik* clientele, and the weight of liquid painkiller he'd need to ease it would collapse the strongest liver. Exile was exile, however dressed.

What remained was to somehow clean the slate, and that was where the problems waited, stacked to save space. He couldn't go to the people who could definitively clear his name, because they wouldn't care to; he couldn't raise the dead to testify on his behalf; he couldn't expect Lamsdorf's remorse to wax strongly enough for the man to emerge from hiding (if he was in this hemisphere still) and risk going the way of his friend Ruben; and he absolutely couldn't hope for Norbert Roth to admit his skills as a papers man. If he was ever to scrape his name from that piece of paper, he would need to go *at* the thing, not wait for it to drop.

He wished now sincerely that his days of going at things had passed. He'd become sanguine, fat in mind (if not nearly in body), regretting the blandness of a life no longer disturbed by splinters. He shouldn't have let the memory of their pain fade so easily. Perhaps he'd succumbed to the national illusion that Germans were being carried on a favourable, rising tide, the weight of all debts discharged by time and strategic amnesia, pretending a cynicism for the *wirschaftswunder* while surrendering to its promise. Like the fellow on the other side of the bars, he'd allowed himself to be persuaded that the jungle had gone away.

At the Zoo cafe he allowed himself the coffee he'd refused earlier and sat with it until it cooled, looking for inspiration among the hairs on the back of the hand that could grow them still. When that failed he ordered another coffee and this time drank it. Fortunately, it was bad enough to deter him from another, and by the time the Zoo Tower clock chimed two he was almost out of the garden and on to Budapesterstrasse, trying to find a bus service that would get him at least part of the way home.

He was standing at the curb, looking eastwards, waiting for a break in the oncoming traffic, when a single option occurred to him. He told himself that he was an idiot and tried to push it from mind, but the idea burrowed down and forced him to consider precisely why it was stupid, and dangerous, and the best proof imaginable of how his mind had atrophied under a regime of too much comfortable living. The answers were obvious, yet the thing persisted, the one palpable argument in its favour being that he had nothing else – nothing at all.

He recalled little of his bus journey to Schöneberg, and more of the transfer to a Lichterfelde service only because he had to search for the correct halt. As he moved among the throng of people on Sachsendamm he felt an irrational grievance, that ordinary lives and schedules could proceed obliviously while his was burdened with a problem for which the only solution appeared to be a form of self-immolation. On the second bus, he offered his best ex-smoker's glare to a man who seemed determined to share his cigarette with his neighbours, moved his legs only reluctantly when passengers tried to ease their way past him and took every disturbance to his tormented reverie as a personal affront. He knew he was being boorish, and felt no need to be otherwise.

The skies over Tiergarten had been grey, but the sun shone down strongly upon Lichterfelde, a further goad to his mood. When he entered his shop, Renate was showing an old lady a battered but working JAZ from the cheap shelf. He ignored all three and went into the back room, removed his jacket and tried to concentrate on his list of pressing repairs, a strategy immediately sabotaged by the newspaper that Renate had placed carefully on his workbench. It was that day's edition of the *Berliner Morgenpost*, opened at page six, and she had ringed a two-column story in blue ink.

New Speculation on Spandau Murders. It was a shameless synthesis of Kleiber's piece (no doubt to save the syndication fees), equally light on facts - at least the headline was honest - and no less damaging to a certain, entirely innocent party. The *Morgenpost*'s daily circulation was at least a hundred and forty thousand copies, so pressure on the police to get off their arses had increased enormously since the kiosks opened that morning. The stress headache that Fischer had been cultivating for the past two hours absorbed the shock gratefully.

He was searching for aspirin when his assistant came into the workshop. 'She bought the clock, Herr Director.'

'Oh, good. Renate have you seen my ...'

'You had a call, at 1.17 pm, from *Kriminalkommissar* Fux. He said can you come to Friesenstrasse this afternoon - perhaps at five o'clock? If not, call him today to arrange another time. He *did* say please, twice.'

Fischer's invisible headband tightened horribly. He had been telling himself that *now* was not the time to decide things - that his thoughts should be more composed, his sense of perspective less skewed, than they presently were. Moving backward from a cliff's edge was never the wrong decision, yet a hand had just shoved, hard, from behind. He closed his eyes, and by the time he had counted fifty pulses in his throbbing head the mundane details that would put into motion his single, awful option had fallen into line.

He went to the safe and removed the fatal, well-padded envelope. From it, he extracted a hundred Deutsche Marks and put them into his pocket. A further thousand he handed to Renate. Then, he placed the envelope in another, larger one and sealed it, and this also he gave to his assistant.

'The thousand is for you.'

Dazed, she looked down at more money than she had ever owned. 'Why? I mean, what for, Herr Director?'

'Back-wages, and your Christmas Bonus.'

'But it's May.'

'I'm going away for a few days. Please keep the shop open until the weekend and make any sales that you can, but take in no repair work for the moment. If I'm not back by Monday, you can decided whether or not to reopen. Keep the envelope until then, but after that send it to Herr Kuhn, in Bremen. His address is in my book.'

Renate's emotions were better hidden than a magpie's thefts usually, but no her face was a model of anxiety. 'Where will you be?'

'It's better if I don't say. If Jonas or Herr Hoeschler ask, just tell them what I've told you.'

'Of course; it's all that I know. And if Herr Fux calls again?'

'Tell him the same, and that I'll make an appointment with him the moment I return.'

'Will you?'

Fischer tried to look mildly hurt, though it probably came over as mildly guilty. 'I wouldn't have said so, otherwise.'

He went upstairs to his apartment and found a small satchel, into which he put the money, a toothbrush and his battered Decca/HMV repair manual. Then he changed into his least best clothes (though hardly distinguishable from those he discarded) and examined the result in the hall mirror. His mutilations did the ensemble no favours, making him look less like a small businessman than a minor criminal or beggar, one whose last meal was a fading memory. Satisfied, he returned to the shop, ignored Renate's silent, open-mouthed reproof and took one of his business cards from the small pile on the counter which never seemed to get smaller. Fortunately, a customer entered at that moment and spared him the ordeal of another interrogation. He waved a goodbye and was out of the door before it could close.

He knew the route by bus, having practiced it in his head many times when darker moods took him. The journey required two changes, and perversely he made them both without inconvenience or delay. Within fifty minutes he was stood outside tall gates; there, his card was examined and returned and he was waved inside before he could re-consider what an hour earlier had seemed to be his inevitable course. After that, it hardly seemed worth the effort.

At the reception he handed over his card once more and told them that the matter was quite important. This raised an eyebrow but he was asked, almost politely, to wait. The *wait* stole almost a further hour, which he bore stoically and almost thoughtlessly. The man who came to break his boredom wore a uniform whose rank he couldn't quite make out, but the one he took him to was a captain. This one was terse, demanding his business without any attempt at pleasantry. Fischer gave him the name and rank, and said that it was important.

'There's no-one here by that name.'

'I assume not. Somewhere else, perhaps?'

'What business is this?'

'His.'

'That won't do.'

'Then give him this message: Otto Fischer, nineteen forty-seven.'

The captain looked at him as if he were an idiot, or a suicide. 'Really? You come *here* with that?'

Fischer held up his satchel, aware that he almost certainly looked ridiculous. 'And a toothbrush. I'm sure he'll be grateful if you pass on the message. If he isn't … well, I'll be *here*, won't I?'

38

For almost three days, Fischer had the cell to himself. Remarkably, it had a view, though to enjoy it required that he drag the bed beneath the small window and almost suspend himself by his nose from the ledge, and everything he could see began at eye-level and rose from there. They provided a blanket and a thin pillow, good bread and acorn coffee at dawn and thick soup of variable quality - but consistent cabbage - in the evenings. Otherwise, he was left alone to meditate, fill his bucket (which was replaced when the bread and coffee came) and consider several other options that had occurred only when the cell-door closed behind him. None of them appealed as much as Buenos Aires, or less than this one.

On the third day he was joined by a young man whose lethal breath and semi-consciousness (he was thrown into the cell) testified to a memorable previous evening, and to the probability either that the building had few cells or that they were extremely busy at present. The following hours were punctuated by sudden, violent bouts of heaving and a heady scent that invited Fischer to reciprocate, but he managed barely to keep his own stomach in check. In the afternoon the boy – still insensible - was dragged out and the floor sluiced with bleached water. When it had dried the smell returned, and that evening's cabbage soup went back to the restaurant kitchen untouched.

The following morning, breakfast came with a bowl of hot water and a razor. He washed and shaved under the close glare of his guard and was then presented with a clean, standard army-issue shirt. He had hardly finished buttoning it when he was taken to an office on the second floor and told to sit at a desk, opposite a colonel.

Disappointed, Fischer hardly heard the first question.

'Have you been treated well?'

'Yes, sir.'

A clipboard was passed across the desk with a pen. Naturally, Fischer couldn't read what was on the attached paper, but he assumed it to be a statement to the same effect. He signed it.

'Have you any complaints?'

He thought about that. 'My shit's changed colour.'

The colonel stood. 'A holiday would do the same, probably. Please wait.'

He sat, squinting, trying to find a spine in the bookcase whose title he could understand, for about ten minutes. When the door opened again he resisted the temptation to turn, but the hairs on his neck's good side rose as if magnetised and remained there even as the gentleman took a seat.

In two years he had aged perhaps five, and the glove on one hand needed little parsing. It struck Fischer suddenly that, in different ways, they'd both been very lucky.

'Hello, Major.'

'Hello, Major.'

Zarubin smiled enough to reveal a full set of teeth still. 'Actually, I've ascended beyond rank.'

'Congratulations. Not a Berlin posting, I assume?'

'Moscow. The Centre isn't fond of letting its senior KGB staff wander too far, for obvious reasons. You mentioned nineteen forty-seven.'

'Yes.'

'I assume you weren't referring to the siege of Berlin?'

'Only a collateral part of it.'

'General Myasnik?'

'Yes.'

'He's very dead, thankfully.'

'I know. But I understand that you recently captured one of his German *kapos* – a man named Thomas Braun.'

'I understand that too, though I wasn't involved.'

'Apparently, Braun squeaked to save his neck.'

'Well, it didn't work.'

'Specifically, he named Mila Henze, one of Myasnik's group of thieves at Tempelhof. And then KGB passed this on to CIA so that they could do something about her.'

Zarubin rubbed his unshaven chin. His blond hair was greyed now at the temples, and his eyes had lost or misplaced their irreverent twinkle. Fischer hadn't hoped for warmth and fond reminiscences, but the slight elbow-room in his grand strategy felt slighter under that distant gaze. He cleared his throat.

'The point is, Frau Henze is married now. To Rolf Hoeschler.'

The eyes didn't give away anything, but the gloved hand began to move, left to right and back again as if searching for something in the dark.

'I didn't know that. Either thing, I mean.'

'You didn't authorize the release of information?'

'I would hardly drag that business from its grave, not having kicked so much soil in over it.'

'I didn't think so. I don't know what CIA's official attitude is to the revelation, but someone at Föhrenweg 19 picked it up and decided to make it private business. He's demanding money from the Hoeschlers, on pain of letting KGB know where she is otherwise.'

Zarubin sat back and stared up at the ceiling. 'Actually, it's not KGB policy to pass on word of any matter to CIA, even if it were to be of benefit to us. Such an initiative would need to be agreed by Moscow beforehand. And it probably wouldn't be.'

'Mila Henze isn't still of interest to you?'

'To my knowledge, no. It's hardly likely, given that she was wholly involved in stealing from the Americans. We don't tend to frown upon that.'

'So, it seems that one of your men in Berlin is making individual arrangements for his retirement, and he has a partner at Föhrenweg.'

'That would be unfortunate.'

'If it's helpful, I have details of the Dortmund bank account into which the extortion monies are paid?'

That brought a laugh, and for the first time Fischer caught a glimpse of the old Zarubin. 'That would be *very* helpful. But I assume you didn't come all the way across Berlin to be of service to KGB?'

'Not *just* to be of service, no. I seem to be a suspect in at least one murder, and possibly more.'

'Really? What company you must be keeping, Fischer.'

'I doubt you can help me with the *one,* but the others ...'

'How?'

'Five dead men were found, in Spandau. I believe you know something about it.'

'I read the newspapers – even western ones. It's part of my job.'

'The men who died, I think they were *volksdeutsche* - specifically, Sudetenlanders.'

'What makes you think that?

'They were – they appear to have been - former members of the *Sudentendeutsche Partei*, the SDP. I'd like to know what else they were.'

'And you think I can help you, because …?'

'Because a Czech execution squad wouldn't be operating in Berlin without KGB permission and assistance.'

39

Zarubin examined his glove for a few moments. It occurred to Fischer for the first time that not only was the man not in uniform but had honoured his old quasi-friend by wearing his American suit, the only palpable legacy of his swiftly-regretted defection. The years had been kinder to the garment than to its owner, probably because it had spent them largely in the dark and company of mothballs. A wise man wouldn't have offered gratuitous reminders to those who had spared his life of why they had needed to toss that coin.

The mouth twitched slightly, as though an inner conversation had commenced. Fischer knew that look - it masked the human equivalent of a wristwatch movement, going different ways but all to a single purpose – in this case, of deciding what would and wouldn't be said. To Zarubin, enlightenment was best doled in clinically-controlled quantities, and not before he had made the correct diagnosis.

'Give me your reasoning.'

Naturally, Fischer would be expected to disclose everything immediately, this being by no means an exchange of equals. He had no objection to that; it was the only way of making his dangerous gamble worthwhile. In any case, why wouldn't he? He was innocent, after all (it worried him that he was beginning to need to remind himself of that fact).

'I've seen a piece of paper sent anonymously to the Police Praesidium at Friesenstrasse with five numbers and the acronym SDP on it. Most people will have forgotten the latter, probably. The Party was wound down after we occupied the Sudetenland in '38 and quite a bit happened after that to take attention elsewhere. I recognized it myself, though I might have dismissed it as one of many possibilities; but the numbers started something in my head. I considered that they might have been party membership numbers, but they weren't.'

'Why not?'

'The lowest of them was in the hundreds; the highest, three thousand and some change. As I recall, the Party had upwards of a million members at its height, so the five men would have had to have been very senior people, and almost certainly older men. I understand that the corpses were of men aged between forty and fifty.'

'So, not membership numbers. What, then?'

'I recalled that there was a bad political odour a few years ago, when Bonn rebuffed an approach from the Czechs. They'd asked that Germans found guilty *in absentia* of committing war crimes on their soil be located and surrendered. Both parties were at fault – us, for trying to draw a line beneath something that doesn't lend itself to lines; them, for being cheeky.'

'Cheeky?'

'Some journalist did a little digging. It came out that the actual number of Germans tried and sentenced by the Czech courts was less than six hundreds, but they had tried to cast a much wider net, hoping to bring back others merely under suspicion of crimes – and, in many cases, crimes that were only laterally to do with the war, given that the Sudetenland German and Czech populations were at each other's throats long before we annexed the territory. Anyway, as you probably know, nothing came of it, but I decided that the numbers on the paper might refer to Czech court or police case files.'

'*Might* isn't *did*.'

'No. But then I was offered an anecdote that placed the murder of which I might be accused with the others. The victim had been followed previously by the man or men who, eventually, killed him. He knew of the risk, but mentioned that he wasn't in danger from *real* Germans. Why would he say that? If they weren't *any* sort of Germans he'd have called them foreigners. So, my mind turned to the SDP once more.'

'A reasonable thesis; but might the men not be … Silesian Germans, for example, chased by Poles for similar crimes?'

Fischer shrugged. 'It's a possibility, but unlikely. We all know that German war crimes committed in the Government-General and annexed Polish lands were chased far more aggressively than those elsewhere, given that this was the geographical nexus of the Final

Solution. Far more men were accused, tried and executed – or escaped to places where German is a foreign language. Again, the numbers on the piece of paper suggest a smaller-scale business. In any case, wouldn't a daring Polish operation that managed to expunge five war criminals be lauded as a triumph? I suspect the Czechs can't do that without embarrassment, given that they've already made a very public face of pursuing the legal course.'

Zarubin nodded slowly, as if he were judging the logic of what he was hearing rather than admitting to anything. 'Assume the Czechs then. Why would you think that KGB was involved also?'

'Because the only Czechs who would or could do this are StB, and they're KGB's favourite child. They wouldn't dream of shitting on your front doorstep, which is what Berlin is. There's also the matter of *how* it was done, which makes KGB's non-involvement unthinkable. Five men were brought, alive, to Spandau, and executed there. They came from somewhere else, and that was either another location in West Berlin – which is unlikely – or ...'

'Why unlikely?'

'Why bring men across enemy territory, to kill them in the same? Why not kill them where they were?'

'They might have been residents of Spandau.'

'They weren't, but I'll come to that. The other possibility – to me, the strong *probability* – is that they were brought from territory controlled by the Soviets or their allies, in which case they had to cross a border. StB might have managed it once on their own, but not five times. You – KGB – waved them through the Staaken boundary into Spandau. You may even have provided the transportation.'

'That would make us very obliging, even to our good friends.'

'There was something in it for you, I think.'

'What?'

'You've heard that the Federal Republic has assumed full sovereignty over its affairs?'

'Nothing escapes KGB's untiring vigilance. I offer my congratulations.'

'Thank you. It's a time of wonderful opportunities, apparently. And a few problems also.'

'Well, you take the good with the bad.'

'As long as we were other nations' pets we could indulge ourselves, everyone fighting to carve a little place under a kind patron. We being Germans, that place was usually an Intelligence Agency. Every Occupier helped set up some sort of service, and various departments in our own Government-in-waiting did the same, all of them working hard to advance their own cause and cack the competition's. Unfortunately for the rest, Gehlen got there first, and with the greatest resources. He's been busy recently, putting himself in Adenauer's best books at the expense of the rest.'

'And?'

'The five dead men were Gehlen agents, weren't they?'

Zarubin said nothing, as expected. Fischer continued.

'Your people made a big thing of Otto John's defection last year – and it *was* big; but I doubt that your feelings about it were unmixed. It meant that his BfV was effectively neutralized, and to the Org's advantage. Gehlen's going to be the Federal Republic's unchallenged Spy Chief, isn't he?'

'I can't see any realistic competition.'

'No, and it's competition that offers the most opportunities to find the gaps and insinuate sympathetic friends. So you probably lost more than you gained with John's defection. But then, along come your Czech colleagues with their polite request to hunt down and kill a few of Gehlen's people, and you see this as a way of embarrassing him, particularly when their pasts come out ...'

Fischer paused as the house of logic he'd been trying to build came crashing down around his ears. It had been there for as long as his problem, as obvious as two noses on the same face, and he hadn't seen it. He looked up and saw Zarubin's old half-mocking smile, goading him to finally understand what this was about.

Why Spandau? Because it was in the British Zone, and the British didn't like Gehlen. Rightly, they considered him a Nazi sympathizer, offering gainful employment and a safe harbour to men who hadn't run but should have; hadn't been hanged but probably deserved it. What better place than Spandau to drop off the physical proof of his association with past crimes and their perpetrators? The British would ensure that anything thrown up by the police investigation would be dragged out into the light, and both Gehlen and his American friends in the CIA would be discredited.

Only they weren't, and wouldn't be. When, in the previous November, Gehlen's other victim, Friedrich Wilhelm Heinz, had gone to Karlshorst with Ruben's list of names it had been too late already. Otto John's defection five months earlier had not only destroyed his credibility but that of the British also. He had been *their* man – given shelter in England during the war, used to bring Nazis to trial and then helped by them to fashion his BfV as an Abwehr-staffed foil to Gehlen's former Nazis. When he made himself a traitor he dragged down the rest.

That's why the police investigation never came close to identifying the dead men. Gehlen used his Bonn contacts to slow things, to withhold men and resources, to keep an appearance of forward movement that was rather the twitch of a corpse, knowing that the British wouldn't – couldn't – push the police to anything like a resolution. If they had tried – and, worse, succeeded - Gehlen could have pointed the finger and said *whatever these men were, your traitor caused their deaths at the hands of the real enemy.*

As upon several previous occasions, Fischer had to stifle an urge to wipe the expression from Zarubin's face with a fist. 'You must have become desperate when nothing happened. The last one was shot, probably in daylight, right at RAF Gatow's fence, and even that didn't get the British off their arses.'

The smile stayed in place. 'I wasn't at all desperate, because my involvement in the business was marginal. In fact, I expressed reservations about the wisdom of allowing it to proceed at all. I was asked my advice, my opinion, and nothing more.'

'You're no longer involved with counter-espionage?'

'I am, very much. Just not in ways you might imagine.'

'Alright.' He could ask questions all day and be further from anything useful at its end. Zarubin's assistance was always eked out like a coarse fisherman's line, and as often as not the hook was bare. Fischer had brought him useful information, but its value had deflated horribly the moment it was out. The trick was to snatch at his sense of obligation before it died quietly in a corner.

Still not sure where to go, he asked a question for no better reason than to keep the conversation going.

'May I ask what your advice was?'

'To ignore the information.'

'The names that Ruben sent to Karlshorst? Why?'

Zarubin pulled a face. 'It wasn't much. To the Czechs, perhaps - which is why we shouldn't have given it to them. They wanted to *do* something, quickly and pointedly. So I said that if it had to happen, it should be done a certain way.'

'Spandau was your idea?'

'No. I wanted it to happen far from Berlin.'

'Why wasn't it?'

'Because those of my colleagues who were happy to help StB worried that if the investigation dragged on elsewhere than here, events would overtake it.'

This at least, Fischer understood immediately. As soon as the Federal Government took charge of its own security affairs they could kill off any exposure, but Berlin remained an enclave, an occupied city where the British – had they the will to do so – could keep the thing alive.

'Your colleagues didn't see that the John affair would undermine British resolve?'

'Yes, but they underestimated the impact.'

'So, they ignored your advice, and failed anyway. You must be pleased about that, at least.'

Zarubin gave him the face again. He wasn't pleased about *any* of it, and Fischer began to wonder, hard, why that should be. Five - perhaps seven - dead ex-Nazis wasn't much, but surely it was part of

KGB's bread-and-butter workload to scrape away the remnants of National Socialism whenever the opportunity arrived on a platter?

Yet he hadn't wanted it to happen. He particularly hadn't wanted it to happen in Berlin. It was therefore a distraction – or worse, an impediment - from or to something else.

'You didn't want it because it attracted attention.'

'Exactly that.'

'Your objection wasn't that it was worthless, but that it wasn't worth – what?'

Zarubin tapped his nose, said nothing.

'Nothing happens in a vacuum. Giving the Czechs what they wanted wasn't your idea, but ...'

Fischer realised that he had allowed himself to dwell too much upon the multiplicity of German Intelligence organizations. The Soviets had only one (GRU could be discounted, because no-one knew what they did, if anything), which inclined one to assume that everyone was pulling the same way, together, in malevolent harmony.

But that was nonsense. Communists were no more immune to personal ambition than anyone else. All the Ministry of State Security had done with its countless restructurings was to bring dozens of conflicting priorities under the same roof. No doubt KGB's directorates defended their personal slopes as vigorously as castellans on adjacent hilltops.

'… it was someone's.'

'It was, yes.'

'And presumably, they thought they could get something out of it – I mean, other than a few Sudetenlander Nazis?'

'Go on.'

'The men died in Spandau, according to the police statements. They were taken there and executed. Why did they go willingly - or at least, without a struggle? Because they thought they were being exchanged. They'd been questioned first by your people, before being handed over to StB.'

'It would have been a wasted opportunity not to.'

'Yet you objected to the operation - so much that you hadn't wanted it to proceed. It might have brought attention, but to what?'

'If I didn't answer that question at the first time of asking, why would I now?'

40

Zarubin wasn't blunt, usually, and Fischer read the warning signs. He was a guest at Karlshorst, a facility from which inconvenient visitors could be misplaced with absolutely no inconvenience. Trying his host's patience wasn't the wisest strategy.

'Let me ask this, then – what did it take for you to acquiesce? What was *the certain way* you said that it had to be done?'

'I told them to make it look like a personal matter.'

'A grudge? Revenge?'

'Yes – which it was, of course. Lamsdorf's friend was using us to achieve his goal. It was perfectly understandable, but I insisted that our involvement be disguised.'

'It was, surely? All you did was hand the information to the Czechs, and they did the rest.'

'If *you* can see that they couldn't operate in Berlin without KGB assistance, I doubt that Gehlen and his people would be fooled. It was not to look like *any* sort of sanctioned operation.'

'But how could you avoid …?'

Fischer paused. There was only one way it might be achieved – to deflect with a pointed finger.

'You lit up Ruben?'

Zarubin shook his head. 'We simply refused to extend KGB protection or logistical support, beyond the unpleasantries. He understood that the thing would proceed at risk only to himself – we were frank about that.'

'That's why his friend came to me, looking to arrange new papers for him.'

'Doesn't that seem a remarkable coincidence, given my involvement?'

'Like Freddie Holleman, I don't believe in coincidences.'

'Ah, Herr Holleman. How is the old scoundrel? Settling well in Trier?'

'Not really.' Fischer frowned. 'But Jens Lamsdorf approached Freddie, who recommended me. That *makes* it a coincidence - a remarkable one.'

'Actually, it doesn't. Having demanded that the operation against Gehlen's men not be seen to be KGB business, I moved to ensure that it didn't.'

'How?'

'By hiring you.'

'What?'

'I proposed that *you* arrange papers for this Jew Ruben. I trust you, Fischer - I trust you to be *discreet*.'

'But … Freddie recommended Lamsdorf.'

'No. Lamsdorf was told to contact Herr Holleman and ask the question – who might arrange papers for his Jewish friend? Obviously, the only correct answer was Otto Fischer. I doubt you would have agreed to help KGB, if asked.'

'But it's still remarkable, that both you and Lamsdorf should know Freddie, and that I be dragged into the business.'

'It isn't, really. I was introduced to Jens Lamsdorf by Holleman years ago - by reputation. Perhaps your friend felt I was using him a little hard at the time, but when I teased him by asking whether he trusted me, he told me that he did – *about as much as he would Jens Lamsdorf at a card table*. It sounded almost like a proverb, the way he said it. I was interested of course, being in the recruitment business, and made enquiries. The trail wasn't too well-hidden – a man who advances by sharp-dealing steps on bodies, many of which don't even require bribing to tell what they know. I found him in 1949, running what he claimed to be an import-export business, in the Saarland, and persuaded him to work for us.'

'How?'

'By threatening to tell the Italian war-booty commissioners where he lived, if he didn't. He agreed, naturally, and once we determined that General Schwerin's infant defence department wasn't going to die in its cradle we ensured that Herr Lamsdorf was in a position to be of service. And he's been so ever since.'

'Is that why he agreed to this charade? Because he had no choice?'

'You're forgetting, Fischer - this whole mess arose because his friend Ruben made it happen. He came to *us*. As I say, we weren't going to let KGB be identified with it, but we – I – told Lamsdorf about you, how you had proven yourself adept at disappearing people. If we wouldn't help his friend directly, at least we could recommend the best of the rest.'

Fischer shook his head. 'I can't believe that I was an obvious choice. How many people in Germany – in Berlin – might have done a better job than me? There must be hundreds, all of them to be trusted not to squeak.'

'Probably. But when I said I trusted you, that wasn't what I meant.'

'What, then?'

'I trusted your competence to do the thing, certainly, and I trusted you not to 'squeak', as you put it. Above all, I trusted you to be at a certain place at a certain time – that is, your premises in Curtius-Strasse when Lamsdorf's friend was obliged to pick up his own papers.'

Zarubin hadn't been able to prevent the Spandau operation, but there was an obvious way to end it decisively. 'You … told the killers where to find him?'

'That would be an uncharitable interpretation. Rather, I ensured that a KGB squad tasked with snatching the assassins before they could do their job were … elsewhere, at the time.'

'Why?'

'I told you – *attention*. Those elements of KGB Berlin who were keen to take this up decided that they could use it to infiltrate Gehlen's operation further. That couldn't be permitted.'

'Who *are* you?'

'Again, it's better not to ask. Think of us as Moscow KGB.'

'So, you let Ruben die. What about Lamsdorf?'

'It seems that the gentleman has used his better judgement. We can't find him, which is a shame. With the Federal Defence Ministry up and running, he was coming into his truly useful period. We'll have to turn someone else, which shouldn't be too difficult. And there's no hurry – it isn't as if you're going to be any sort of military threat for a while, even wearing your new NATO badges.'

Fischer told himself that he shouldn't be surprised. Dealing with Zarubin had always made him feel a little like a tethered goat in tiger country. The pain was a little deeper this time only because he'd persuaded himself that he'd escaped, climbed the fence and had a clear run. It seemed that there was no point at which *enough* was considered to be so.

He rubbed his face, the good and bad halves. It was a despicable business, but he was safe, probably. From what Zarubin had told him, just about everyone in Central Europe regarded the dead men as done business, not to be troubled further. If he was ever permitted to leave this building the only remaining barb would be a fat envelope, its contents as soiling as pieces of silver. He could and should probably bear the guilt of it; he deserved at least a little anguish.

Zarubin was checking his watch. He needn't have come from Moscow, if the purpose was merely to arrest a prying, troublesome German. So why had he?

'I have a final question. No, two.'

The Russian rubbed his head wearily. 'Why not a fucking debate? I have nothing more pressing on my schedule.'

'What did these men do? I mean, what connected them, apart from their ethnicity?'

'Theresienstadt.'

'Oh.'

Theresienstadt - National Socialism's model camp, the place where happy Jews laboured lightly, ate well and enjoyed a range of improving cultural experiences under the avuncular eyes of their hosts – or at least, they did when the Red Cross was allowed in for a matinee performance. At other times, the best that might have been said for the place was that it possessed no industrial-scale extermination facilities. For those, the Jews had to be sent elsewhere, and were.

'I assume that Ruben had family there?'

'His father - made to stand to attention, apparently, for the length of a winter's day. He and several hundred others died of exposure before sunset came.'

'The five men were guards?'

'They were *something*. I didn't care to ask more.'

'I was told that Ruben was given information on them by another Jew, one who lives in Rome.'

Zarubin seemed to come awake slightly. 'Now, this is what some people might call irony, or tragedy - or comedy, possibly. The Roman Jew is named Murmelstein, and he's very special.'

'In what way?'

'He's breathing. He was a *Judenältester*. Do you know what that is?'

'A traitor to his own kind.'

'Dear me, Major, you're as unforgiving as the Israelis – their nickname for him is Murmelschwein. In fact, he's said to have saved thousands of Jewish lives, though yes, he did this by cooperating with the Nazis. He was the head of the *Judenrat* at Theresienstadt. How he escaped the last-minute evidence-removal exercise I can't say, but he's the only man to have served as an *ältester* who survived the camps, anywhere in Europe. As you can imagine, he hasn't been welcomed back into the warm embrace of his community.'

'Where's the irony in that?'

'At the Surrender he was seized by the new provisional Czech Government on suspicion of being a collaborator. They kept him for almost a year, tried and failed to build a plausible legal case and then released him. He moved to Rome - where, for a while at least, he worked for the Vatican.'

'Alright. That's a little ironic.'

'I didn't mean that. While he was held by the Czechs they had every opportunity to squeeze him for information about Theresienstadt – its personnel, operations, the lot. They didn't, for Christ knows what reason, and he didn't volunteer anything, presumably because he might have been digging a hole for himself by doing so. This whole Spandau business wouldn't have been necessary, had his interrogators done their job at the time. It was left to the man named Ruben to take up the thread and avenge his father. The irony is that Murmelstein had been allowed to leave Czechoslovakia only upon the clear understanding that he owed StB. As a frightened man, otherwise entirely friendless, he took this to heart, and when Ruben approached him he was careful to ask their permission to tell the young man what he knew. They gave it, he proceeded, StB took the chance they'd squandered in '46 and then KGB – me – closed the loop. So, Murmelstein continues to be both the Good and Bad Jew, despite his best intentions.'

'But it was you who let Ruben walk into a bullet, not Murmelstein.'

'If you wish. I wouldn't have chosen to, had I thought there was a better way. There wasn't. Nor, I should say, was there any chance that you wouldn't play a part in it.'

'What do you mean?'

'My coming here today is by way of an apology.' Zarubin lifted the gloved hand. 'While I was losing these, I was encouraged by my manicurists to give a full and frank account of my American vacation and miraculous reappearance in Moscow. Of course, part of that story was how I got into and out of Berlin on a day when everything else was falling into shit. Acute pain has a way of suppressing discretion, and I'm afraid that I named you and what you did for me. When I told you that *I* decided to involve you in this business, I wasn't being entirely honest. It was suggested to me - by men who still look wistfully at my other hand's intact fingernails - that you participate. They liked the way you moved – quickly, and quietly. Best of all, you're not anywhere near other KGB. We didn't want Karlshorst to remotely suspect that we were going to expunge the Spandau operation from history. Our own personnel have a bad habit of talking to each other.'

'Again, who *are* you?'

'Exactly who you think we are, but tasked with something so utterly essential that nothing – *nothing* – can be allowed to put it at risk. It might be of consolation to know that you've helped tremendously.'

'Then you owe me an answer to the second question.'

'Do I? Ask, please.'

'We've spoken of five dead men in Spandau. I've heard that seven died, but two of the corpses were removed before anyone could examine them. Why the discrepancy?'

'An accounting error.'

'What?'

'The Czechs accounted for rather more former Theresienstadt employees than was convenient.'

'Those two ...'

'Were turnarounds, *double agents*, as the Americans say, working for us as well as Gehlen. Had the police managed to identify them we might have been embarrassed, their histories doubtless being as despicable as their brethren's. We got them out quickly – a risky operation, but fortunately Bonn, Gehlen himself and the senior ranks of Berlin's *Landespolizei* were all equally content not to have more of these inconvenient murders advertised than necessary.'

'So I needn't really have worried about being implicated?'

'No, but you weren't to know that. Again, I apologise.'

It sounded genuinely like remorse - an over-reaction, surely, to what had been at most an inconvenience and the cause of several bad nights' sleep? Zarubin hadn't put Fischer's name on that piece of paper, so why would he be kicking himself for it?

Fischer's stomach got the message a moment before the head had fully decoded it, and lurched slightly. 'My help – it wasn't *that* tremendous.'

'No, it wasn't. I mean, not yet.'

'Not … this was a *test run*?'

Zarubin nodded. 'Believe me, it's not my choice – I don't *have* a choice.'

'But I don't know anything, or anyone. What use am I?'

'You're ex-Luftwaffe Intelligence, ex-Gehlen Org and a respected and respectable businessman, resident in the very eye of a coming storm. Do you have any idea of the quality of our typical local agent? Of course you do, you've seen the same on your side - outcasts, bankrupts, sexual deviants, psychotics - men whose filthy pasts and present habits make them pliable, and not remotely reliable. When I was obliged to introduce you to my interrogators I swear that their eyes all but lit up. They regard integrity as a thin but precious seam - always to be sought out, to be secured, to be mined. I really *am* sorry, Fischer.'

When a man hears the shutters come down on every conceivable exit, he flings himself into the dusty corners, looking for some neglected strategy, a key to fit a lock whose mechanism he can't even made a start on understanding. But Fischer's head wouldn't work; it felt as if several bottles of brandy were doing their business, slowing him to a bleary halt. All he could think about was not being where he was, as soon as possible.

'Can I go?'

Zarubin seemed slightly dumbfounded by the question. 'Of course you can. Someone will be in touch.'

'When?'

'I don't know, truly. Karlshorst will make that decision, not Moscow. If it's any consolation, you'll be treated properly - royally, even. God knows, they won't want to squander you.'

41

Melchior Fux couldn't recall when he had last eaten as well as this, if ever. The menu – a somewhat redundant document, as everything on it was served up – ran to eight courses, any one of which would have put a modest appetite out of commission. The other sixty or so diners were probably more familiar with this sort of excess, belonging as they did to a profession that had never allowed the collective navel to rasp against the spine.

He had hoped to sit next to his friend Ernst Beltze, but the seating arrangement had been preordained by name-cards placed precisely between quantities of cutlery. It hardly spoiled the evening; the gentleman to his left was an interesting fellow who could talk about his work in layman's terms and seem genuinely interested in police work, while the one to the right interrupted occasionally with jokes that were extremely funny and so tasteless that Fux wouldn't have repeated them in a dockers' canteen.

The lowest buttons on his shirt were threatening to part when an old fellow with Hindenburg whiskers stood and proposed a series of toasts, after which chairs shuffled and diners waddled around to seek new company. The Joker excused himself and was replaced by Beltze, whose normally ruddy face had acquired mottled maroon highlights.

'Melchior! What about the *Poulet Breton*? Delightfully rustic, wasn't it?'

Fux had no idea which of them *Poulet Breton* had been, but he'd enjoyed everything put in front of him. 'Yes, very much, Ernst. Thank you for inviting me.'

'Ach.' Beltze waved it away. 'It's good to have someone here who doesn't want to talk cadavers. How's the family?'

'Very well. Freda goes to middle school in the autumn.'

'Already! Where does the time go, eh?'

The conversation was interrupted by port being passed around the table in the English manner. Fux helped himself to enough to wet the bottom of his glass; Beltze almost filled his, then took a generous swig and smacked his lips.

'Do you know, I can actually feel my head crunching as I swallow it? Tomorrow's going to be Hell.'

That was as much small talk as either man had. Fux re-read the menu to put the experience into context while his friend cupped his glass and carefully examined the contents. Eventually, he cleared his throat and spoke quietly, though the volume of a dozen conversations around the two men made him almost inaudible.

'Have you put by that business yet?'

'Business?'

'Don't be obtuse.'

'I have, Ernst. Most definitely.'

'You aren't just saying that?'

'No. In fact, I've solved the mystery to my entire satisfaction.'

'How?'

'By sitting on my arse and having the answers come to me. I received a letter – well, a brief note, typed and unsigned – that cleared everything wonderfully.'

'Anonymous?'

'Yes, though I know perfectly well who sent it, and he must know that I know. Presumably, he didn't want his name on anything.'

'The same name as on the famous piece of paper?'

'Yes. I invited him back to Friesenstrasse for another conversation, but he either ignored it or chose not to accept. To be honest, I was going to take no for an answer and drop it all at that point.'

'Very wise.'

'But then he sent the note. I'm still wondering why.'

'Perhaps he thought your persistence deserved something.'

'Or he was tired of being pestered about something he knew or suspected was no longer my business to chase.'

'So, what was the answer?'

'Really, Ernst? You want to know?'

'Christ! Of course!'

'The dead men had pasts. Their executioners were tasked with retribution. Everyone from Adenauer down believes that what happened was either justified or too embarrassing to admit to – particularly at the moment, when everyone is watching and wondering what sort of Germany emerges from the Peace Treaties.'

Beltze frowned. 'The Israelis, you think?'

Fux glanced around. 'The note didn't specify, but that's my assumption.'

'They've never done anything like this before, have they? I mean, so blatantly?'

'I don't know; but as the World forgets what was done to the Jews, some of them must be thinking they'd better do something about it.'

Around the room, the first verse of *The Hunter from Kurpfalz*, hesitantly taken up, gradually strengthened to an almost tuneful assault. Beltze, his lips tightly pursed, examined his port for a few moments and then turned to his friend.

'Did I ever tell you I wanted to be a writer?'

'Eh? No.'

'I was studying medicine at the Humboldt, my first year, and getting pretty sick of it. It was my parents' idea, of course – a doctor son, it's better than membership of a yacht club, and only a little more expensive. Anyway, I began to drop classes and took up hanging around the Romanisches Cafe, spending my allowance on black coffees and intellectually soaking up the company. You won't believe it, but one day Berthold Brecht excused himself to me and asked if he could take a spare chair from my table to his! Of course, I had no sharper *bon mot* to hand than *by all means*, but I felt bathed in glory for all that.'

'How long did this decadence persist?'

'About three months. My father made it clear that I was perfectly welcome to enjoy the artistic life, and in suitable penury. Naturally, I was soon up to my elbows in bowels once more. The thing is ...'

Beltze shuffled his chair a half-metre closer, until he and Fux were almost in kissing range.

'... my memories of that time are some of the fondest, and they were formed among more Jewish culture than Tel Aviv could provide on a Friday night. I look at that hopeful, naive young man and see someone as yet uninfected by the filth that followed. How can that be, though? How could genuinely decent men and women do what we did?'

'Oh God, Ernst. It was the times ...'

'*We* were the times! The gentleman from Linz wouldn't have gone further than his outside privy if we hadn't felt what he said in our bones. We ignored, then overlooked, then rationalized and then participated efficiently. For years I told myself, well, at least my unit never knowingly killed a Jew for *being* a Jew, but what mitigation is that? If we'd been given new orders we'd have carried them out in a moment, and thought nothing of it. We – all of us - put armour between our souls and what we knew to be wrong or right, and *now* ...'

His hand swept over the general *gemütlichkeit*; '… we say it's all in the past anyway and Germany must look to her future. Look around, though. That one, there ...'

Fux couldn't be certain, but Beltze's finger appeared to indicate a stocky, bald laughing man at the head of a table in the middle of the room;

'… that's Heinz, a lovely man – he'd do you a favour in a moment and beg you to think nothing of it, for all that he lives in a mansion. Also, he served with one of the *einsatzgruppen*. Richard, there, he crosses the line every week, volunteering five hours' free clinical work at the Children's Hospital in Weissensee. During '43 he was the doctor attending torture sessions at Gestapo HQ in Vilnius, keeping captured Jewish partisans alive during their interrogations. I know this because he told me. He also expressed regret, that such *necessary* operations had to take place. My own war service was far nobler, of course. I treated only our own men, keeping them fit and healthy for the arduous task of digging large trenches and filling them with local civilians. I sleep well, most nights, and think very little of it. We've all found a perspective, a sufficiently distant view to make unspeakable events fade to the pleasing greyness of *regrettable but necessary*. We're decent men, we tell ourselves, and decent men survive indecencies intact.'

Beltze shook his head. 'I sometimes wish God existed, to make me dread what I've seen and done. But He doesn't, and every year I feel myself floating a little more towards a state of indifference. If *we* can forget, who will remember?' He drained the last of his port and smiled. 'Except, perhaps, *Mossad*. Thank you for telling me, Melchior. You've made me feel a little better about feeling better.'

Afterwards, Fux decided to walk home. He was troubled by what he'd heard, and couldn't help but think of his own history. He had been a Pioneer, a front-liner, for whom war service had mostly passed burrowing beneath enemy fortifications or in an extended crouch (a posture that protected him as much from his own side's ordnance as that of the Soviets). There was no obvious stain upon him from that time, but was that enough? He had never believed the official line that the enemy were sub-human, and that theirs was a struggle for civilization itself; but he'd understood that soldiers required a degree of motivation to be killers. He had passed by any number of smoking blackened holes where villages had only recently stood and thought it a shame, but told himself that that was what war did, always. He recalled almost pitying the huddled groups of captured soldiers waiting to be taken to the rear, but had never bothered to wonder why there were so few of them, ever. There was no law that said a man was required to examine his conscience, but a readiness not to do so was a form of moral failure, wasn't it?

Never having studied philosophy or listened to sermons, Fux had no answer to this. He thought about asking his wife's opinion, but it was a bad idea, easily dismissed. She hadn't cared to know anything about his war service (though she was grateful for his safe return), and even now worked hard to ignore any revelation regarding war crimes and their German authors. In any case, he told himself, a soul's condition was its owner's business alone.

By the time he reached his home, he was irritated that the matter had dulled his appreciation of the evening's fine food. The mood didn't last long, however. His two daughters weren't yet in bed, a small concession to the excitement raised by a looming holiday. The following morning they would help to pack up the family's six-year-old Ford Taunus, and then Father would point it at Ruhpolding. The journey would take almost two days (the worst it the closely-watched transit across the DDR), but once over the border and into Bavaria they would play the camping game, looking for the best place to pitch that evening (chocolate for the daughter who spotted it), and the second day would be a series of easy stages punctuated by tea- and meal-breaks – an adventure, even for the two adults. These were the best twelve days in any year, and they started tomorrow.

The past had no chance against that sort of present, and by the time Freda and Mathilde had been coerced into their beds, Fux had declared a truce with his conscience. What had been done in Spandau wouldn't be punished, but earlier crimes had been - by murder. It was a moral conundrum even knowing what to think, and if he gave it the attention it deserved he would forget to pack something vital for the holiday. If, two weeks from now, he still felt like torturing himself about matters he had no power to change, fine - for the moment, little blessings crowded out the larger shadows.

He would have liked to thank Otto Fischer, though. He was obviously still deep in the Intelligencer's game and owed Fux nothing, yet he had taken he trouble to give both enlightenment and reassurance that the best place for a sensible *kriminalkommissar* was as far as possible from the whole business. It was a great pity that the man wore his own war so starkly; clearly, he was someone who had met the bill for it in full, the interest compounded cruelly.

42

Three days on a standard Gulag-issue bed had given Fischer's spine an appreciation of its age, and in his own bed once more he slept for a full ten hours. On Sunday morning he rose late, tried to read Saturday's *Morgenpost* as he ate breakfast and didn't even think of checking his workload in the repair-room. Renate had left a note – a thesis, rather – regarding the items she had taken in and sold in the past few days, and he didn't doubt that the ledger would tally precisely with whatever funds sat in his safe. At any other time, these little felicities would make for a pleasant morning, and today they lifted his spirits about as much as if his death sentence had been delivered on scented notepaper.

He was too preoccupied to let the loud knock on the shop door disturb him. Without bothering to put on shoes, he went downstairs and saw Rolf Hoeschler, nose pressed against the glass, hand over eyes, trying to find life inside.

He opened the door. Hoeschler seemed nervous, or anxious, and given that it was likely to be his one pleasant task before bed-time, Fischer decided to put him out of his misery.

'Rolf! I was going to come and see you later.'

'Were you, Otto? That was a kind thought. Listen ...'

'I have news for you. About your problem.'

'Oh! What's that?'

'You don't have one. You need to 'phone your CIA friend and tell him that you know he's in … what are Americans in, when they collaborate?'

'Um, cahoots, I think.'

'Really? That he's in *cahoots*, then, with someone on the other side. That KGB are aware of it, and that he's probably got a few hours at most to find some way out of Berlin not in handcuffs. Tell him not to bother about the bank account; it's Sunday anyway, and Karlshorst have probably made an easily-traced transfer into it by now to taint the pot for when CIA come looking. You might want to wish him well in his future endeavours. And then hang up.'

'You don't think KGB will come after Mila?'

'I know they won't. I've had it from a friendly horse's mouth.'

'Wh … not *Zarubin?*'

'The gentleman himself. He's senior KGB now.'

'Christ! Was there ever such a lucky bastard?'

'Mostly lucky. By the time he'd convinced them of his patriotism, the fingernails on one hand had gone. No Soviet defector ever goes home to flowers, even if he brings the means of toppling Beria.'

'Still, a promotion. He probably thought the price cheap.'

'Probably. So, you can go to Frau Knipper's and reclaim your wife. She must be mad to get home.'

Hoeschler swallowed visibly. 'I went to see her. An hour ago.'

'You risked it? I mean, there was no danger, obviously, but you didn't know that.'

'She called me, earlier this morning. I told her there might be a 'phone trace, but she said it couldn't wait. Otto ...'

'Rolf, you've gone quite white.'

'She told me that something's been *wrong*. The atmosphere in that house was always a little strange, but her landlady and your pretty assistant have been arguing for the last few days, and it's worried her.'

'Argued about what?'

'You, I think, though most of it was whispers, apparently.'

'Oh God. Hopefully, Renate's been putting in a very bad word for me.'

'I don't think it matters now. Mila couldn't sleep last night. At dawn she got up to make herself some tea. The kitchen door was wide open, and no-one was in the garden, so she went to tell Frau Knipper.'

'A burglary?'

'She's gone.'

'Eh?'

'Absconded. Mila saw the envelope, your payment from that fellow, last Wednesday evening. I think Renate took it from the safe.'

'No, I gave it to her, to hold for me. I've been away.'

'Well, the arguments must have been about what to do with it. Mila's second thought was for Renate, but the girl was in her bed still, asleep. When she heard what her mother had done, Mila almost had to tie her down. She was going to go straight to the police.'

Fischer stared at his friend. 'Christ, she mustn't do that.'

'It's strange, I agree. But why not?'

'What if they catch the woman?'

'Oh, right. Anyway, Renate said it must be Albert Preisner's fault.'

'Who?'

'Apparently, he's been working on Frau Knipper for years. Lives three doors down, a widower. He was Waffen SS in the old days, with the *Frundsberg* Division. He courted the woman before she was married, and now he's back on the scent. I didn't know what to think, so I went and knocked on his door. No answer.'

If Fischer had entertained any rational thoughts that morning, they had been upon the matter of his blood-money and how it might get a man out of Berlin before Karlshorst came knocking. It wouldn't need to be Buenos Aires – if he could get as far as France, he doubted that KGB would bother to follow. Without that envelope, though, the bus fare to Potsdam and a light lunch afterwards would probably clean him out.

At least the last vestige of his guilt had fled with (or rather, been abducted by) Frau Knipper. If his head had been in better fettle he might have laughed at the romantic thought of two middle-aged Nazis making for a border with their loot. He put his hand on Hoeschler's shoulder.

'Call Mila now. If Renate picks up the 'phone, let me speak to her. She isn't to do anything until ...'

'Until what?'

'Never mind. Just tell her she still has a job.'

'That's very decent of you, Otto.'

'Not really. The alternative is to advertise for new help and then sit through a dozen interviews, pretending to believe what I was hearing. To be honest, if I'd thought this was going to happen I might well have walked the envelope around to the Knipper house and added whatever was in my pocket.'

While Hoeschler was on the 'phone, Fischer examined a blank section of shop wall and considered the future He'd worried about being marked as a war criminal, when all the while he was being recruited as a peace-time one – or at least a traitor to half of his kind. KGB could play him for years, squeezing out every little use to which he could be put and then allow him a spy's retirement, to be enjoyed briefly, his back against a post. No doubt the remuneration would be risible, the hours irregular and poorly notified, the holiday and sickness benefits foregone by mutual agreement.

Hoeschler was frowning as he replaced the receiver. 'Do you really think that Smith is finished with us?'

'I can't see how he can survive what's coming. Without his CIA badge he's nobody. Unless he's a fool he'll be running already.'

But that was nonsense, of course. Like Otto Fischer, Herr Gregory Smith would discover that he had been recruited by KGB, and upon much the same terms. He might even live to get the opportunity to flee across the line before his old employers smelled the proverbial American rat. The Soviets liked to parade their big successes, after all.

Naturally, he couldn't say any of this to Rolf Hoeschler, who was regarding him with almost plaintive gratitude,

'Well, that's a hell of a weight off, God knows. Thank you, Otto.'

'I didn't do much, just ask questions.'

'It was enough, certainly. But what about *your* problem – that piece of paper and the poor dead fellow?'

It was difficult, but Fischer managed a smile, and was almost certain that his voice didn't betray it. He told himself that a little dishonesty, honestly displayed, was useful practise for when he took up his new career. As he did so he noticed a small pair of pliers on his workbench, his favourites to pry off difficult, tightly-fitting wristwatch backs, and it occurred that they would be an excellent tool with which to relieve former Major Zarubin of his remaining fingernails, should the opportunity ever present itself.

'That's gone away, too. It's all worked out wonderfully.'

Author's Note

General Zarubin's fear of drawing 'attention' to KGB operations in Berlin reflected a deep concern for their star agent at that time, the British traitor George Blake. During 1955 he was posted there by MI6, and charged ostensibly with 'turning' Soviet and DDR personnel. In reality, he was passing a stream of information to KGB, including details of Operation Gold, a CIA/MI6 scheme to build a tunnel into East Berlin to tap telephone lines used by Soviet Military Intelligence. Fully informed of this from its inception, KGB allowed it to proceed to completion (without informing either GRU or Stasi of its existence) and then access unaltered Soviet Intelligence for almost a year, rather than risk Blake's true mission being discovered by their interference with the operation. For the same reason they also left in place during this period Western agents in Soviet institutions whom Blake had betrayed to them. Only after he was transferred out of Berlin did KGB and Stasi 'discover' the tunnel and close it down.

The byzantine manoeuvres between the Intelligencers Reinhardt Gehlen, Otto John and Friedrich Wilhelm Heinz are well-documented. The defector John returned to the Federal Republic in late 1955, claiming to have been abducted to the East by KGB. His defence failed, and he spent eighteen months in prison. For the rest of his life (he died in 1997), he tried vainly to clear his name.

The 'bad Jew' Benjamin Murmelstein's record before and during his time at Theresienstadt has been debated strenuously. There is no doubt that he collaborated – specifically, with Adolf Eichmann to clear Jews out of Vienna, and later as the concentration camp's senior elder; but there is evidence also that he worked to save Jewish lives. Following his release by the Czechoslovakian authorities he lived in Rome until his death in 1989, following which his son was forbidden to recite the *Kaddish* for him.

29725558R00227

Printed in Great
Britain
by Amazon